FLIGHT

THE NARAVAN CHRONICLES 5

ISABO KELLY

FLIGHT

Published 2018 by T&D Publishing
Cover design: © 2017 EJR Digital Art
Interior book design © 2018 T&D Publishing
ISBN-13: 978-1-944600-14-3 (Trade Paperback Edition)

This is a work of fiction. All of the characters, places, organizations, and events portrayed are either products of the author's imagination or are used fictitiously. Any resemblance to actual persons, living or dead, business establishments, events, or locales is entirely coincidental.

First printing T&D Publishing edition: October 2018
For information, contact T&D Publishing www.tanddpublishing.com

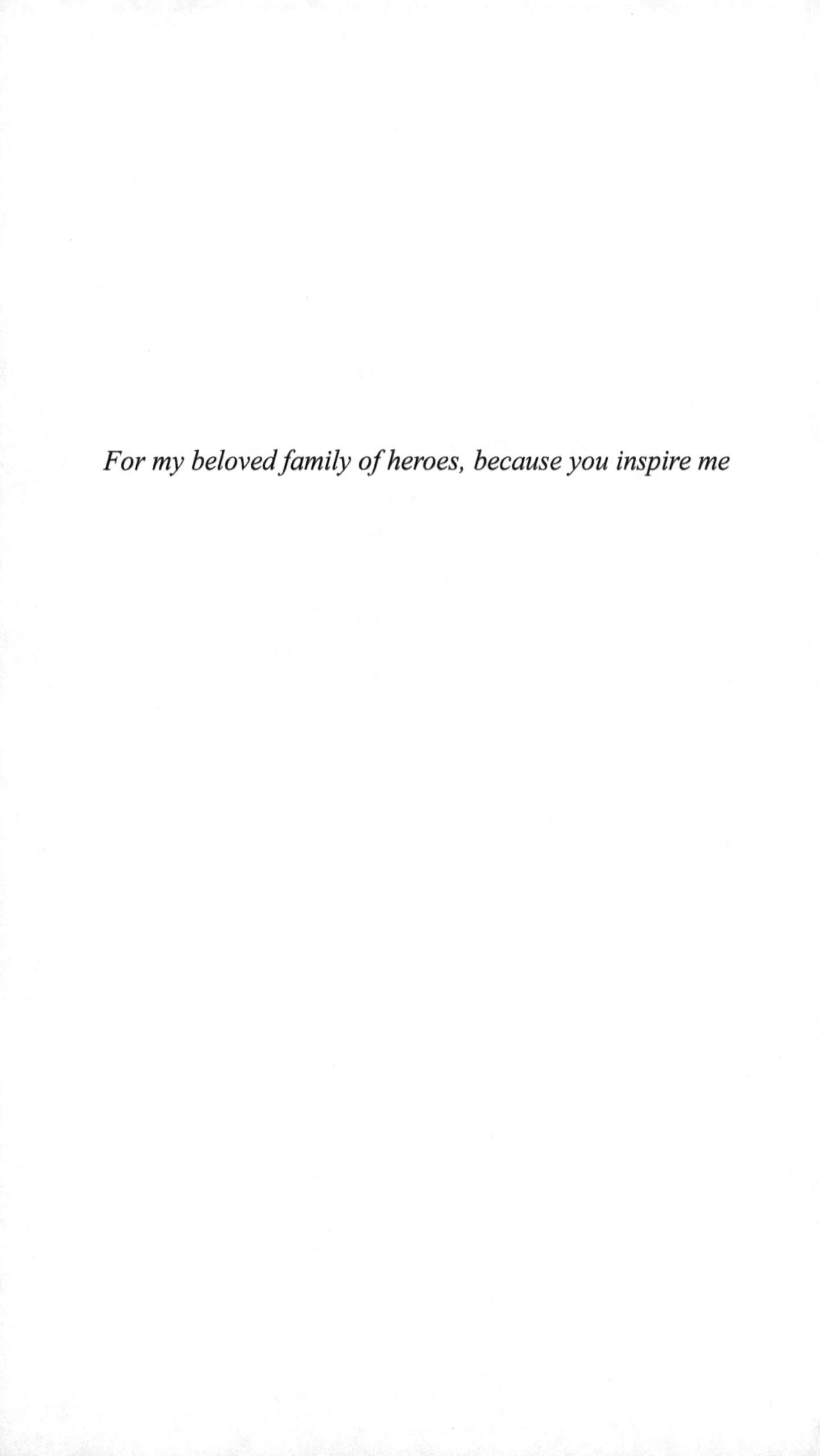

For my beloved family of heroes, because you inspire me

"Fantastic job, Reilly. Best story yet." Tom Rafferty leaned back in his chair, his heavy frame making the wood creak.

"Thanks, chief." Reilly tipped an invisible hat to the head of the network and grinned.

Breaking the news of the Shifter city to the citizenry of Narava had been a coup, something that made a reporter's career, and they both knew it. Up to that point, the native residents of Narava—called Shifters by the humans colonizing this planet—had been hunted relentlessly, and their extermination was sanctioned by law. Shifter support groups defied that law and tried to protect the Shifters, claiming they weren't as dangerous as the government claimed.

Reilly had gone into this last assignment with no real opinion on the Shifters, one way or the other. After breaking the story, things had changed.

Everything was changing.

"Now you need more," Tom said. His thick jowls rocked as he leaned forward and dropped his forearms onto the top of his desk.

"What'd you have in mind?" Despite a slight sting of annoyance that this particular accomplishment couldn't be savored for long, a pulse of excitement started in Reilly's gut. Excitement for the hunt, the next big story.

Tom smiled, and his eyes narrowed. "Kira Farseaker and David Cario."

Well that was definitely *more*. "You mean the two people not even the government has been able to track down in more than a year? The two most elusive people on the planet?"

"The two people responsible for starting all this," Tom confirmed. "You get that interview, Reilly, and you can mark yourself a journalistic legend."

Legend had a nice ring to it. "It's gonna take me a few months."

"No problem."

"And I'll probably have to go off-planet. No way those two are still here or someone would have found them by now. Or their bodies would have turned up."

"True. And you're approved to go off-planet. Just keep me informed. Usual channels."

"You need Farsearker and Cario here on Narava? Or will a recorded interview do?"

"It'll be a better story if they're here. Epic if they return to Narava. But I'll take what I can get. So long as we're the first ones to have it. The *only* ones to have it." Tom lowered his chin, his dark eyes serious. "The exclusive, Reilly. Don't stop until you've got the exclusive."

"You got it, chief. I'm on it."

Tom smiled and leaned back in his creaking chair again. "Legend. You'll be a goddamned legend!"

CHAPTER ONE

Clare O'Malley squeezed her eyes shut and ducked her head as glass shattered against the wall near where she took cover behind an upturned table. Cursing under her breath, she fired her blaster around the edge of the barrier without looking. She didn't care if she hit anyone and her blaster was on high stun because she didn't want to actually kill anyone. But she did not want the mayhem to get any closer to her hiding spot.

Getting shot in a bar brawl was not on her list of things to do tonight.

What *was* on her list was getting Raf Tygran to fly her off-planet. Her plan didn't work unless Tygran agreed to the job. Unfortunately, the Binnean clan fight had disrupted their negotiations, putting a real crimp in her efforts.

"How long are they going to keep at this?" she shouted to the man next to her as she fired into the melee again.

"Until most of them are dead," he answered with a shrug.

She glared at the cocky spaceship captain, and he flashed

her a quick, sexy grin. Raf Tygran was dangerous, and not just because he was a smuggler and reputed pirate. The little tingle of interest dancing in her stomach didn't bode well for their ongoing negotiations. She had to stay sharp if she wanted this to happen and getting distracted by his grin would put her at a disadvantage.

But she had bigger things to worry about in that moment.

"Who the hell let t'Pree clan into a t'Kalb clan bar anyway?" she snapped, not really expecting an answer.

"Either someone who didn't know anything about Binneans—"

"Who doesn't know this?" she interrupted, then ducked again as more glass shattered nearby.

Everyone knew you couldn't put two Binnean clans in the same space. It was chemistry, science. Something to do with pheromones. You put two clans together, you got violence and mayhem. And a lot of dead Binneans plus a lot of dead and injured innocent bystanders.

Most of the time, the huge, fur-covered beings went out of their way to avoid other clans. They wore signature insignia and clothing. Each clan had a different range of fur colorations. They ensured their businesses were clearly marked with the owner's clan. They even had special negotiators, the tek'la, who weren't affected by the pheromones and so could move between clans, ensuring they could conduct trade without creating chaos.

Humans couldn't have worked with Binneans for decades without knowing the fundamental fact that putting two different clans together was disastrous. Everyone *knew* this.

"Or someone wanted to start a fight," Tyran finished, sending a hail of blaster fire into the ruckus as a few bolts fired from across the room scorched the wood floor in front of their table.

"Why would anyone want to *start* a Binnean fight?" she asked.

"Got me." He ducked and put his back to the table. "But if we stay much longer, our chances of getting out in one piece go down. A lot."

"I'm ready to leave whenever you are."

He grinned again and nodded to her left. "The fighting's moving away from the front door. Stick close to the wall."

With a deep breath, she dropped the thin strap of her small purse over her head so it hung across her chest, checked the charge on her blaster, then nodded. Tygran looked around the table one last time, gauging the movements of the rolling mayhem, before moving out.

They both fired randomly into the fighting as they scrambled around the edge of the room. A human man dropped back into Tygran after being punched in the face. The smuggler pushed him off and fired a few shots at the Binnean who'd thrown the punch. The giant, black fur-covered being dropped to the ground stunned.

"Nice shot," Clare shouted as they continued toward the front door.

"So long as he doesn't remember it when he wakes up," Raf shouted back. "I know him."

She actually laughed. "You are in trouble."

"Wouldn't be the first time," he said.

With a snort, she shot and stunned the two Binneans charging toward them.

"Getting a little dicey out here," she said as adrenaline

roared through her blood and more than a little worry tightened her grip on her weapon.

"Then stop playing and get a move on," Raf said, sprinting toward a banister near the door that provided some semblance of cover.

Clare followed at low run, cursing the height of her heels and the tightness of her skirt. She hadn't gotten dressed for this meeting with a blaster fight in mind.

From their new position, they were within a few meters of escape. A handful of mostly Binneans fighting with fists and knives blocked their way.

"Now what?" she said against Raf's ear to be heard over another loud crash and the shouting.

Raf fired a few shots behind them, guarding their backs, a slight frown creasing his excessively handsome face. He took a few moments to study the fist fight blocking their exit, then grabbed her free hand and tugged. "Move!"

Resisting the urge to scream, Clare ran with Raf right at the fight. As they neared, Raf fired two quick shots and Clare followed his lead by shooting into the mess of bodies. The Binneans scattered, leaving the door free.

They flew out of the bar into the cool, humid air of the Docks. Still holding her hand, Raf raced down the cobbled walkway, through an alley and only slowed to a walk when they were several blocks away from the bar. Finally, he stopped and Clare took the opportunity to catch her breath.

Raf glanced down at her shoes and grinned. "You run good in those. Thought I might have to carry you."

With a crooked, cocky smile of her own, she dipped her head in thanks. "Have to be prepared in the Docks." Though, to be honest, if she'd know the night was headed in this direction, she would have chosen a lower heel.

She glanced around to get her bearings. The Docks was a city built on the Dreic Sea and designed to look just like the Earth city of Venice, Italy. It was beautiful here during the day, with gorgeous stucco buildings fronted by wrought iron and stone balconies and slow-moving canals between tree-lined, cobblestone walkways.

But at night, more sinister characters came out. Standing around opened her and Raf up to attack from some enterprising thief. And they still had negotiations to finish. She couldn't get off-planet without Raf Tygran and his ship. Everything, all the months of effort, depended on convincing him to take this job. Which meant they had to find a new—preferably safer—place to talk.

"Where to now?" she asked.

Raf raised his brows, then glanced down the nearest alley.

At the end of the narrow corridor between pale stucco buildings, Clare could just see the black waters of one of the many canals that snaked through the city. The cool air was tinged with a faint hint of fish and seaweed—and a few fainter, less pleasant odors she didn't want to think about too closely.

"Come on," Raf said. "I know a place. Much quieter than a bar. We can finish our conversation there."

She let Raf put a hand on the small of her back to guide her, but the feel of his warm fingers against her bare skin made her stomach dance dangerously. Damn him. He was doing this on purpose, to distract her in an effort to get a better deal. She knew it. He knew it. It might have worked on another woman, or even on her under different circumstances, but she *needed* this deal. She had no intention of letting the gorgeous pirate keep her from getting off Narava by the end of the week.

There was a reason she had this particular dress on—washed silk, long skirt slit up the sides to her hips, cut out back. The long sleeves and high neckline did nothing to make this dress look modest and the blue color made her pale skin glow. All of her look was very specifically designed for this meeting. To distract *him* so *she* could get the deal done for the price she could afford.

She refused to waste all that effort by losing her focus just because Raf Tygran had a killer smile and was quite possibly the most handsome scoundrel she'd had the pleasure of meeting.

He led her across a small bridge, down a barely lit alley, and out into an open courtyard painted soft orange from the light of iron lamps spaced throughout the center of the area. The ground floors of the surrounding buildings were fronted by stone arches, hiding the actually entrances. The spaces under the arches were black this time of night, casting a sinister face on an area that would look quite charming in daylight. A cool breeze intensified the fish and seaweed scents from the sea, and a shivered crawled up her spine. She didn't want to call the sensation fear. But it was skirting close.

"Stay to the center of the courtyard," Raf warned.

"I caught the movement," she murmured. In the darkness under the arches, shadowy shapes hovered. Waiting for pray.

She adjusted the blaster she still carried so it caught the light of a nearby lamp. The glint of metal was enough. The dark figures froze, or disappeared. She wasn't sure. But the threat emanating from their surroundings seemed to ease.

She noticed Raf also had his blaster in plain view and smiled, wondering what they looked like to the Docks' denizens.

Raf was dressed in tight black trousers, a black long-sleeved shirt, and a fitted, steel-colored flight jacket. But he had a kind of light, rugged handsomeness that didn't scream deadly. His blond-brown hair was short, but still brush his collar. His blue eyes sparked with mischief rather than threat. Even the way he carried himself, the confidence he exuded so effortlessly, came across as more playboy than assassin.

Yet he held his blaster like an old lover and had had no trouble using it during the bar brawl. A careful visual assessment right after they'd met had confirmed he carried at least two more concealed weapons—a knife in his calf-high boot and a second blaster at the small of his back. There was much more to Raf Tygran than was apparent at first glance. And Clare found herself…curious.

As they made their way out of the courtyard and onto a walkway at the edge of the Dreic, she breathed in deeply of the murky, salty scent and forced her mind toward logical thoughts. She needed Tygran. She couldn't finish what she'd started without him. She had to keep her focus on the goal, on the negotiation and the job.

But a small part of her was still very much aware of the heat from his palm warming the bare skin along her spine.

He took another cobbled street, away from the sea and back toward the center of the city. Crossing another bridge, down a narrow alley, they came out into a small, dead-end square bracketed by tall, unadorned brick buildings. At the far side of the square was an ordinary brown door with a large brass knocker shaped like the head of an Earth camel. There weren't any other distinguishing features. Not even a series of buttons and speakers for ringing the occupants of the building.

She gave the door a dubious frown. "You know how to get in, I take it."

He grinned and swung the brass ring hanging from the camel's mouth three times without once actually hitting the door. Then he set it gently against the frame, careful not to make any noise. He stepped back and a second later the door swung open.

"Good trick," she said, trying not to laugh at his self-satisfied smirk. "If you knock the ring against the door what happens?"

"Nothing," he said. "You're ignored."

He guided her into the interior with his hand at her back again. Inside, they were greeted by dark wood, lots of dark leather, and patterned rugs on hardwood floors. Smoke was thick in the air and the walls were lines with what looked to be real leather-bound books. A fireplace against the far wall flickered, burning real wood. High-backed leather chairs were scattered throughout the room, singly or in small clumps around inlaid tables. Men in suits from various centuries, from modern to ancient Earth, occupied most of the chairs, many of them holding cigars and brandy snifters. An androgynous looking droid in shirtsleeves and a vest manned a small bar at one corner of the room.

"Very Victorian-era Earth," she commented as Raf led her to a couple of unoccupied seats.

"Fashioned after the old men's clubs of that time period," he confirmed.

She'd noticed immediately the lack of women. "It's not an issue me being here?"

"Given most of the old farts can't take their eyes off you, I'd say no one will make a fuss."

"Well then." She returned her blaster to her little handbag and settled into a chair, crossing her legs so the entire room got a view of the full length of her thigh. "Shall we continue our talk?"

Raf grinned and dropped into the seat across from her, his posture deceptively relaxed. He sprawled with his legs stretched out and crossed at the ankles, his arms draped loosely across the armrests, his blaster already returned to the shoulder harness he wore under his jacket. Yet she was sure, if needs be, that blaster would be back in his hand in the blink of an eye. Maybe even faster than she'd be able to get hers from her purse, even though she'd spent months practicing. The thought that he was ready for instant action was sobering. Yet his underlying alertness made her feel safer, more comfortable.

And that was even more sobering.

"Now about my fee…" he started, his eyes narrowing.

"I've offered all I'm allowed to pay," she said. "You're not getting any more."

"Ah, but you won't find another ship that can take you where you want to go. I've been there. Twice. And returned. Not another living soul can say that—outside of my crew of course."

"And yet you can't get there again without the information I have," she said. "I can always give the coordinates to another pilot. There are a lot of ships willing to take me anywhere I want to go for the fee I've named."

"Not one as good as the *Ebisu* and her crew."

She might have laughed at the boast if it weren't true. Tygran and his crew were so notoriously good at what they did that despite having warrants for their arrest issued on most civilized planets, they still came and went with impunity. It had taken her more than a month of research to find him and arrange this meeting.

And as it happened, she did need *him* specifically.

Because she didn't actually have the coordinates to get where she needed to go either. She could only get them from Nathan Longfeather.

She'd met Longfeather while working as security for a Shifter support group. The mercenary was suspicious, secretive, and stubborn. But Clare had helped his wife, Dr. Ti'ann Jones, which in turn helped Clare gain Longfeather's trust. Even then, it had taken Clare months to uncover of the existence of Kierna'Rhoan. The secret planet was a family legacy that only family members could locate. It wasn't on any space charts and was far enough off the main trade routes it was impossible to stumble across on accident. There was no way to find it without help. And Longfeather had only agreed to cooperate and give her the coordinates if she could convince Raf Tygran to fly her there.

So she needed Tygran. If he insisted on more money, which she didn't have, or simply refused to take the job, she was screwed.

She stared at him while the droid from the bar brought them two snifters of Binnean brandy and set the drinks on their small table. She hadn't noticed Raf ordering anything, but somehow she wasn't surprised either. After the droid left, Clare took her time sipping her drink as she weighed her options. She had one desperate card she could play, one gambit Tygran wouldn't expect. But playing this ace could backfire.

As she let the sharp, sweet taste of the brandy slide down her throat, she decided the risk was worth it. "You're still having trouble with the Leeches. Aren't you?"

He tensed subtly and his fingers tightened around his glass. He stared at her through narrowed eyes as he took another drink. Silence stretched between them, broken only by the sounds of crackling wood in the fireplace and the quiet shuffling of the other men in the room.

She didn't dare blink. She needed him to believe she'd let the Leeches know where he was. She needed him to think she'd follow through with her unspoken threat. The fact that she'd never really do that to anyone wasn't going to get her what she wanted.

After what seemed a silent eternity, his posture relaxed again and a sexy grin lifted his mouth.

"Deal," he said.

She worked hard not to let him see her releasing the breath she'd been holding.

But he must have noticed because he chuckled. "Worried?"

"Maybe a little," she allowed.

"You should be. I don't like threats. Any more than I like Leeches."

"But you're still going to take the job." She made it a statement. He'd agreed. She wasn't about to let him back out now.

"I'm still taking the job." He nodded. "I'm curious now."

"Curious?"

"You wanted *me* for this," he said. "You're right, without the coordinates, I'm no better than any other pilot. But you were willing to threaten me to get me to agree. I find that interesting."

She tried for a casual shrug. "You're the one who said it. You're the best. And you've been there before. And the Leeches are your weakness. I'd be a fool not to take advantage of every one of those points."

"And you're no fool, are you Clare O'Malley."

"No," she said, very seriously. "I'm no fool."

His expression turned thoughtful, considering. She didn't like that look. Raf was no fool either.

Unlike so many of the others she dealt with, Raf lived in the underbelly and played with bad people. He was still alive, despite that. Despite the Leeches hunting him and civilian governments on most planets after him. He was going to be a hard man to hide from. If he started digging, he might well uncover her lies. Everything she'd done, everything she'd worked for all these years, required her to disguise her real self. Her life depended on keeping her secrets. Especially from a notorious smuggler she couldn't trust.

Which made Raf Tygran a very dangerous man indeed.

CHAPTER TWO

She was a liar.

Raf had known the instant she smiled at him that the first words out of her mouth would be a lie.

"I'm Clare O'Malley."

Lie.

He studied her over his brandy, watching her watch the room. In general, he loved liars. They were so reliable, so predictable. There was a security in knowing someone would *always* lie to you. You knew where you stood with dishonest people.

And in his line of work, he spent a lot of time with the less than honest. So the fact that Clare O'Malley wasn't actually this woman's real name didn't bother him. The fact that she lied so well didn't bother him either.

It did, however, intrigue him. And it was the intrigue that was going to get him into trouble.

The fact that she was stunning didn't help. Curly red hair, which she'd attempted to tame into an updo, sexy-as-all-hell chocolate eyes, kissably full lips. And most enticing, an adorable line of freckles across her nose. He was beyond tempted to run his finger along those freckles just to see how she'd react.

He let his gaze dip lower, to the tight silk dress covering her outrageously curvy body. They hadn't discussed it, but he knew she'd worked as a stripper here in the Docks before taking her current position with a Shifter support group. He'd lay money she'd earned a fortune with that body.

He was as used to working with beautiful women as he was liars. He loved them both. But this one…

This one was going to be trouble.

"This place," she said, motioning around with her drink, "is it…known for what some of these places are known for?"

"The kink upstairs is significant," he confirmed. "But consensual here. No slaves. No abuse."

"You're sure?" She raised her brows at him.

"I am. I wouldn't frequent the place otherwise."

Her disbelieving look might have offended a lesser man. But he wasn't known for his honesty, and he expected people to treat him that way. If they didn't, he'd get nervous. He did have a moral code, though, for what it was worth.

He tipped his still mostly full glass of brandy in her direction. "You're thinking, why would a smugger care?" he said. "I don't smuggle slaves. And I don't condone abuse."

"Okay. Sure." She shrugged as if it made no difference.

But when she took a hurried sip of brandy, he grinned. She cared. She liked that he hadn't brought her to one of the other kinds of men's clubs. So she was a brilliant liar, but she couldn't hide her emotions completely.

He liked that very much.

She set her empty glass down on the table and smiled at him. It was a calculated smile, designed to be sexy and sly. He liked that too, even knowing she was doing it on purpose. Playing games with Clare O'Malley, whoever she was, was proving very entertaining. The flight to Kierna'Rhoan was going to be fun.

"We're done for the night." She stood, straightening her tight skirt down over her hips. "I'll contact you with the meet up location."

He rose, making no effort to hide the fact that he was staring at her curves. "You don't want another drink?" he asked, just to see what she'd say.

"I'm good. I have other mischief to get up to."

Lie. He loved it. "Fine. I'll walk you to the Grand Bridge." The bridge that brought visitors from the mainland into the city was a beautiful stone structure that hid as many nighttime dangers as any other part of the Docks. Tourist only traveled here during the day for a reason.

"No need." She patted her purse and the blaster hidden inside. "I can see myself safely home."

"I insist." He slipped his hand around her elbow. "If something happens to you before you can relay our deal to your people, I'm out a substantial fee."

He watched her try to suppress her smile.

Back out in the cool air, he led the way toward the Main Canal, and a relatively safe route out of the Docks. He pulled out his blaster, though, keeping it in his free hand. Just in case. When he glanced down, Clare had done the same.

"I suppose you're used to the night life here," he commented.

"As used to it as anyone can be."

"But not one of the predators."

"Not one of the prey either," she said very firmly.

His turn to smile. "No. No, you aren't. Where'd you learn to shoot so well?"

"My mom." She shrugged. "Thought it'd be a handy trait. She was right."

So. Close to her mother at least. Interesting tidbit of truth, that. He considered pushing for a little more personal information but consoled himself with the fact that he'd have a couple of weeks on the *Ebisu* to dig deeper into her secrets.

He was looking forward to it.

To test her, he moved in a little closer, their hips bumping slightly as they walked. She didn't move away. But he felt her arm muscle flex and then relax under his grip. Breathing deep, he caught her scent beneath the other less pleasant smells of the Docks. A hint of something spicy, like cinnamon, mixed with a soft musk. Not something typical, not a familiar perfume or even a soap he recognized. More intriguing.

As they neared the Grand Bridge, he turned to study the side of her face. She very carefully didn't look at him.

What would she do if he kissed her?

Probably a bad idea. She still had her blaster in hand. But those lush lips of hers were a hard temptation to resist. Still, he'd likely be shooting himself in the foot if he tried it, putting an end to any chance of taking her to bed on the flight to Kierna'Rhoan—and he was definitely interested in taking Clare O'Malley to bed.

He should let her go without trying anything.

He wasn't going to. But he should.

When they hit the far side of the Bridge, he faced her. "You have transport?"

She nodded. "I'm good from here."

"You are good," he murmured. "Contact me tomorrow after midday. I'll be occupied before that."

"A woman?" She raised her brows.

"Work."

She waited for details and he let her, watching as she struggled against an instinct to ask more. It was a natural instinct, and he'd purposefully played into it, just to see what she'd do. Finally, she pressed her lips together and nodded. She glanced toward the parking area.

"Fine. After midday," she said.

"You sure you don't want me to walk you to your transport." While most of the criminal activity stayed within the Docks, beyond the reach of Capital's Guards' jurisdiction, a mugging in the parking area wasn't unheard of this late at night.

"I'm sure," she said with a smile. She waved her blaster slightly. "I'm a careful girl."

She was an adrenaline junkie if he'd ever met one, a woman who liked to take risks. But from the sharp look in her eyes, he'd bet she calculated each risk so she'd come out on top. He'd have to challenge her to a poker game.

"Goodnight," she said after another pause. "And thanks for…"

"For?"

"For the brandy." She grinned and started to spin away.

Yeah, he wasn't going to resist. He hadn't released his hold on her yet so he used his grip on her elbow to spin her back to him. She barely had time to blink before he pulled her close and settled his mouth gently over hers. He didn't hold her in any other way, giving her a chance to back off. He expected to feel the nose of her blaster against his ribs. But as the moments ticked past, her mouth softened under his, her breath sighed out, and Raf lost sight of everything but deepening the contact.

He moved his hand from her arm to her bare back and pressed her tighter against him, angling his head to settle his lips more firmly on hers. She opened her mouth first, but he didn't refuse the offer. He slid his tongue across hers, tasting the brandy and sweetness. Her breasts rubbed against his chest with her breathing, creating a delicious friction he wanted more of, only with a lot less clothing between them. But just getting this kiss, without her shooting him, was more than he'd hoped for, and he savored it, savored her.

Right up until she eased her mouth from his.

Her eyelids were heavy, her breathing uneven, her lips wet and still a dangerous temptation. Orange light from the Bridge reflected in her brown eyes. He couldn't seem to find his easy smile or any pithy comments. Staring at her was too enchanting, and he didn't want that silent moment to end.

She broke first, with a small smile and a slow blink. "What was that for?" she murmured.

"Seal the deal," he said, surprised to hear his voice was gravely and harsh. She had a more serious effect on him than he'd anticipated.

"Thought we did that with the brandy," she said.

"I like this way better."

Her eyebrows shot up. "You do this with all your clients?"

His smile returned at her only half-feigned shock. "Only the ones who've escaped Binnean bar fights with me."

She chuckled, a deep, sexy sound, and pushed out of his arms. "I'll talk to you tomorrow."

She turned toward the parking structure, giving him an excellent view of her bare back and beautiful ass. Her hips swayed as she walked, a calculated effort he as sure, but even knowing that, the movement kept his attention rapt. He really hoped no one decided to mug him because he wouldn't be able to think enough to put up a fight.

She waved a hand over her shoulder, without looking at him, and disappeared into the dark night. He smiled. The next few weeks were going to be fun. And trouble. So much trouble.

So much wonderfully interesting trouble.

CHAPTER THREE

"She's got him," the shadowy figure said, his voice altered to further disguise his identity over the vid-comm.

Terrance Samuels would have smirked at the man's precautions given Terrance already knew who he was. But the informant provided good information, so he let the man have his illusion of anonymity.

"They just sealed the deal tonight."

Terrance considered the news. "Did you find out when they leave?"

"Two days."

Terrance glanced at the vid-screens across from his desk, the myriad of broadcasts playing out from every part of Narava, the wealth of information hidden in all that reporting. "And how many did she book passage for?" he asked.

"Just herself and some cargo."

So, Clare O'Malley was off on some secret mission on her own. He'd expected her to travel with at least one other person from James Monroe's Shifter support group.

"Any clearer idea where she's going? Or what she's going to do?" he asked his source.

The man shook his head. "Nope. But she needed Tygran and his ship for some reason."

Terrance nodded. He had an idea why Tygran was so important to O'Malley's mission, but it wasn't anything his source needed to hear.

Terrance had spent months tracking Monroe and Longfeather's people, on his own, without Senator Johnson's knowledge. After that debacle with the Shifter city, he didn't trust the senator's instincts anymore. And Johnson had kept something from him. The senator had had another source feeding him information from the paleontology dig, a source who'd uncovered the city when Terrance hadn't been able to. That grated against Terrance's pride. But it also presented a puzzle. Who exactly tipped Senator Johnson to the city's existence?

In his effort to uncover the secret source, Terrance had found a few tantalizing hints—a mysterious Shifter, murmurs of the outlaws Kira Farseaker and David Cario. Never enough information to draw any conclusions, but the teases were enough to keep him following the trail.

And now Clare O'Malley, security for James Monroe's group of Shifter supporters, had booked passage with a noto-rious smuggler. A smuggler who, it was whispered, was responsible for getting both Kira Farseaker and David Cario off-planet. It had taken a lot of time and money to uncover that particular rumor, but the effort had been worth it.

Monroe had taken over Farseaker's Shifter group. That created a tie between Farseaker and O'Malley. Tygran had likely gotten Farseaker and Cario off Narava. Another tie.

Terrance was almost positive now that O'Malley was being sent to get Farseaker and Cario. The discovery of Lost City had changed things on Narava. Monroe probably thought Farseaker could return safely and add her weight to the anti-extermination battle. But Senator Johnson wouldn't bother with anything as changeable as the law when it came to Farseaker and Cario. He wanted them dead and would make sure they were assassinated if they ever turned up again.

That wasn't Terrance's concern, though. What he needed was someone on Tygran's ship, someone who'd keep feeding him information. He didn't dare let O'Malley off-planet without being monitored. And he couldn't go himself because she knew him, at least she knew one of his covers. He still had too much to do on Narava anyway. But he was accustomed to managing multiple lines of information gathering.

Information was his business.

He stared for a long moment at his source. "Tygran still has problems with the Leeches?" he asked.

"Yeah," the man said. "They've got a huge price on his head. Fortunately for him, no self-respecting bounty hunter wants to deal with the Leeches."

"And fortunately for us, there are some hunters without any self-respect."

"Huh?"

"Never mind. Your usual fee will be deposited by morning."

"Thanks, sir. Anything you need, you know where I am."

Terrance disconnected, switched to a second coded communications line, and sent a written message to FarMore

Station. No time to waste putting his plan in place. He needed someone on Tygran's ship. And he had just the spy.

CLARE LET herself into her cozy apartment, turned off the security mesh and ordered the lights up to a nice subtle hue. With a sigh that might have been more groan, she kicked off her heels and headed for her bedroom. The silk dress was beautiful and had served its purpose. But she couldn't wait to get into something more comfortable.

In her bathroom, she slipped into soft, well-worn pajamas, reorganized her unruly red curls into a ponytail, and washed her face. When she looked into the mirror, she blinked.

"Well hello there, Reilly."

She touched her reflection and smiled. She'd been playing Clare O'Malley for a while now. Sometimes she felt like she was losing herself in this particular character. The differences were subtle, most of them in her eyes and her facial expressions. She'd stuck closer to her natural appearance for the Clare persona because she'd wanted something easier to maintain after the last couple of characters she'd assumed—one as a man and one as a woman significantly older than Reilly's biological age. Both personas had taken time each day to ensure the physical camouflage was right. Her current external appearance was easier to maintain and slip into daily, but she had to look closely to distinguish between herself and Clare. And when she looked in the mirror, as often as not, Clare looked back.

Seeing herself again was a relief.

The Clare persona had gotten her into a lot of places and helped her break some of the biggest stories on Narava. She quite liked Clare, actually. The woman was strong, sexy, confident, and could kick ass when necessary. It was weird to play someone like that, to know that person *was* her on more levels than usual, and yet be able to detach from Clare so that Clare was her own person.

In all the years of undercover reporting, this was the first time Reilly'd had so much trouble separating from one of her characters. Clare was going to have to disappear soon, after this final job, because if she didn't, Reilly might.

With a groan, she pushed away from the sink and headed back to the sitting room. *So maudlin. Get a grip.*

Tired. She was tired. Late night, tense evening…of course she was exhausted. She needed some sleep. This job wasn't in the bag yet. She still had to get to this mysterious planet where Kira Farseaker and David Cario were hiding. And then she had to convince them to return to Narava— where they were still wanted criminals. No easy task. But she had a plan. She'd get the story.

She always did.

She was on her way to the kitchen for a cup of herbal tea to take to bed with her when her private vid-comm dinged. It was the line only her family and her boss knew about. She stared at it, considered ignoring it, but it could be the chief. She didn't dare ignore that.

Settling onto her oversized couch—Clare's couch—she flicked on the screen. Her brother's beloved face stared back with raised eyebrows.

"Emma, you're looking puffy. Have you eaten enough today?" he said without preamble.

"Nice to see you too, Dr. Reilly," she greeted with a heavy dose of sarcasm.

"I'm serious."

She rolled her eyes, but did take a moment to count up her caloric intake. Her genetic condition necessitated she eat an exact number of calories each day, not more, not less, or she ended up suffering some pretty serious medical complications. With a wince, she realized she hadn't eaten enough, even with the Binnean brandy thrown into the mix.

"I'll have a bar before bed. I promise," she said.

"You haven't been managing your condition well over the last few months. You can't ignore it."

She groaned. "Yes. Yes. Yes. I know." Sean was also her doctor, something that was both convenient and extremely annoying. Sometimes, she just wanted him to be her older brother. "So what's new? You calling just to check on my diet?"

"Mom wants you to come to dinner next weekend. The whole family's going to be there. John and Donal are bringing their partners into Capital especially for it. Caren's making her famous trifle." He wagged his eyebrows, knowing her weakness for her sister's trifle.

"Wish I could," she said. "But I'm going to be working."

"You're always working. You need a break. And family time. We've barely seen you in the last year and half."

"You know what I do. That's necessary sometimes."

"But you used to make time for us," he said.

She stared at him, refusing to feel guilty. He'd missed many family meals while getting his M.D. Of all their siblings, Sean understood being career-driven best. Which was why he was top in his field, just like she was top in hers.

He blinked first, which gave her a punch of satisfaction. Nothing like besting Sean in a staring contest.

"Fine," he said, grudgingly. "I'll let Mom know you're working. She's going to expect a call, though. And you better have a good excuse."

"Is cracking an even bigger story than the last story I broke a good enough excuse?"

His dark brown eyes, so close to her own, sparked with curiosity. "Anything you can talk about yet?"

She shook her head. "Don't dare. But you'll know it when you hear it."

"We are proud of you. You know that, right, Emma?"

Her chest tightened. "Thanks, Sean."

"Don't forget to eat that bar. And whatever you're doing, wherever you're going with this story, do *not* forget to keep your calories balanced."

He gave her his stern doctor look, which she rolled her eyes at again, and she disconnected with promises to eat and to call their mother.

She dropped her head against the back of the couch and stared at the ceiling. Probably good he'd called to remind her to eat. When she got very deep into a job, it wasn't unusual for her to forget for a day or two how careful she needed to be. Until the side-effects started to show.

Pushing off the couch, she trudged back to the kitchen for a nutrition bar. Her condition was such a pain in the ass. Always having to think about food, calorie intake, never being able to just eat—or not eat—when the mood struck. If she ate too much, she lost a lot of weight and risked death. Too few calories a day, though, and she put on excessive weight so fast she could also suffer dire health consequences.

Only a very specific balance kept her from tipping into dangerous waters. All because a couple of relatives two generations earlier wanted to be skinny.

Genetic tinkering before doctors and scientists knew the consequences. And she suffered for it. She wasn't the only one, though.

A little shiver crawled along her spine as she took her bar and tea back to her bedroom. She couldn't consider genetic tampering without thinking about the strange being who'd started out an enemy and become a weird sort of ally.

E.

The name he gave himself. Part Shifter, part human, something completely new and different. And dangerous. The result of human tampering.

As it turned out, E was as important to her story as the information about the Shifter city. She hadn't been allowed to break the news about him. Yet. But everyone involved in discovering the city as well as the Shifters living there had agreed, E should go with her to meet Kira and David.

A part of her that she wasn't proud of recognized that bringing E to Kira could be a disaster and *that* story would be amazing. She didn't like that mercenary aspect of her personality, but it did make her a great reporter. Over the years, she'd lost more and more of her shame and reservations. The cost for her success.

"Too late to regret it now," she murmured as she crawled beneath the covers. She was damned good at her job. The best. And she'd worked her ass off to get to this point. She couldn't regret that. Even if her soul felt a little damaged. There'd be time for fixing those small holes when she retired.

When she retired a *legend*.

She finished her bar and tea, read a bit more of the novel she was in the middle of, then ordered the lights off and the curtains closed. The sun would be up soon. She had to get some sleep. Day after tomorrow, she'd meet with Nathan Longfeather and Jasmine Farseaker, introduce them to Tygran, and begin the trip that would finally *finally* see her to the prize. She had a lot to do. Clare had a lot to do.

Despite her exhaustion, excitement still made her stomach dance and kept her awake for a bit longer. She was so close now. The culmination of months of work. The story that would solidify her as a journalistic legend.

She was smiling when she finally drifted into sleep.

CHAPTER FOUR

RAF STUDIED CLARE, STANDING A FEW METERS AWAY IN quiet discussion with Kira Farseaker's two cousins—a big mercenary named Nathan Longfeather and a tall, slim woman named Jasmine Farseaker. Clare looked serious, intent, and fully focused on the conversation. Instead of a slinky dress and heels, she'd donned more practical pants, a leather jacket, and boots that wouldn't punch holes in the grass. Her mass of curly red hair was pulled back into a messy ponytail, and she wore an obvious blaster holstered at her hip.

And despite wearing an outfit not designed to seduce, she still looked just as dangerously enticing as she had the other night in the Docks.

Even as he stared, the remembered feel of her full lips under his rose up to taunt him. Given they were about to start a new mission, being distracted by his client was probably not the best of ideas.

Not that he'd ever been accused of having *good* ideas when it came to women.

He glanced away, taking in their surroundings, trying to focus on something other than Clare's mouth. They were standing in Kira Farseaker's massive backyard…well, Jasmine's backyard now. The last time Raf had been here, he'd been helping Kira and her crew, including a number of Shifters, load onto his ship for the trip off-world. Jasmine hadn't changed the place much. There was still a vast swath of open, grassy land dotted with thick cops of trees, all dominated by a spectacular mansion. He knew firsthand the extensive lands hid an underground bunker where Kira and her Shifter supporters had worked to protect Narava's native species from the government exterminations. He idly wondered if Jasmine had left the bunker intact.

Not far from where they stood, his ship sat, a giant silver bird in the middle of the huge expanse of manicured lawn. The *Ebisu*, his home and his baby for ten years now, was an awkward sized ship—too large for an ordinary intraplanetary vessel, but too small for typical interstellar cargo or travel transports.

She was, however, the perfect size for a smuggler's ship.

With a crew of twelve plus a half dozen droids, *Ebisu* was the most successful and notorious outlaw ship in the galaxy. Satisfaction in his ship and his crew swelled. They'd earned every last ounce of that success. And notoriety. There was no place in the universe he'd rather be than on the *Ebisu*.

A small movement drew his attention away from his pride and joy, back to the quietly talking group a few meters away. Clare tucked a few thick strands of red hair behind her ears as the grass-scented breeze played havoc with the riot of curls. It was entirely too easy to imagine burying his fingers in all that thick fire, to picture pulling her close, watching her dark eyes drift shut, tasting her mouth again… Despite knowing he was too interested in her every move, he couldn't bring himself to look away from her this time. Not even for the sake of his own sanity. For about the millionth time since meeting her, he wondered who she really was. What was she hiding? And just how long would it take him to uncover her secrets?

"Curiosity killed the cat," Sonia said from his side.

He frowned down at his co-pilot and second in command of the *Ebisu*. Sonia Shen-mae was one of the few people in the universe he trusted completely and without hesitation. She knew more about him than any other living human, which wasn't always good. She was family. Better because his real family had been horrible. And she and Raf had each other's backs.

She only came up to his shoulder, barely, despite the giant purple high-heeled boots she wore. But his Sonia made up for her short stature with a huge personality. Dressed in skintight red pants, a complicated white top with straps and buckles he couldn't begin to guess a use for, her black hair up in a series of braids and decorated with tiny bells, her blaster on one hip, a wickedly sharp dagger tucked into her boot—she was the image of a prosperous pirate. An image she cultivated very carefully.

"Cat?" he said, turning his glare into a charming grin and pressing a hand to his chest. "You've always called me a dog. Can't have it both ways."

"Cat, dog, whatever. You're an animal."

"So are you."

"I'm not the one looking to sleep with our new passenger."

"That would be fun to watch, though."

"Ha. You wish." Sonia smacked him on the arm, none too gently. "She's trouble, Tygran. You know it."

He rubbed his arm, soothing the sting from Sonia's slap. "They're always trouble."

He looked back at Clare just as she pushed more hair behind her ear with an irritated swipe. Though he wouldn't admit it to Sonia, *ever*, she was right. Clare was going to be more trouble than his usual female interests. He couldn't put his finger on why, but years of smuggling had honed his instincts to a fine point. And this woman was going to be a complication he shouldn't indulge.

He would. But he shouldn't.

"You should have charged her more," Sonia said with a sharp hand gesture.

Raf dipped his head, conceding the point.

Clare finished her conversation with Longfeather and Farseaker and then all three joined Raf and Sonia.

"We good?" he asked, making sure to meet Longfeather and Farseaker's steady gazes, giving his best impersonation of a trustworthy ship's captain.

Longfeather nodded. "Kira trusted you enough to take her to Kierna'Rhoan. Jasmine and I will trust you to go again."

Raf raised a brow. He didn't miss the fact that Clare was left out of the trust loop.

"There's just one thing," Clare said.

Raf felt the other shoe dropping. There was always one more thing.

"I'm not the only one traveling," Clare finished.

"The deal was for one passenger and two cargo containers to Kierna'Rhoan." Raf glanced between

Longfeather and Farseaker. "Which one of you has decided to go?"

"Not us," Longfeather said.

"Why not?" Sonia asked, crossing her arms over her chest, all suspicion and defiance.

"I'm too busy with security at Lost City," Longfeather said.

Raf had heard that the mercenary had settled into a more or less permanent job of security liaison with the newly discovered Shifter city. The idea of a Shifter city peaked Raf's curiosity. If he got back to Narava after this job, he wanted to get a look at the place. Shifters building cities. Who would have guessed?

"And the government keeps too close a watch on me," Jasmine said. "At least elements of the government. I can't disappear or they'll have an excuse to enter the property."

Since Jasmine was Kira's cousin and had inherited the mansion and lands, the people still after Kira probably hoped Jasmine would lead them to her. Fat chance of that. But there would be hints on the property, and maybe even evidence of Kira's association with the Shifter support group—the ones after her hadn't been able to actually *prove* that allegation even if it was common knowledge on Narava now. He understood Jasmine not wanting to risk the Guards having an excuse to get inside the property and potentially find things better left hidden.

Raf glanced around the wide open landscape and raised his brows in question. "So… Are we waiting on this other traveler? We've only got a small window where our clearance code will work before we'll have to buy another. That'll cost you more. Hard to get a smuggler's ship out of here with clean codes."

"Second passenger will cost more, too," Sonia added.

Raf smiled. She was so mercenary. He loved having her on his crew.

Clare frowned and glanced at Longfeather. "There's something you should know first," she said. "Something that affects the way this passenger will travel. Then we'll introduce you to him."

"Don't tell me you're trying to bring a Shifter with you," Raf said. "Unless they can pull the same trick as Kira's group, that's not going to work. I can't get a Shifter through the detector rings."

"And we're not gonna try," Sonia said. "Too damned risky. We take enough risks with you as is."

"He's not a Shifter," Clare said. "Exactly."

Well that didn't sound good. "Meaning?" Raf asked.

Before she could answer, a form rose up from the grass a few feet behind Jasmine. The form twisted and bent, finally resolving into the shape of a man. A man who looked exactly like…

"Ennoren?" Raf said, gapping at the ghost. "What the hell? You're dead."

CHAPTER FIVE

Raf's brain couldn't resolve what he'd just seen, the
fact that a man who looked like Commander Ennoren, the
former *head* of the Shifter exterminations, just shifted like
one of Narava's native species…

Oh, this was so not a good thing.

"What's going on?" Sonia demanded. "He's fucking
dead. How's he standing here? How'd he shift? No way am I
letting that freak on the *Ebisu*. Fucking hell."

"Sonia," Raf warned in an undertone.

She fell silent but her lips pursed in a stubborn pout, and
the bells she'd woven into her complicated hairstyle jingled
with her chin jerk.

Raf was more concerned with the *thing* standing behind
Jasmine, staring at them with unblinking blue eyes.
"Someone needs to explain," he said. "Now. Or no one is
boarding my ship."

Longfeather glanced at the creature that looked like
Ennoren—pale blond hair, narrow thin face, sharp blue eyes

—then met Raf's stare. "He's called E," Longfeather said. "He's…different."

"No shit," Raf said.

"Shifter Research Center developed him," Clare said softly. "They built him genetically."

"Meaning?" Raf asked.

"We're only guessing," Nathan took up the tale. "My wife and her partner aren't geneticists but they have a strong working knowledge. We think they used Ennoren's dead body and inserted Shifter DNA to develop a new being. That new being is E."

"I was the fifth," the thing called E said.

Sonia jumped, just a little at the sound of E's voice. Raf kept himself from reacting outwardly, but only barely.

The thing's voice was soft and halting, and while it was hard to tell because it had been a few years since Raf had heard Ennoren speak, he'd swear E didn't sound anything like the now-dead commander. E's voice was both harsher and gentler all at once. Raf couldn't put his finger on it exactly, just that the sound was unique. And it was really weird hearing that unfamiliar voice come out of a familiar face.

"So, you're Ennoren reborn?" Sonia asked E directly, covering her surprise with arrogant bravado now.

"No. I am myself. Commander Ennoren is dead."

"Near as we can work out," Longfeather said, "this is more like breeding a new life. But the commander's dead body was used as a template as well as contributing some genetic material."

"Fucking Frankenstein," Sonia muttered.

"That's why this work is illegal," Clare said.

"Why haven't we heard about him then?" Raf demanded. "How is this planet not screaming with news of the Shifter-human… What are you? A hybrid?"

E tilted his head down and slightly to the left, giving Raf the impression E was nodding yes without actually nodding.

"Of a sort," Clare said. "And Narava isn't up in arms over this because no one outside of his creators at SRC, the Shifters of Lost City, and our group knows about him. He made himself known to us during the initial discovery of Lost City."

"We humans and the Lost City Shifters decided to keep news of E quiet for the time being," Longfeather said.

"To avoid political chaos," Raf guessed.

"And an all-out war," Longfeather said very seriously. "The news of Lost City was enough for Naravans for now."

Raf could see that. The Shifters were a hugely volatile topic on this planet. Their extermination had been government sanctioned for a long time, decades in Naravan time. The discovery of Lost City had altered the direction of the winds on the extermination debate—a change that began with Kira and David more than two and a half years ago—and now most of the population was against the killings. But the debate continued and nothing had been settled. If the population learned of E, fear might drive them back toward wanting to destroy all the Shifters on the planet. And from what he'd heard, the Lost City Shifters weren't passive and harmless like ordinary Shifters. They weren't likely to allow themselves to just be slaughtered without retaliating.

Given that Shifters could be anything, anywhere, and without a detector humans wouldn't know, Raf didn't give the human population high odds in that kind of a war.

"But the bastards who did this," Sonia said, nodding at E. "They'll do it again. What's stopping them? It's gross. Those assholes should be stopped."

"That's being investigated," Longfeather assured.

Raf narrowed his gaze and studied the mercenary. "Investigated, huh? Privately?"

Longfeather nodded. "Quietly. Don't worry. We have no intention of letting this kind of experimentation continue unchecked."

Longfeather looked pretty serious. And since Narava wasn't Raf's home planet, this wasn't his business anyway. He'd leave policing Shifter experimentation to the locals. What he was most concerned with was how this affected him and his ship.

"We won't be able to get him off-planet," he pointed out the obvious again. "Not through the detector rings."

Without commenting, E suddenly shifted shapes. Where the strange man had stood, now a solid, large transport container sat in the grass, looking for all the universe like an ordinary metal box. A blink later the thin, blond man had returned. His light blue eyes were serious and devoid of anything Raf might call emotion. E blinked slowly, but that was the only show of expression on his otherwise neutral face.

Raf sucked in a sharp breath. "Kira said that mutation only happened in a single line. And they got that entire line off-planet when they left."

Most Naravan Shifters could only change into organic shapes. And detectors could identify a Shifter in any organic form. But metallic, non-organic shapes could elude detection —primarily because the mutation which enabled Shifters to take a non-organic shape was new, and as far as Raf understood, confined to a single line. E shouldn't have been able to change into a metal box unless somehow the Shifter DNA used had come from the right line.

"We're not sure why he's able to take non-organic forms," Longfeather said. "E doesn't know either. There are several possible explanations, and until we get our hands on the original notes on E's development, we won't be able to say."

"I take it someone is looking into that, too," Raf said.

Longfeather nodded.

Something, some almost imperceptible movement, drew Raf's attention to Clare. Her gaze was sharp, her body seemingly relaxed, but he could practically feel the tension coming from her. Excitement maybe? He couldn't be sure. But whatever it was, talk of E's development was of specific interest to her. Clare was part of the Shifter support group that discovered Lost City, which meant she already knew all this about E. Why the excitement?

More questions for the mysterious woman.

Raf returned to studying E. "You want to bring something that looks like Ennoren to Kira. That seems like a stupid idea. She's gonna shoot him again. Mind explaining why you want to take him along."

Clare exchanged another look with Longfeather, and Longfeather nodded at her to explain.

"The head of my group," Clare said, "he thinks Kira needs to know about E as well as Lost City."

"Why?"

"Because I have her image in my head," E said.

Raf straightened. "A memory?"

Clare shook her head. "After a lot of work with other Shifters, we're certain it's not a memory. The images of Kira and David Cario were planted in E's mind."

Raf's temper, usually well controlled, started to heat. "I am not taking an assassin to Kira." He glared at her cousins, wondering why they'd agreed to this mad plan. How could Kira's former associates *want* to send an assassin to her?

"He's not programmed to respond to Kira or David in any particular way," Longfeather assured. "We've tested him. A lot."

"We would never put Kira or David in danger," Clare said.

Her sincerity surprised Raf for some reason.

"Still don't know why he has to come along," Sonia put in. She looked E up and down with a snarl. "Doubt Farseaker will want to meet a science experiment that looks like her ex-husband."

"Who she killed," Raf added.

"We've discussed all this a lot," Clare said. "Among people closer to Kira than you. We aren't doing this on a whim. Kira needs to know about this, needs to know what was done with her ex-husband's body."

"So send her a fucking vid-note," Sonia said.

"She won't believe unless she sees him in person," Clare said. "And E needs to meet Kira in person. He needs to learn where his human genes came from. She's the best person to tell him that."

"Why? Why any of this?" Raf wasn't buying it. There was some other reason behind this. Something they weren't telling him. And he wasn't allowing E on his ship without an honest explanation. There was only so far his love of liars went, and it didn't extend to unnecessarily endangering his crew. They only got paid enough for necessary levels of danger. "You're running out of time to make the departure window. Truth now or we're leaving."

Longfeather raised his brows and looked at Clare expectantly.

"We have to get E off-planet," Clare said.

"His creators are looking for him," Longfeather said. "And it looks like someone else, outside of Shifter Research Center, has learned about him too. There's a separate party on the hunt. We don't want either getting their hands on him."

"They would not survive it," E said with absolutely no sign of emotion.

Longfeather glanced at E, then faced Raf. "And if they somehow managed to survive and reclaim E, they might… finish his programming."

Raf stared at Longfeather. "You mean turning him into a full-blown assassin."

"He's already an assassin," Longfeather said. "We just don't want him focused on anyone in particular."

"And what makes you think he won't kill off our entire crew if he feels like it," Sonia spat. She half turned so she was facing Raf without losing sight of E. "We can't take him, Raf. He's too dangerous."

Raf turned his stare on E. The thing stared back without blinking. "When you 'made yourself know' to Longfeather at Lost City," Raf said, "what were you doing?"

"Hunting Shifters," E answered.

"Did you kill many?"

"I killed no Shifters."

"Who did you kill?"

"Soldiers. The ones that came to destroy the city."

"Why?"

E paused for a long moment, as if thinking. "Nathan Longfeather wanted the city and the Shifters protected. He wanted Ti'ann Jones protected. I was helping. I could do what he could not."

Raf raised his brows. Not exactly the answer he expected. "So if Nathan Longfeather tells you *not* to kill my crew, will you listen to him?"

"I have no reason to kill your crew, Raf Tygran. Unless they attempt to kill me."

"He'll be okay," Clare stepped in.

Raf heard a very slight edge of desperation in her voice, just the barest hint of it. This trip was important to her, Raf knew that already, and she was desperate to keep him from backing out.

"He just admitted to killing humans," Raf said.

"He doesn't just kill randomly," Clare said. "He has to have a reason."

"He was hunting Shifters. Why should we believe he won't try to kill the Kierna'Rhoan Shifters?" Raf said.

"I do not hunt Shifters anymore," E said. "I…need them. To learn what I am. Why I am this way."

"He wants to talk to the Kierna'Rhoan Shifters," Clare said, "not hunt them."

"And we do need him off-planet," Longfeather said. "You're right to think he's dangerous. He is. Very. And right now, he's able to choose how to use his abilities. He's chosen to side with us, not to go back to his creators. We need to keep that balance."

"I should have charged you double," Raf said to the

group in general. "Triple."

"Quadruple," Sonia said.

"You get me back from Kierna'Rhoan," Clare said, "and there will be more money. I promise."

Raf almost smiled. She was bluffing. Not quite a full-blown lie, though. She wanted to be able to fulfill that promise. She just wasn't entirely sure she'd be able to. She was good, she hid her truths well, but he was so used to reading people's expressions, she couldn't hide completely from him.

Longfeather spoke up. "I realize this wasn't part of the original deal. To be honest, I didn't think Clare would convince you to take the job. We had another plan in place for E. But this will work out better."

"What was your alternate plan?" Raf asked.

"Get him off-planet with one of my associates. A Binnean," Longfeather said.

"Why is my ship better?"

"I'm not sure E would do as well on Binnea," Longfeather said with a shrug. "Given their aggressive natures. We want to keep E out of any potential conflicts. He steps into the wrong situation and he's going to defend himself. The Binneans won't be happy with an outsider killing them while they're trying to kill each other."

Given the bar fight the other night, Raf could appreciate this line of logic. It also jibbed with the rumors about Binnean clan difficulties arising lately. That bar fight was no accident. Dropping something like E into that kind of charged environment could be disastrous.

"Wouldn't have to take him to Binnea," Raf pointed out. "Your associate could take him anywhere."

"Not for long," Longfeather said. "Eventually, E would

reveal himself, rumors would spread, word would get back to Narava. There aren't any other shape-shifting species in the known galaxy. There are very few places we can keep him hidden."

Raf took a slow breath and crossed his arms over his chest. He saw the logic. He also knew he wanted more money to take E onto his ship. "This is a lot more than we signed on for. If we do this, it's gonna cost. Triple the agreed fee."

Clare opened her mouth, but Longfeather raised a hand. "Done."

Clare's eyes flared wide. So. She hadn't realized Longfeather would pay more. She'd been left out of at least some of this part. Longfeather said he didn't think she'd be able to arrange this job in the first place. He didn't trust her. Not fully. Yet he was going to give her access to the Kierna'Rhoan coordinates. Why?

He started to ask, but Sonia nudged him in the ribs.

"Time," she said shortly, then turned on her ridiculously high heels and stalked back to the ship and the already-lowered starboard landing ramp.

She was right. They were out of time. He'd just have to grill Clare on board.

To Longfeather, he said, "You have the details on paying me. If the money doesn't show, I'm dropping them both off at the nearest space station. If E does anything I feel endangers my crew, I'm shooting him out into space."

"Fair enough," Longfeather said.

E's head dipped forward, his chin tucked back. Clare looked like she wanted to say something but was biting her tongue.

"The money will be transferred within the hour," Longfeather said. "I understand the importance of getting paid."

Raf nodded. Longfeather's work wasn't all that far removed from his own. "Deal then." He gestured to Clare and E. "Board. E, someone will show you to the cargo hold. You need to be shifted before we take off. If we get caught by the detectors, I will not hesitate to turn you over."

E gave him another one of those chin tucked looks without any readable emotion in his expression. But he walked toward the ship without argument.

Clare hesitated. "Nathan has to enter the Kierna'Rhoan coordinates."

Ah. Raf wondered why Longfeather would give that information to someone he didn't trust. The answer was, he wouldn't.

"My navigator will meet you at the nav-system," he said to Longfeather. With a smile, he added, "And I'm assuming you have a kill that will activate once we arrive."

Longfeather shrugged. "You'll have enough left to get back to familiar space when you leave Kierna'Rhoan. That part of the nav-coordinates will self-destruct once you're on your way."

"And I'm sure Kira's hacker, Pat, will double check to make sure that happens," Raf said with a chuckle. Pat and Sonia had a volatile *thing* which was infinitely entertaining. Yet another reason Raf was looking forward to returning to Kierna'Rhoan. And so was Sonia even if she wouldn't admit it.

Longfeather murmured something to Jasmine then

headed toward the *Ebisu*. Clare raised a brow at Raf, and he gestured her toward the ship with an extended arm.

She smiled and fell into step beside him. Having her so close started a low hum of awareness running through his skin. He'd been right about her. She was trouble.

Good thing he loved trouble as much as he loved liars.

CHAPTER SIX

They'd just cleared the detector rings when Clare noticed a tension spreading through the crew.

She'd been led to a small sitting area for takeoff, and Raf promised to return for a "chat" once they'd left the system and safely made their first jump. The sitting room was a more comfortable space than she'd been expecting on a smuggler's ship. A padded, U-shaped couch took up the center of the room, large enough to fit six humans or three Binneans comfortably, and a round activities table with a computer console embedded on the top sat in the center of the couch's curve.

Clare glanced briefly at the console but was too restless to take advantage of the various entertainments provided. To the left of the arched opening into the room was an auto-cooker unit set into the metal wall, on the opposite side a small fridge stocked with drink canisters. None of the drinks or autocooker snacks appealed to Clare just then as her own tension tightened in her gut.

Despite the cozy space, despite finally being on her way to Kierna'Rhoan, she couldn't relax. She paced circles around the couch as she waited for them to get through the last barrier between her and her destination. A barrier that wouldn't have been an issue except that they had E aboard.

When the announcement came over the internal ship's comm that they'd cleared the detectors, Clare took her first deep breath. If she'd subscribed to her father's religion, she might have even thanked a deity for the smooth passage. Her relief only lasted for a few minutes before she noticed the sudden uptick in movements by the crew past the sitting room.

She stepped out into the corridor and stopped the first crew member to pass, a short human man with dark hair and pale leathery skin. "Is something wrong?" she asked.

The man gave her a worried look. "The captain'll have to say, miss."

Before she could question him further, he ran off down the corridor, toward the rear of the ship. She tried a few more crew members on her way toward the flight deck, but they all gave her the same response. Nerves and instincts had her checking her blaster's charge before returning it to the holster on her hip.

When she got near the nav-system room, just outside the main flight deck, she heard Raf's voice seconds before he stepped into the corridor.

"You're sure this will work?" he asked the tall human man following him out of the room.

"Yeah, we'll still be able to pick up the right jump course even with the detour," the man with Raf said.

"Detour," Clare said. "What detour?"

Raf frowned when he noticed her. With a bare nod to his navigator, the man disappeared back into the small cabin holding all the navigation equipment.

"We'll still get you to Kierna'Rhoan in good time," Raf told her when they were alone. "But we need to make a stop first. I have something I have to take care of."

"What?"

"Don't worry about it. It won't affect your trip."

She slapped a hand on his shoulder as he started to turn away and swung him back to face her. "Listen, with what Nathan has agreed to pay you, I deserve an answer. We didn't discuss any detours. I need to get to Kierna'Rhoan soon. Too much time has passed already."

She realized she might have said too much when his expression sharpened. But rather than grill her, he heaved an exaggerated sigh.

"We're going two days out of the way," he said. "Tops."

"Where?" She watched him calculating how much to tell her. "I'm going to figure it out when we get there anyway. No point in lying. Besides, I'm good at digging up information. If you don't tell me, someone else will."

"Not if I tell them not to. My crew does what I say."

"You're missing the point that as soon as we land, I'll be able to figure out where we are." She narrowed her eyes. "Two days out of the way. That's got to be FarMore Station, Deven, or somewhere in the Kyoto system. Anywhere else would take too long to reach."

Raf shook his head. "Shit."

Clare raised her brows and put her hands on her hips, waiting him out.

"Fine," he said. "We're going to FarMore Station. Just a

little business to take care of."

"Business?"

"Private business."

"We're not paying you for private business."

"And I'm not charging you for the detour."

She huffed. The man was as stubborn as she was. She considered changing tack and trying for a more seductive approach, but she had a feeling Raf would see right through that. He was too adept at that angle himself. She scowled as frustration dug at her gut. She wasn't this easy to stymie under most circumstances.

Damned handsome pirate playing havoc with her priorities.

"Okay." She made a show of giving in reluctantly. "But if this takes longer than two days, I'm telling Nathan to deduct it from your fee."

"Not afraid I'll leave you behind?" he asked. "Take the money and run?"

"Nathan will take the entire fee back then. Trust me, he's got resources."

Raf chuckled. "I have no doubt. I know who I'm working with before I take on a job."

She almost smirked in reaction to that, but years of practice kept her eyes narrowed in irritation. "Don't play with me, Tygran. I'm serious. More than two days and I'll make sure your fee gets cut."

"Don't worry," he said with a confident shake of his head. "Two days. Tops."

"Hmm." She looked him up and down, making her doubt clear, exaggerating her irritated acceptance. Then she returned to the sitting room to plan.

Once they landed at FarMore Station, she'd be able to ferret out the reason for this detour. Her curiosity wouldn't allow anything else. Hell, she might get another story out of it. She'd never been one to pass up a good opportunity for another lead—even when she was in the middle of landing a legend-making story.

If she'd hesitated, she'd never have been in place to break the Lost City news. She'd been working the mob family story in the Docks when she'd met James Monroe, current head of the Shifter support group Kira Farseaker had left behind on Narava. Clare had had no idea where that first brief meeting would take her, but she knew getting inside a Shifter support group could be invaluable.

She hadn't known at the time she met him that Monroe headed Farseaker's group. Never could have imagined going to work for Monroe would lead her to an *actual* Shifter city. Before the discovery, she hadn't even known Shifters could *build* cities. But she'd taken advantage of the opportunity Monroe presented—he needed someone to head his security, but someone who wouldn't look like obvious security—and her instincts had led her to the biggest break of her career.

Listening to her instincts now, she had a feeling this little detour might also yield some interesting results. Even after she brought Farseaker and Cario back to Narava, being a legend didn't mean she'd be able to rest on her laurels. She'd still need the next story, the next break.

A part of her wondered when it would be enough. Would she ever be satisfied and able to relax? Sometimes she thought she wanted to. She knew she needed to leave Clare O'Malley behind soon. But did she want to stop with the undercover investigations?

Her gut was clear on the issue. Not yet. Not when there was still so much left to discover.

As she settled back into the comfortable couch in the sitting room and toyed with the cold drink canister from the small fridge, she smiled. Curiosity had always been a strong motivator, as well as a powerful drive to achieve greatness in her field. In some ways, she wasn't so different from her friend Ti'ann—Nathan's wife. Dr. Ti'ann Jones' curiosity had led her to science and drove her to discover and uncover mysteries, even when doing so was dangerous. Before meeting the scientist, Clare wouldn't have thought she'd have anything in common with someone like Ti'ann. After they'd single handedly tried to prevent the destruction of Lost City in one of Ti'ann's mad plans, they'd formed an unexpected bond.

She was surprised how much she cherished that friendship, because outside of her family, she didn't really have any close friends. Her job didn't allow for maintaining relationships for long.

She was going to miss Ti'ann when she had to let Clare O'Malley go.

The pain that triggered shocked her, so she forced her thoughts back to the reason she was passively sitting in this room instead of dogging Tygran's steps. She needed a plan. Raf was right. If he told his crew to keep the reason for their detour a secret, they would. She'd still make a few quiet inquiries, but his crew had already proven they'd defer to their captain. Her best option was digging deeper once they landed at FarMore.

She hadn't been to the space station before, so she didn't have any sources to tap. Turning to the computer console imbedded on the activity table, she did a search for the station's schematics. If Raf asked why she'd done the search, she'd just tell him she was looking for ways to spend her time while she was stuck there.

As she hunted for a good place to unobtrusively find information, she suddenly remembered E. Damn. She should probably check in on him now that they were beyond the detector rings.

She stared at the sitting room door and nibbled her bottom lip. E was fascinating. And she was happy to bring him along on this trip because it was yet another juicy element to add to her story, but the guy gave her the creeps. His face rarely displayed much in the way of emotion. He could turn himself into a dragon if he wanted to—a fucking fire-breathing dragon! Or a laser cannon. Or…anything. He was still pretty bad with human language, especially anything figurative. And he looked like Commander Ennoren.

She gotten close to the commander once, during another story. Not close enough for the then-head of Shifter extermi-nations to notice her, but she'd had to work in his circle for a few weeks. The commander had been pretty terrifying in his own right. He was a fanatic and fanatics scared the shit out of her. They were unpredictable and entirely too passionate in their causes. Ennoren's cause had been killing Shifters.

He'd be horrified to know what had been done to his body.

With a shiver, she refocused on the screen in front of her. As soon as she found a few places to collect information on FarMore, she'd go check on E. This wasn't stalling, she told herself. She needed to do her research now, just in case Raf decided to restrict her access to the ship's computers later.

She found two possible places to pick up good gossip—one pub near the docking bays and another one not far from the Paradise casino. Information had a way of leaking out when inebriation or serious financial losses were involved. Or both. There were always tantalizing bits of information floating around docking bays, so that was an obvious place to start. The casino districts on FarMore would provide a lot of opportunity too, but she wouldn't have time to be in too many places at once. Since Paradise was one of the largest casinos, she'd try someplace near there first.

And if she found any enticing leads, she'd follow them.

Once she'd memorized the layout of the station, the location of the pubs, and double checked the most recent stories about the station so she knew what she was getting into, she turned away from the console and contemplated the corridor.

Time to check on E.

Without conscious thought, she touched the blaster at her hip, reassuring herself it was there. Though given what E could do, she'd never get to the weapon in time to protect herself. A blaster was likely useless against E anyway. But its presence gave her some measure of comfort.

She recognized she was still stalling when another few minutes had passed and she had yet to stand. She was getting soft. Shaking her head, she pushed off the couch and headed toward the cargo bay. She wasn't even sure if E had changed back to his natural shape yet.

Or if Raf had warned his crew about E.

Shit. That could lead to some awkward situations if the crew weren't prepared. She changed direction and went in search of Raf again.

CHAPTER SEVEN

Clare found the sexy pirate coming out of the flight deck. "Is E a secret or have you told everyone?" she asked without preamble.

Raf's brows rose and a crooked grin tilted his mouth. The look was a little too charming for her peace of mind.

"No secret," he said. "Couldn't keep a secret like that on this ship if I wanted to. Which I don't."

She nodded. "Good. I was going to check on him but… Well, anyway, I'll go check on him now."

"Tell him not to disrupt my crew's work or I'll confine him to the hold."

"You tell him that," she muttered, not able to hide her discomfort with E.

That earned her a narrow-eyed stare. He put his hands on his hips and studied her for an uncomfortable moment during which she tried desperately not to squirm.

"Don't like him either, huh?" Raf said.

"It's not that I don't like him. He actually saved my life

once. Kind of. It's just… Ennoren? Of all people he's got to look like Commander Ennoren? It's creepy."

"Agreed. You have some personal experience with the commander?"

"Not directly."

When she didn't explain further, he shrugged. "How'd E save your life?"

"He turned into a dragon," she said, still awed by the sight of that giant creature from Earth mythology spitting ropes of fire from the sky. She blinked and refocused on Raf. "When the government was quietly trying to destroy Lost City, Nathan's wife and I found ourselves in a position of trying to stop attack ships from getting off the ground. Just us and our blasters against trained soldiers. And Ti'ann is a horrible shot. Stupidest damned thing I've ever done."

"Gutsy though."

"Ti'ann is crazy." She smiled fondly. "Anyway, we weren't very successful, as you might guess, and then suddenly this dragon descends out of the skies and wipes out…everything. Machine, human, everything in that clearing was crisped." She shivered. "E did it for Ti'ann, to protect her because Nathan would want her protected. For some reason, E has formed a kind of bond with Nathan and none of us are going to argue with it because it means E is on our side."

"Bad kind of enemy to have," Raf agreed. "Especially if he can wipe out a contingent of soldiers and their ships so easily."

"Which is why we try to stay on his good side."

"You worried about him on this trip?"

She stared at Raf, wondering if she should lie. Then

decided truth, in this case, would be to her benefit. "I wouldn't ever let your guard down around E. His sense of right and wrong is…flexible."

"Well then he fits right in with this crew."

The comment startled a laugh out of her. "Okay, fair point. But really, just be careful. He's so unique he's impossible to predict. So far, he's been an asset."

"You think he'll hurt Kira?"

"No. No one would have let him travel to her location if they thought that. E is curious about her, but he has no interest in hurting her."

"Good," Raf said, "because if he did, I'd have no problems launching him into space." He frowned. "Would he survive that?"

"No idea. And I'd rather not have to test it. If he did survive, he'd be pretty pissed afterward."

Raf tilted his head and his brows rose. "That wouldn't be good."

"You want to talk to him?" she said, then bit the inside of her cheek. She couldn't believe she was asking him to come with her, like she needed his protection or something. Raf was no better equipped to defend himself against E than she was. She, at least, had seen what E could do first hand. She'd more likely be the one protecting Raf. But still… Having him with her while she checked on the Shifter-human hybrid seemed more comforting that it should have been.

To her chagrin, Raf seemed to realize her intent and his sexy smile teased her. But he didn't torment her or draw out his answer.

"Sure," he said. "Got a few things I'd like to ask him

anyway." As they turned back toward the cargo bay, he added, "And you."

"Me?"

"Yes, Ms. O'Malley. I think we have a few things to discuss."

"Can't imagine what." Her stomach danced a bit but she hid the reaction. "Unless you're going to tell me why we're detouring to FarMore."

He snorted. "Persistent, aren't you?"

"No more than you'd be."

He shrugged in agreement. "Let's just say I have some older business to deal with."

"I should be worried, shouldn't I?"

"Probably."

He spoke with a complete lack of real concern for her worry and that made her grin.

"Why you?" he asked as they reached the lift that took them down to the hold.

"Why me what?" She frowned.

"Why are *you* the one going to get Farseaker and Cario? You're not related. You're not one of their original group. I'd guess they don't even know you."

"What makes you think that?" She kept her tone neutral, mildly curious, attempting not to give more away than she wanted to.

"I know you started working with the Shifter support group under Monroe."

She grunted. "You know more than you should." But she'd half expected him to dig into her background. That was why "Clare O'Malley" had such an extensive history.

"Docks is a hot bed of good gossip when you know who to ask," he said.

"I know," she muttered. As the lift doors opened, she made a show of admitting, "I wasn't part of Kira's original group, that's true."

"So why you? Why not Monroe, or someone else Kira would know personally? She's got no reason to trust you. And to top that off you're bringing something that looks like her dead ex-husband. You're gonna be lucky if she doesn't stun you and send you back without even speaking to you."

That was the part of all this that had taken her so long to set up. Raf was right on every point. Why her? She'd spent months not only convincing Monroe that Kira needed to know about Lost City—the easy part of the whole business— but convincing him *she* was the one to go bring Kira back to Narava.

Then she'd had to talk Nathan around to her side. Without him, she could never have gotten to Kierna'Rhoan, even if Monroe approved, because Monroe didn't know where Kira had gone. They'd arranged that on purpose so he couldn't give her away, even if the government arrested him. The only thing Monroe knew was that Kira had left Narava with no intention of ever coming back.

Nathan had been the key. And he in turn had required Raf. But before that, she'd had to convince them *she* could be trusted to do this.

Because her logic had worked on the others, she gave those same reasons to Raf. "I don't have any ties to Farseaker or Cario. Even if I'm tagged as part of a Shifter support group now, I don't have a direct relationship with Kira and

David. So why would I be the one sent to bring them home? Your very question is the reasons I'm the perfect candidate."

"You think the people looking for Kira won't consider you're going off-planet to find her?"

"That's why I went off-planet with a smuggler." She grinned, her flirty grin, and blinked slowly up at him. The look had felled stronger men. And she wanted Raf distracted from his line of questioning. If he felt he had the answers, he'd stop digging, and she needed him to stop thinking about all this.

He smiled back, that look that said he knew more than she wanted him to. "You don't think anyone knows you're gone?"

"Not yet. I've gone to a lot of trouble to make sure it looks like I'm still on-planet for at least another week. By that time, anyone interested won't have any idea what's happened to me."

"You didn't come to me just because I could get you off-planet without anyone knowing."

"You knew that already. I needed you." She decided to give him a little truth to keep him distracted. "Nathan insisted you were the pilot. If I wasn't able to convince you to take the job, he wouldn't have given me the coordinates to Kier-na'Rhoan."

Raf barked out a laugh. "I knew it. I knew you couldn't go to another pilot."

"Yeah, yeah. You were right. And here I am on the way to where I need to go. So it's all worked out. You even ended up with triple the fee."

"Which brings us to our current destination." He stopped outside the cargo bay and faced her. "This…thing I've carrying aboard my ship. This is a big deal. That he even exists."

"Yeah, it is," she said.

"Who's really after him? Longfeather said other parties besides his creators were looking."

She considered prevaricating. She only "officially" knew the answer to this because Nathan thought she was Monroe's security—which she sort of was, even if that was just her cover. But again, a little truth could keep Raf from seeing the lies, so she shrugged.

"We don't know exactly. Just hints. But from what we've uncovered, we think they've got government connections, maybe worked for the government during the Lost City incident. This hunt, though, they're doing without government sanction."

"How do you know that?"

"Because someone from the government is trying to figure out who they are, too."

Raf's brows rose. "You know who the government people are?"

"We're pretty sure Senator Johnson is heavily involved."

"His aide was blamed for the attack on Lost City."

She nodded. "But have you seen the man in interviews? He wouldn't have done anything without the senator's approval. Unfortunately, the senator is incredibly smart and he's covered his involvement well. There's no actual evidence to connect him to his aide's anti-Shifter efforts."

"Johnson is on record as still being adamantly for the continuation of the exterminations. At least he was until Lost City."

"You know a lot about Naravan politics," she commented.

"I know a lot about what's happening anywhere I do business. It's how I've survived so long."

She lightly tapped the bay door. "Shall we go see how E is doing?"

He frowned at her change of subject, but nodded. As he swiped open the door, though, he murmured near her ear. "We'll talk about this more later."

Well hell. Her attempt to keep him distracted wasn't working. When his hand settled at her back to guide her into the bay, her stomach tightened. The chemistry between them was no small thing, which made all this a lot more complicated. Playing him was never going to be easy, not with his years successfully maneuvering through the criminal class, but the way she kept getting distracted every time he touched her was muddling her thinking, opening her up to making mistakes with him.

Although…

She considered the spark between them, and that it went both ways if that kiss the other night was any indication. If she seduced him, she could keep him from asking too many questions. From the way his fingers flexed against her back, inching just a little too low to be polite, she was sure he'd allow her to take him to bed.

The question was, could she do it and not get overly involved?

She only ever used her sexuality in a surface way while she was on a job, as a distraction. But she didn't randomly sleep with people who were important to one of her stories. Too much could go wrong. She could be found out. She could cross one of the few ethical lines she'd promised herself she wouldn't cross to get the job done.

She could fall in love.

No, she was better off not going the route of sleeping with Raf. Flirtation and teasing were one thing. Opening herself to anything else… She didn't dare take that risk. She had too many other things to juggle.

As she and Raf got deeper into the bay, one of the most dangerous of those other things emerged silently from behind a large cargo container not a meter away.

CHAPTER EIGHT

CLARE SUPPRESSED A SHIVER, THE REACTION SHE ALWAYS GOT when coming face to face with E, especially this close to him. His gaze remained steady on her and Raf. Not even a hint of emotion showed in his expression. Her gaze dropped briefly to his arm—an arm Nathan had told her E had shifted to a laser cannon—before she jerk her attention back to E's face.

"How are you?" she asked, forcing a pleasant tone. The cool, recycled air of the cargo bay felt several degrees colder as she tried to hold E's gaze. "Any problems with the take off?"

"No."

She waited a beat for more but she knew E was a…man? …of few words, so she went on. "You can come out of the bay now if you like. And the captain has a few questions for you."

E looked at Raf and tilted his head down. His thinking pose. "You are a pirate?"

Raf chuckled. "Smuggler is the word used most often."

"Smugglers have no honor."

"Depends on the smuggler. We have a code. Of a sort."

"Like Nathan Longfeather? He was a mercenary. But he had a code."

"Just so," Raf said with a slight dip of his head. "And you, Mr. E? Do you have a code of honor?"

"I am only learning the meaning of honor. I had a code, which was given to me by the scientists at SRC. But I have decided I don't wish to follow that code."

"Can't say as I blame you for that," Raf said. "What code do you follow now?"

"I am still deciding."

"Well, that can't be good," Raf said.

"He's been following Nathan around a lot," Clare said, trying to deflect some of Raf's tension, obvious in his tightening shoulders if not anywhere else. "And spending time in Lost City," she added. "He's learning from them."

Raf considered E for a silent minute. E stared back without blinking. Clare hated when E did that. It made him look so obviously *not* human. Although, since he wasn't human…

A hand gesture from Raf broke the staring contest. "I'll show you around the ship."

Since she hadn't gotten a tour yet either, she wasn't about to miss this. The *Ebisu* was a fantastic 12KZ, small enough to maneuver on-planet, large enough to carry cargo and passengers. Perfect for smuggling. She was sure there were hidden compartments, and secrets everywhere, and it was almost impossible for her to resist her natural curiosity for uncovering those secrets.

Raf was obviously proud of his ship, pointing out the

highlights as he took them through the public areas, including a comfortable canteen that felt more like the kitchen in a house, and the state of the art navigation system. He did not give them a tour of the flight deck or the engineering systems. She wasn't surprised, though she wondered what made him think E couldn't get into those areas any time he wanted.

E, for his part, listened closely and actually asked a few questions. She hadn't thought about it before the tour, but this was his first time on an interstellar vessel. And he showed a great deal of interest in everything to do with the ship. Mostly the tactical capabilities and weapons, but also the mundane things like hold capacity and jump interval requirements.

"It will take us two weeks to reach our destination," E said in a way that was a question without being a question.

"Actually," Clare said, "we have to detour. To FarMore Station."

"Why?" E asked.

Clare raised her brows at Raf.

"I have another bit of business that needs to be taken care of," Raf said. "Last minute stuff."

"Will you require my assistance?" E asked. "I am very good at…many things."

Raf actually stopped in his tracks halfway back to the sitting room where he'd first settled Clare and turned to stare at E.

"You know, I just bet you are good at a lot of things," he said, considering the Shifter-human hybrid with narrowed eyes.

"He's not here to work for you," Clare put in. She didn't trust that look on Raf's face. "He's a paying customer."

"He offered," Raf said.

"That doesn't mean you should take him up on it," Clare said. "Remember, we're supposed to be keeping him a secret. Everyone in the galaxy knows about Naravan Shifters. They'll recognize what he is. He'll draw too much attention."

"I won't if I do not shift in front of others," E said.

"Then what use are you?" Raf asked. Not rudely, but with genuine curiosity. "What do you do when you aren't shifting?"

E tilted his head down again and didn't speak for long moments. Finally, he said, "I am very good with weapons. Even ones I do not shift into."

Raf whistled at that admission. "You can shift into weapons? Like blasters?"

E dipped his head once. "Any weapon."

"That is some impressive talent, E," Raf said. "Shame we can't use it."

Clare glared at Raf. The way he said that last sentence made it sound like he didn't entirely believe it. But using E's Shifter skills would be disastrous.

"We're not paying you to bring attention to us," Clare said. "I mean it, Tygran. E's existence needs to be kept a secret." Until *she* got the chance to break his story. No way was she letting word of him leak out before she was allowed to present him to the galaxy. She'd been working that angle for too long. This was her story.

Raf raised his hands in surrender. "No need to get excited, O'Malley. I was just considering his talents." He faced E. "Thank you for the offer. But we won't be on the station long enough to need your help. This is just a quick stop to take care of a little issue, then we'll be on our way."

"You ever going to admit what that 'little issue' is?" Clare asked to distract Raf from E's talents.

"Nothing to worry about," Raf said.

In a way that made Clare worry.

"E," Raf said, "I'll show you to the cabin we've had made up for you."

He looked Clare over, his expression dropping into a lazy grin she should have found annoying but instead found kind of sexy. Although she wasn't about to let him know that.

"You need any help settling in? Unpacking?" he said, his voice low.

"I'm just fine," she said firmly. If she wasn't going to seduce him for her own ends, she sure as hell wasn't going to let *him* seduce *her* to suit his plans.

"You know where to find me if you need anything," he said. "Anything at all."

Clare scowled at his back as he and E walked away. The man was a scoundrel with a capital S.

Despite telling himself to wait for Clare to come to him, Raf still found himself wandering the ship, well after everyone but the night crew had gone to bed, looking for her. He went to her cabin first—dangerous, that—and when he didn't find her, went to the common areas of the ship.

He found her in the canteen, talking with one of the technicians. Delilah had been with the *Ebisu* for years, almost as long as Sonia. Raf had a soft spot for the older woman with her scarred soul running deeper than the facial scars she refused to give up.

His protectiveness asserted itself for a brief moment while he eavesdropped on their conversation. He didn't take kindly to people trying to use or abuse his crew. But it was clear Clare was just chatting in a friendly way, no hunting for information, no attempts at manipulating Delilah—not that anyone could. In fact, Clare was busy regaling the technician with a colorful story of her time as a stripper in the Docks.

He finally stepped into the canteen with a smile for both women. "Gossiping about me, are you?"

Delilah rolled her pretty green eyes at him. "So arrogant. How do you get away with it?"

"I'm very handsome," he said. "I'm supposed to be arrogant."

That earned him a snort of amusement and a soft smile. Delilah had been through a lot in her childhood, things she never talked about these days and had only admitted to him and Sonia once, a long time ago after a substantial amount of alcohol had been consumed. But the smiles had been few and far between when Delilah had first joined the *Ebisu*. Now when she let one slip, it made his heart happy.

Delilah and Clare were sitting at the canteen's long, rectangular metal table, a place that could accommodate the full twelve-person crew, including the three Binneans. A couple of long benches and a scattering of padded chairs were arranged haphazardly around the table, magnetic feet keeping everything secured to the floor but still moveable —couldn't have loose furniture on a ship that might lose gravity suddenly, but he liked flexibility in the common areas. Delilah and Clare were at the far end of the table, in a couple of the chairs, close enough to talk easily, two mugs between them. The rest of the canteen was empty, and the lighting was low and intimate, adjusted for the late hour.

Delilah glanced between him and Clare then rose slowly to her feet, taking her mug of what looked and smelled like coffee—but knowing Delilah probably had a healthy shot of Binnean brandy in it—to the kitchen.

"Got a few last things to do before I sleep," she said as

she set the mug into the cleaning unit. "Goodnight, Captain. Night, Clare. Thanks for the stories."

Clare nodded her goodbyes and waited for him to take Delilah's seat across the table from her.

"You're up late," he said. "Ship's time throwing you off?"

She shrugged. "This is my first time off-planet. I'm enjoying the experience. I can sleep when I'm an old lady."

"If you get to be an old lady."

"Well, if I don't, I won't regret missing the sleep the way I might regret savoring life."

He touched a pretend hat brim. "Fair enough. Must admit, I feel the same way."

"That's not why you're up late."

"No. Captain's the last to sleep. First to rise." He paused, then grinned. "Well, outside of the night shift."

She chuckled and ducked her head, breaking eye contact. The move gave him a chance to study her unobserved for a few seconds. She really was stunningly beautiful. Pale, rosy skin, that riot of red hair, sharp, dark brown eyes. But that smattering of freckles across her nose… Sexy as all hell.

When she glanced back up, he didn't try to hide his perusal. "What's a stripper from the Docks doing working as security for a Shifter support group?"

She raised her brows and shrugged. "I'm an ace shot."

Said without a hint of boasting, he noticed, so it must be true.

"And I don't look like I should be security," she continued. "Gives me an edge."

Ah. Some pieces fell into place. "You were working security when you were stripping, weren't you?"

She smiled. "Wondered if you'd figured that out."

"Who?"

"The owner of the club. A big bad among his particular family. I was protecting his girl-on-the-side. She worked there and was getting threats from one of the other families. They were trying to get her to talk out of turn."

"Ah. And I take it she didn't want to turn spy."

"Oh no, her loyalty could be bought. But she didn't want to end up dead."

"Did she hire you or did her man?"

She slid down in her seat and toyed with the smooth metal of the tabletop, considering a spot he couldn't see.

"She approached me first," Clare said. "He agreed to the hire. He didn't know the part about her loyalty being flexible, obviously. He just thought she wanted his protection. In fact, he liked that she went to him. And he loved the idea of an undercover bodyguard."

"Why not just obviously be her bodyguard?" He watched her closely as he asked. She wasn't looking at him and he wondered if she was purposefully leaving something out of the story. Funny. He was used to reading people. And he knew Clare wasn't totally honest. But he was having a hard time figuring her out. There was a lot more there. Lies on lies intertwined with enough truths he couldn't quite tell them apart.

The challenge of her eased through his bloodstream like a shot of old-fashioned whiskey, dampening his resistance, heightening his thrill-seeking impulses.

"The boss didn't want me to be obvious," Clare said, "because he wanted to draw out the individuals from the other family threatening her. If he put an obvious guard on her, the rival family would know he was onto them. At that point, she becomes useless and the rivals either kill her outright or back off."

"What happened in the end?"

She tilted her head and finally met his gaze. "She was safe right up until the moment a skirmish between the two families started. Then she escaped off-planet, without her man's help or knowledge. I quit to go to work for Monroe and his people. And a small war broke out between the families."

"I remember that. You got out just before things got bad. Good timing."

"It was Tilly's timing, not mine. I'd have still been there protecting her if she hadn't run away."

"And her man didn't blame you?"

"He couldn't. Tilly ran when a second guard was watching her. Not my shift, not my fault."

"There was more than one of you?"

"Of course. Can't be on guard for a full cycle every day." She lifted the side of her mouth in a crooked smile. "I knew she'd run, though. She didn't tell me directly. So I could be perfectly honest when I said I had no idea what she'd planned. But it was obvious she was getting rabbity."

"And you're sure she didn't defect to the other family? Or wasn't killed?"

"Oh, I'm sure. She was good enough to drop me a quick vid-call once she was safe. We got friendly while I was protecting her."

"I bet you have that effect on people. They get to know you, start to trust you…" He was baiting her, just to see what she'd say. There was something slightly off in her story, but he just couldn't put his finger on it.

She snorted and met his gaze. "Do you trust me?"

"I don't know you that well yet."

"You don't strike me as the trusting type."

"I'm not."

"So what type are you, Tygran? I get a feeling there's more to you than just the handsome pirate."

He straightened and grinned at her compliment. "See, I knew you thought I was handsome."

She rolled her eyes. "Since I don't want to add to your arrogance, let's just say you're not terribly difficult to look at."

He preened a little just to see her smile, which she tried to hide. Then said, "You and Delilah seemed to get along well. Not everyone can talk with her so comfortably so fast, or her with them. She's careful of people."

"She's a nice woman. Strong. I like her."

"The fact that she sat here with you speaks to her liking you, too. That can't be good for me."

That earned him an outright laugh. "You are something, Tygran. You got anything to drink around here? I could use a little more than the spiked coffee Delilah was drinking." She frowned, as if considering, then groaned. "I need some food, too. Don't suppose you have anything easy, a nutrition bar maybe? I'm not really hungry, but I need the calories."

Her phrasing sparked his interest. He went to the kitchen cabinets and dug up a nutrition bar. After tossing it to her, and appreciating her reflexes when she caught it effortlessly, he pulled out a secret bottle of Deven whiskey from a high storage locker filled with infrequently used utensils. He got two glasses from another cupboard while Clare finished off the bar in quick, efficient bites.

When he poured out her drink, he said, "Sorry if that wasn't to your taste."

"What do you mean?" She lifted her glass and sniffed, savoring, before taking a drink. "Oh wow. What is this? I've never had it before."

"Deven whiskey."

She whistled. "Expensive."

"That's why it's hidden from the rest of my crew," he said. "You didn't seem to enjoy that bar much. I could have gotten you real food."

"No, it's not that," she said. "I just wasn't hungry."

"Then why eat?" He studied her as she continued to take tiny sips of the whiskey, her eyes closing as she inhaled deeply with each drink. He liked the way she savored it, giving the expensive alcohol its proper reverence. And he couldn't help but wonder what else she might savor in just that way.

"As I said," she broke into his reverie, "I needed the food. Now it's your turn."

"My turn to eat?" He raised his brows.

"Your turn to tell me something about yourself."

"I don't recall agreeing to an exchange of information."

"Why did you get into smuggling?" she asked.

"The usual reasons."

She waited him out, eyebrows raised. He was tempted to remain silent just to keep her curious, but he had a feeling her curiosity wouldn't be so easily deterred.

"Money," he said. "Lots and lots of potential for money."

"Easier ways to earn."

"I had a talent for this work. And they always say if you do what you love, the money will follow."

"I thought it was 'you'd never work a day in your life'."

"That too."

"So… You don't work, and you make money?"

He grinned. "Actually, I work pretty hard."

"And the money?"

"Depends on the job."

"I think there's more to your story," she said, her eyes narrowed.

"Why?"

"You're handsome."

The comment startled a laugh from him. "True enough. But why does that mean there should be more to my story?"

"Handsome can do a lot for you. You didn't have to go into smuggling to make money."

Smart woman. That was one of the many questions he had for her, too, considering how stunning she was.

"I grew up on Jenolon," he said, matter-of-factly. Something he'd spent years working on—being able to say his home planet's name without any hint of the resentment and anger he felt toward the place. The bitterness that mixed with a strange melancholy in his gut never showed in his tone or expression anymore.

Her eyes widened. It was universally acknowledged by those who didn't grow up on Jenolon that it was one of the worst planets in the galaxy to live on. Second only to Gy'lee —the planet with an atmosphere that killed most humans, or mutated the few that survived into Leeches. Given the effects of Gy'lee on humans, having Jenolon in the same category spoke to the cesspool his home planet was. From Clare's expression, she was well aware of all the rumors about the place, too.

"How did you even get off Jenolon?" she asked. "I thought the inhabitants rarely left."

"Almost never," he agreed. He sipped at his whiskey as he thought back to those early years, things he'd prefer to forget. "I got lucky."

"You wanted to leave?"

"From the time I was nine years old. I stowed away on a ship that need repairs when the only inhabited planet nearby was Jenolon." He leaned back in his chair. "Poor sods couldn't get out of there fast enough. So when they discovered me, they were perfectly happy not returning to that place just to get me off their ship."

"How old were you?"

"Fourteen."

"A kid."

"Old enough." Almost too old. Almost beyond help. But he didn't say any of that out loud. "The captain of that first ship was kind. I got lucky with that, too. Not all captains are that way with stowaways." He rolled his glass back and forth between his palms. "He taught me the trade."

"Smuggling?"

He nodded, smiling a little at the memories of Captain Bael drilling him on the life or death necessity of secret-keeping.

"And your family on Jenolon?" Clare asked. "Ever seen them again?"

"They wouldn't want to see me again after I left. Once you're exposed to the outer galaxy, you're no longer considered pure enough to touch 'the sacred ground'."

Her nose wrinkled. "Zealots."

He agreed with her assessment.

"You did get lucky, though," she said. "Lots of stories about runaways not doing so well."

And he'd been thanking that luck every day since his escape.

But because his early years were not exactly his favorite topic, and he was starting to feel the creeping moroseness that came with those memories, he decided to get back to discussing Clare. He'd rather think about the mystery of her than anything to do with Jenolon.

"How about you?" he asked with a deep, cleansing breath, followed by another sip of the fiery whiskey. "You grew up on Narava. Still have family there?"

"Huge family," she admitted with a very genuine smile.

So that was a truth. Interesting. "How many?"

"Two older brothers, one younger, and three younger sisters."

He whistled. "Wow, that's some family. How'd your parents manage so many small humans?"

"My mom was very organized. And brave."

"You love them. Had a good childhood." He didn't need to ask, it was obvious in her voice.

"Yeah. Good childhood. Lots of noise and love and support."

He liked the way her expression softened when she talked about her family. Her full mouth turned up just a little. Her eyes took on a distant look. In that moment, he was pretty sure he was looking at the real woman beneath the Clare O'Malley mask.

He was tempted to probe deeper, maybe even see if he could get her real name. But before he could, she blinked and the mask fell back into place. She pursed her lips, studying her now empty glass.

"Guess I'm more tired than I thought," she said. "Whiskey went right to my head." She set the glass down and braced her hands on the table to lever herself up. "Thanks for the drink and the chat, Captain. Have a good night."

He remained seated but leaned farther back in his chair to meet her gaze. "You too, Ms. O'Malley. We reach the station mid-day tomorrow ship's time. If you're inclined, the shopping is pretty spectacular."

She chuckled. "That sounds tempting. Think I will explore a bit."

He grinned and tipped his glass at her in goodbye as she sauntered out. He didn't even pretend he wasn't watching her ass as she went. His smile widened when she put an extra swing in her hips. She was some woman.

Whoever the hell she was.

CHAPTER TEN

FARMORE SPACE STATION WAS MIDWAY BETWEEN NARAVA and Deven, within easy range of Binnea, and only two jumps from the Kyoto system, putting it in an ideal location to receive a lot of galactic travelers. It was as high tech as a space station came, had an "open and neutral" policy, which meant anyone from anywhere could board the station. And because of that open atmosphere, FarMore was a bastion of both pleasure seekers and the business-minded alike. The station boasted some of the best casino resorts in the galaxy. It was also an ideal place for those who wanted to conduct business that may or may not be entirely legal. While FarMore abided by Trade Law outwardly, and had their own security force to ensure things remained peaceful on the station, no one dug into the details of the business being done here *unless* it caused trouble.

The set up was absolutely ideal for an information hunter like Clare.

After Raf and Sonia left the *Ebisu* with two of their

human crew and one of the Binneans, Clare made her way to the pub near the docking bay to gather gossip.

She'd dressed in her "prosperous mercenary" clothes—fitted black pants tucked into chunky boots that could crush a man's throat, a tight silky blue shirt to show off her cleavage under a heavy black faux-leather jacket accented with silver studs on the shoulders and arms. She kept her blaster prominently strapped in a holster at her hip, and by the time she'd cleared the *Ebisu's* exit ramp, she had slipped into an appropriate attitude and walk that would add to the illusion of her being a mercenary. She'd be able to move around the station and listen in on conversations without being noticed or bothered in this guise.

Out of habit, she listened to people talking around her as she crossed the docking bay toward the main station corridor, attention primed for any interesting tidbits of information. The really good stuff didn't come until she'd reached the pub, though. Once there, she'd barely ordered a drink before she heard people talking about the Leeches.

"Hate their kind," a woman said, then spit on the floor.

"Can't believe anyone carries them after what happened on the *Venture*."

"Terrible. I hear it was Binneans brought them in this time."

"No way. Binneans are too attached to their tech. No way they'd risk Leeches aboard."

"What self-respecting human would transport them?"

"I hear they're developing tech they can manipulate."

"Na. I hear it's drugs."

"Drugs? What the hell are you talking about?"

"Drugs. They're drugging humans to get them to do what they want."

"It's money, you morons. Plain and simple."

"Some people will do anything for enough credits."

"You hear Tygran just landed?"

"Shit."

"I'd love to see that face-off."

"What they got against him?"

"You didn't hear? They've been after him for years now."

"Why?"

"He refused to carry them."

"So does everyone else."

"No. Apparently he made the deal, took their money, then refused to transport them."

"I hear he gave the money back."

"I hear he killed a bunch of them and that's why they're after him."

"No, that's that other guy. The one they call Mouse."

"Yeah, he's the one! He's been killing Leeches for years. Got a real vendetta against them. No one knows why for sure."

"Ha. Why not? I'd kill them soon as look at them, too. Disgusting mutants."

"They've started taking women from the smaller colonies."

"That's bullshit."

"No, I know a family, lost their daughter and two female cousins to a Leech raid."

"Bullshit. They aren't the bogyman. Just mutants."

"Well, I'm not going anywhere near them."

Clare's heartbeat doubled as she sat quietly sipping her

beer, her back to most of the people talking, and absorbed the conversation. Tygran must have known the Leeches would be here. He was still alive so it wasn't like the Leeches could catch him out easily. He probably checked before landing anywhere to make sure the mutants weren't in the area. Right?

Or was he here because of the Leeches?

She finished a second beer as the gossip ebbed and flowed, until the chatter started to repeat things she'd already learned. Then she made her way to the pub near Paradise casino. On her way, she studied the station's population. There was an undercurrent of unmistakable tension, which surprised her given the size of the place and the sheer number of visitors who came and went.

But if Leeches were aboard…

Back in the early colonial period, when humans were attempting to make homes on new planets and moons, often without enough research on the environments of those new places, a few mistakes happened. The most significant mistake was the attempted settling of Gy'lee. After only brief exposure, the atmosphere mutated human DNA and the result was death. Or a Leech. More often than not, death. In fact, for any human without a Y chromosome, it was always a death sentence.

Over the years, Leeches—who considered themselves a new species rather than mutant humans—could only "reproduce" by kidnapping humans and exposing them to the planet, a process which killed significantly more of their victims than it mutated. Usually, they raided outer systems that weren't as tightly tied in to the trade route planets. Occasionally, they took individuals quietly off less reputable space stations. And sometimes, one of the smaller, human populated trade planets would send their most deplorable criminals to Gy'lee, the criminals so hated an ordinary death sentence or on-planet punishment seemed too easy.

Clare had never really understood that, though, and considered it pretty short-sighted. Because if the criminals didn't die but instead mutated, then you had a Leech even more deadly dangerous than the ordinary humans who'd turned Leech.

That meant all kinds of trouble.

Maybe it was the threat of Gy'lee that mattered. The threat of that kind of death—or worse, life—might be enough to curb the worst crimes in systems with less effective law enforcement. Personally, she'd prefer getting shot out an airlock into deep space than being exposed to the Gy'lee atmosphere. Both would be a death sentence for her, but she'd die quicker and less painfully in space. She couldn't even imagine what the punishment of Gy'lee might mean to someone who could be turned Leech.

Even in the warm circulated air of the station, Clare shivered, her stomach tightening at the thought.

By the time she reached the second pub, she'd heard talk of the Leeches being on the station several more times. She didn't learn anything new about them, or their reason for being on FarMore, but she did pick up more whispered gossip about Binnean clan conflict, and a possible war. Apparently, there had even been a fight on the station at Paradise Casino not all that long ago. Just like on Narava, rival Binnean clans didn't go near each other under normal circumstances because of the violent reaction. Humans most certainly worked to keep the clans apart so they didn't become casualties in the conflict. Some of the gossip claimed the fight on FarMore was purely an accident. Others said it had been planned—a way to initiate a war on Binnea.

All the talk reminded her of the bar fight she and Raf had ended up in that first night in the Docks. If that fight wasn't some strange fluke accident, if it had been something planned because of rising clan tensions… A jump of adrenaline made her pulse beat a little faster, and she filed away the rumors for future reference. A clan war on Binnea would be a *great* story.

Most of her career, she'd focused on Naravan-based news. But being on FarMore, seeing the sheer possibilities, all the stories she could expose, not just to the population of Narava but to the entire galaxy… Excitement danced in her gut. Talk about legendary. Crack the most significant stories ever on Narava, then move out into the galaxy for more. No one in the history of undercover journalism would be able to compare to her successes.

Tempting. So very tempting.

But first she had to get to Kierna'Rhoan and finish what she'd started.

Once she was satisfied she'd learned all she could for the time being, she headed back toward the docking bay and the *Ebisu*, keeping an eye and ear out for word of Tygran. She had no idea where he was on the station and hadn't seen him or any of his crew in her wanderings. But the station was huge so that wasn't surprising. Because of the Leeches, though, she took a circuitous route around the station, passing through as many of the public corridors as she could.

After passing through the largest of the station's shopping areas, she realized she wasn't seeing any Leeches either.

Leeches were impossible to miss. They were incredibly tall, skeletally skinny, white skin, yellow eyes. And they usually wore heavy robes that kept their bodies from coming into contact with anything around them. A requirement on a space station.

A Leech's touch destroyed anything that contained an electrical current. They fried almost all tech, which made interacting with most modern places difficult. And they destroyed human tissue at a cellular level on contact. They fed through their touch, soaking up the electrical currents and converting them to chemical sustenance. When that feeding happened on tech, it could be anything from inconvenient to deadly—especially aboard a space station or ship. When the feeding happened with a human… Clare's stomach turned at the thought so she didn't follow it. There was a reason the mutants were called Leeches.

She searched a few more of the popular public spaces, including one of the huge gardens in the stations exterior level, a lush place full of manicured greenery and an over-head screen that gave the illusion of a sunny spring day on a planet like Narava, complete with warmth and the deliciously delicate scent of flowers. The garden was full of wandering FarMore visitors, but still no Raf or Leeches.

There'd been so much talk and worry about the presence of the mutants on station, she couldn't believe she hadn't seen any sign of them anywhere. Not even whispers that the Leeches had passed through any of the places she'd visited. She hadn't even spotted one of their human emissaries—those few who were willing to work for Leeches for signifi-cant financial rewards.

Her heart beat harder, anxiety churning in her gut. This

couldn't be good. Something was wrong. Something felt very wrong.

She returned to the *Ebisu*, hoping she was seeing trouble where there was none. But once back aboard the ship, her anxiety only increased.

"They were due back an hour ago," Delilah, the technician she'd chatted with the night before told her.

The woman's face was pinched with worry, making the scars bisecting her face whiter and more obvious in her olive-toned skin. Creases bracketed her mouth, and she tugged unconsciously at her dark blond hair near her temple, a gesture Clare hadn't seen from her when she'd been relaxed.

"Has anyone heard from them?" Clare asked. "No messages?"

"Nothing."

"The Leeches are on the station."

When Delilah didn't react, Clare knew Tygran had told his crew what this diversion was about even if he'd refused to tell her.

"Does he have a contingency plan in place?" Clare asked. "If you don't hear from him in a certain period of time, what are you supposed to do?"

Delilah frowned, settling her hands on her hips. "We're supposed to go looking for 'em."

"When?"

"Said to give it a half cycle."

"And if you can't find them?"

"Get the *Ebisu* out of here. Back to...to a safe place."

That gave Clare pause. "What were you supposed to do with me and the other passenger?"

"Captain said to make sure you were safe, take you with us. We'd get you home as soon as it was clear."

Clare straightened her shoulders. People didn't surprise her very often. She'd have laid money Raf would order his crew to dump her and E on FarMore, that he'd consider them one complication too many when the crew was on the run. Yet he'd told his people to keep her and E safe.

She shook off the moment of shock to focus on the situation at hand. "I've been all over this station, and I haven't seen any sign of Tygran, the crew with him, or the Leeches. Something's wrong. I'm sure of it."

Delilah swallowed visibly and looked down a corridor deeper into the ship. "My nerves have been jumping since we landed. So've others. There's something wrong about all this."

"We need to go find your captain. We can't wait even a half cycle."

Delilah hesitated. "Captain said to wait."

"What if he's in trouble?"

"That's why he brought Sonia."

"I'm sure she's skilled enough to handle almost anything," Clare said, "but we're talking about creatures that can kill with a touch. We have to go look for them."

Delilah nodded and turned back toward the interior of the ship. "I gotta talk to Euan—he's in charge when the captain and Sonia are both off ship."

Clare nodded but sighed heavily. That would take time. Time her gut told her they didn't have. A low level of panic was making her nerves jump. She'd lived on her instincts for years. They were sharp and usually knew things before her conscious mind did, so she paid attention to them. Those instincts were why she was so good at her job, why she always managed to get out of trouble before her cover was blown, how she'd survived even extremely deadly situations.

Now those same instincts were saying Raf Tygran was in a world of trouble.

She hesitated a beat, then took off at a trot to find E.

CHAPTER ELEVEN

WHEN CLARE ENTERED THE ROOM E HAD BEEN GIVEN, HE was standing in the middle of the small space, facing the door as if he'd been expecting her to walk in. The scene gave her a moment's pause. But she decided to ignore her shiver of unease for the sake of expediency.

"Tygran is in trouble," she said without preamble. "I need your help."

E tilted his head down and stared at her for a long moment. Then said, "I thought you wanted me to remain aboard the ship."

"I did. But this is a unique situation."

"You would like me to shift?"

"Maybe just a little so you don't look so much like Ennoren but still look human. Can you do that?"

Without a word, his face started to melt and reform. Clare swallowed hard against the stomach-churning reaction caused by watching his shift. She hadn't found it so hard to watch actual Shifters change shape. In fact, that was kind of fascinating. And happened too fast to be gross. But with E, with this melting and reforming of a face that looked human, she had trouble keeping the bile down.

When he was done, a different man stood before her, but only slightly different. His hair was a few shades darker, his features broader, his mouth and nose both thicker, his skin still pale but not the translucent white of E's usual complexion. In fact, there was a hint of gold that reminded her of a Shifter's natural skin color.

"That's so weird," she muttered. "Okay, you'll do like that. Do you have a weapon?"

He raised his arm and his hand shifted to a large blaster.

"Right," she said. "Keep that trick in your pocket until we need it."

His head dipped and he tucked his chin back, a slight frown moving his mouth down. "Keep what in my pocket?"

"Sorry. I mean don't shift your hand to a blaster until it's necessary." She turned back into the corridor then stopped and spun back, pointing a finger at E. "*I'll* let you know when it's necessary."

He blinked once in response. After months of dealing with E on and off, she recognized that gesture as the closest she'd get to agreement.

Before leaving the ship, she swung past her own cabin and collected two more blasters—a second to carry in her hip holster and one small one she could slip into a holster inside her boot. After a brief pause, she also slipped a multipurpose knife into her other boot. She wasn't trained to use the knife as a weapon, but she'd found over the years that the present from her father had come in handy in unpredictable ways.

Fortunately, weapons weren't prohibited on FarMore, so

she could carry them without risk. One of the best things about the station was the top of the line shields which took advantage of Binnean molecular scanning technology to close off any breeches almost instantaneously. Clare had never understood how people could live on a station surrounded by the vacuum of space without that level of shielding.

Once back into the public corridors with E, Clare realized she had no real idea where to go to find Raf. She paused and put her hands on her hips. "Damn."

"What is the problem?"

"I know he needs help," she murmured. "But I don't know where he is."

"If there is a computer access port, I can find him."

"You can use computers?" She wasn't sure why that surprised her.

"I am skilled in many things."

"Of course." She searched for a public port and found one a level up from the docking bay.

She kept watch on the flow of inhabitants passing them as E's fingers danced across the computer panel. She prevented her foot from tapping with impatience by will alone.

"There is a section two corridors away and one level up," E finally said, "which has been blocked from access. We will find the captain there."

"You're sure?" She glanced at the screen

"Yes. They have put up a privacy shield. No other area of the station has been secured against monitoring. And I confirmed he is nowhere else on the station."

"What did you tap into?" she asked warily.

"Security logs and monitoring."

Her brows rose. "You can do that?"

E turned to face her. Without his expression changing, she still got the impression he was giving her an incredulous look. Since it was an emotion—one she could relate too—she smiled.

"Sorry," she said. "Didn't mean to doubt your skills. Let's go."

On the way to the location E had identified, she gave him the rundown on Leeches. "Don't let them touch you. I have no idea how your body heals from injuries or what their touch will do to you. I've never heard of them getting near a Shifter. But it's better to be safe and just not let them come into skin contact with you."

He nodded once.

"How do you heal from injuries, by the way?" That bit of information would come in handy going forward. "Other Shifters have to return to their natural state and regenerate the cells if the injury is serious enough. If they aren't killed."

"I have never been injured," he said with his usual lack of emotion.

"Never? How's that possible?"

"I am too strong and superior. There is no other being capable of hurting me."

She shook her head, not sure what to say to that, or how to feel about it. "Just don't take any chances with the Leeches, okay? Even if you can recover from their touch."

When they neared their target, Clare took in the surroundings. The corridor, one of many in a maze of conference rooms, was bracketed by clear walls beyond which were the sparsely decorated meeting areas. Some of the walls were smoked so the meetings inside were private, others remained clear so she could see inside.

"Which one is it?" she asked E. They all looked the same to her and several were smoked for privacy. She couldn't tell at a glance which had the full privacy shields up to prevent any type of monitoring.

E nodded to a door near the end of the corridor. The walls were smoked, the door's locking panel blinked red.

"You're sure?" she asked.

He didn't respond, just walked to the door.

"So, how do we get in?" she asked aloud, studying the lock.

E looked at her, then knocked on the door.

Clare blinked and almost laughed.

Two beats passed before the door opened. A man she didn't know looked out, his expression blandly curious. He was about her height, with black hair and dark brown eyes, wearing the blue and silver jacket associated with Leech emissaries.

"We have this room booked for another two hours," he said, his voice unremarkable and even. "Is there something I can help you with?"

"We're from the *Ebisu*," Clare said. She cocked her hip, settling into a sexy, easy-going stance. Even with the guns, people tended to underestimate her if she was busy throwing around her sexuality. To her satisfaction, the young man's gaze dropped to her breasts and stuck there for a moment longer than was polite. She took a deep breath and watched him swallow visibly.

"You're with Captain Tygran?" he asked without looking up at her face.

"Yes. We have a message for him. I know he doesn't want to be disturbed, but this is important. You mind?"

The man shook his head, then seemed to remember himself. He blinked and finally brought his roaming gaze back to her face. She smiled, and he blinked again.

"Uhm. Can you wait here one moment, please?"

"Sure." She shrugged and leaned casually against the door frame, effectively preventing the door from being resealed.

The man didn't seem to notice. He turned back into the room, leaving Clare free to eavesdrop on the conversation.

Unfortunately, she didn't hear much but some whispers. She caught Tygran's name and "important" from the man. A hissing, "How did they find us?" Then some sharp but very quiet words passed before the door opened abruptly.

Clare stumbled back a few steps in her hurry to get away from the Leech.

Just being in such close proximity to one made her heart rate triple and her stomach tighten. The mutant looked her over, spared a glance at E, then focused on her again.

"You look fecund," he said from the depths of the cowl pulled up over his head.

"I'm just here to deliver a message," she said around a suddenly dry throat. What the hell could a Leech want with her "fecundity"?

"You may pass your message to me. I will see Tygran gets it."

She wondered if the Leech thought she was stupid. If he did, she could use that. "Tygran's eyes only. Sorry. Have to tell the captain myself."

"He will be finished with this meeting in another few hours. Come back then."

"Can't. Needs to hear it now. He'll fire my ass if I don't deliver this." She tried for a casual shrug but knew her nerves made the gesture jerky and uneven. She couldn't seem to control her pulse, despite years of practice. Her hands started to shake so she fisted them and crossed her arms.

The dark cowl turned toward E briefly again, then back to her. "One moment."

The Leech disappeared into the room and Clare took a deep breath. Neither she nor E spoke in the few moments that the Leech was gone, then he reemerged with the young man who'd answered the door. The young man held a hand scanner. He moved the blocky instrument in a long, sweeping arc, scanning her from head to toe. The box beeped a few times. Then the young man tucked the scanner into his jacket pocket and nodded to the Leech.

"You may come in," the Leech said.

Clare swallowed. She did not want to actually go into that room and be cornered by a bunch of Leeches.

She glanced at E. "Stay here. I'll be out in a minute." She held E's gaze and hoped he understood her underlying meaning. *Come in and get us if I don't come back out right away!*

Then she followed the Leech into the room.

CHAPTER TWELVE

RAF FELT LIKE HE'D TAKEN A BLOW TO THE STOMACH WHEN he watched Clare walk into that room just ahead of Beyvir. What the hell was she doing here?

He'd been asking himself the same question for the last few hours—what the hell was he doing here?

At least no one had tried to kill him yet. But they'd separated him from Sonia and the others almost immediately. And Beyvir, the Leech in charge, had been "negotiating" with him since they sat down at the long conference table in the otherwise bare room. It was more Beyvir lecturing him and Raf barely getting a word in, but at least he was still alive.

He watched Clare taking in the room, noticing the absence of his other crew.

"What?" he snapped at her, letting irritation out to cover his worry, hoping Beyvir wouldn't notice the worry.

Clare sauntered over to him, letting her hips swing and her sexy red curls bounce and sway. For just a blink, he forgot she was doing that on purpose and got caught up in her performance. She was dressed in ass-kicker black leather, her blasters strapped very obviously to those luscious hips, looking every bit the security guard/mercenary she purported to be on Narava. But she had a tight-fitting, low cut shirt under the leather jacket that showed off her magnificent breasts in a way too obvious to ignore. And the slight smirk lifting her gorgeous mouth, the riot of red curls, the way she ambled through the room… She was like a magnet for his gaze. Impossible to look away.

When he realized he was so caught up her he'd forgotten to pay heed to his surroundings, he fisted his hand to refocus and turned his attention on the others in the room. Five Leeches in total and three human "assistants", all males. Every gaze in the room followed Clare.

Huh. He almost smiled. Clever trick. Clever woman. He'd seen Sonia do something similar. But his co-pilot was harder and sharper than Clare. Despite her outward attitude and attire, Clare was all bounce and curves, inspiring an entirely different set of fantasies.

She stopped close and met his gaze before leaning close to whisper in his ear. "Your crew is worried. I've got E outside. You should have told me what was going on."

He watched the others as she spoke, making an effort to ignore the feel of her breath against his skin. He turned his mouth to her ear to reply. "I got more than I expected. Is the rest of the crew coming? You shouldn't be here. They want women."

He felt her shiver even though they weren't touching.

"I told them I had a very important message for you," she whispered. "Do you need out of here? E can help."

"Thought you didn't want him off the *Ebisu*."

"Desperate times," she muttered.

He straightened and faced her. "You sure that's what they said?"

She nodded, playing along without a moment's hesitation.

He faced the head Leech. "Gotta end this negotiation, Beyvir. Emergency."

"We're not finished here yet."

"*I* never intended to start this in the first place." He noticed Clare straightened almost imperceptibly and any hope of keeping this business to himself seemed to slip away. She was too perceptive. Worse, he would have to admit he was tricked into a face to face with Leeches. He should have known better.

The only good thing was they were actually talking a truce, in between all the lecturing. If this got settled, he wouldn't have to worry about them on his trail anymore. But things hadn't been going well. The few times he'd been able to speak had been met with dismissive rebuffs, and one or two threats.

"I gotta go," he said, pushing up from his seat at the table. "We can finish this at a distance. As originally planned."

"I'm afraid not," Beyvir said.

Hell. He knew they'd been playing him. Couldn't trust a fucking Leech.

The message he'd received had said he'd be met by an emissary. That he'd be negotiating a truce via vid, the emissary serving as intermediary, like a neutral tek'la on Binnea. Raf had been assured there would be no Leeches here in person. He'd even checked with a contact that Leeches weren't scheduled to be at FarMore before he arrived—a contact he had some very serious words for if he survived this. Being on the run from the mutants was really cutting into his bottom line, so he'd jumped at the chance to end their hunt and finally come to a truce.

More the fool him.

"We're going," he said, staring into the blackness under Beyvir's cowl.

"You still owe us, Tygran."

"We've covered this ground before. A lot. What made you think anything had changed?"

"We were assured by a third party."

He narrowed his eyes. "You were misinformed." And so was he. But he'd be pissed about that later. "Since we're still at an impasse, I'm leaving. Now."

One of the human men reached inside his jacket and before Raf could blink, Clare had her blaster in hand, aimed steadily at Beyvir.

Well, well, Ms. O'Malley.

"You heard the man," she said. "Negotiations have broken down. Time for us to go."

"But your presence has changed everything, woman."

Oh oh. That was really not good. "You got one of those to spare," he murmured to Clare, tilting his head toward her blaster. She had a second one on her hip but opposite him and reaching around her might hamper her movements.

"One in my boot," she said, her tone even, no sign of the earlier sexy attitude she'd entered the room with.

As he started to lean over to get the blaster from her nearest boot, the human reaching for something in his jacket moved again, and Clare shook her head.

"You take that weapon out," she said, "I kill your leader. Hands in the open. Now."

Raf was impressed. She hadn't even glanced at the man. Her entire focus was on the head Leech, exactly where it needed to be to keep them from getting killed. He sure did like this woman.

He slid her blaster out of her boot holster and stood. "Now," he said. "So we don't cause a ruckus on the station, you're going to step aside. We're going to leave. And things go back the way there were." Which wasn't what Raf wanted, but it looked like the only option right now.

Beyvir stared at them from beneath his cowl, the yellow glow of his eyes just barely visible in the well-lit conference room. The entire cowl dipped to the side as he moved his head. And then he stepped toward them instead of back.

Clare hit him with a solid blaster stun. Stun didn't have the same effect on Leeches as it did on humans, but the shot hurt him and he fell back with a hissing cry.

Everyone else in the room swarmed forward, closing in on he and Clare just as the door to the room slammed open and E, his hand now a laser cannon, stepped inside. Raf gave up on ending this quietly. He started firing at anything in a robe.

"Get out," he shouted at Clare and they both charged the open door.

E covered them with random streams of deadly shots from his cannon.

"Nice trick," Raf commented.

"Where's everyone else?" Clare asked as they hit the hall at a run.

They left E at their backs to keep the Leeches and their humans occupied—or to kill them. Raf wasn't sure which the strange Shifter-man would do.

"This way." He wove through the spider web of corridors full of conference rooms until they reached the place he'd left his people.

They barged in without announcing themselves and in a surprisingly synchronized effort, stunned the three humans guarding his crew.

"Nicely done, O'Malley," he said with a half-grin. "Sonia, get your ass in gear. Why the hell are you still standing there?"

"Fuck you, Captain," Sonia said with an answering grin as his people took to the corridor, moving fast.

"Get to the ship and get it ready for takeoff," he said to Sonia. "Make sure we've got all the clearances. I don't want a hole put in the hull because of an unauthorized launch."

"And you?" Sonia asked.

"I'll keep the Leeches occupied, to give you time for the clearances."

"You be onboard in half an hour or we're leaving you behind."

"Don't you dare take off in my ship without me." He clapped Sonia on the shoulder. "See you soon." He realized as he watched Sonia trot off that Clare wasn't following. "You too, O'Malley. Back to the ship."

"What about E?" Clare asked.

"I get the feeling he can take care of himself. But I'll go find him."

"I'm going with you. Don't argue. You'll just waste time."

He opened his mouth to do just that, but then the low sound of hissing caught his attention. More Leeches, heading their way. Whether E had left anyone alive or not, there were more on the station than those in the room with him. Time to draw them off his people.

"Don't let them touch you," he said, in a pointless warning.

"Gee, ya think?" she answered.

He grinned, despite the danger, and moved toward the sounds of the Leeches.

CHAPTER THIRTEEN

RAF AND CLARE TURNED A CORNER IN THE CONFERENCE room labyrinth and came face to face with three Leeches.

"You wanted their attention," Clare muttered then fired three quick blaster shots and turned to run the opposite direction.

Raf grabbed her arm and led her to the right instead. He knew these twisty corridors well. They were designed to be difficult to get out of so he'd made a of point of memorizing the layout. He was counting on the Leeches being less familiar with the territory.

"Hope you know where you're going," Clare muttered as she kept pace. "I'm completely lost now."

"Got it. This way." He stayed just far enough ahead of the Leeches to keep their attention, never quite running but occasionally moving into a trot. They passed a number of humans and Binneans along with some of the station droids. Outside of a few sideways looks, no one raised any alarms. Either the earlier blaster fire was being ignored, which he doubted given the security unit on FarMore, or it had somehow been missed.

Or security was on the way and just hadn't found them yet.

When he got a little too far ahead of the Leeches, he moved Clare into a doorway and paused to wait for them.

"You don't think they know you're leading them around?" she asked. "What's to stop them from breaking off and going straight to the *Ebisu*?"

"They've been after me for a while now. They get very fixated on me and it keeps them from thinking more strategically."

"Hope you're right."

He frowned. He had been in the past, but the Leeches had a way of complicating his life in unexpected ways. When another few moments passed and the ones following still hadn't come into view, he started to worry Clare was right.

Shit.

He hesitated a heartbeat, then said, "Let's get back to the ship. They've disappeared."

She grunted in response, a noise that carried a world of unease.

Couldn't say as he blamed her. His nerves were jumping like a ship without stabilizers in on-planet turbulence. He hunted the corridors ahead and around them as they made their way back to the conference area entrance. From there, they had to cross through a public shopping space and then down into the docking bay. If they got that far without seeing a Leech, they'd be home free.

Unfortunately, Raf figured he must have used up all his really good luck when he'd escaped his home planet all those years ago, because they'd barely stepped out into the shopping corridor before he spotted two more Leeches. Damn damn. He didn't want to lead them back to the *Ebisu* on the off chance the bastards didn't know where it was docked, but he was running out of time. The Leeches headed their way, the crowd falling back to give them plenty of room. No help there.

He made his way toward the nearest lifts, hoping to lose them that way. These two Leeches didn't seem to have a human emissary with them which meant they couldn't operate the lift themselves. Before Raf could reach the tentative safety, though, another two Leeches stepped into the corridor to block his path. Again the corridors cleared before them. Even the station droids seemed to vanish and security was nowhere to be seen.

Great. Just great. No one wanted to mess with a Leech fight. He couldn't blame them. He didn't want to be in the middle of one either.

Where the hell was security? This couldn't be good for business.

Clare pulled him back toward one of the shops just as its security doors descended, blocking them from entering.

"This is not good," she hissed.

"Yup." Now that the corridors were virtually empty, he took aim with his blaster and sent a few jolts into the approaching mutants on their left while Clare fired at the ones on the right. "Where the hell is E? He'd be very useful about now."

"You're asking me?" Clare said.

"What was that about a fire-breathing dragon?"

"We better hope he doesn't pull that trick on a space

station or there will be more problems than Leeches to worry about." She fired again.

"But it would be fun to see." He shot an approaching mutant dead center in the chest. Even at high stun, the Leeches were only knocked backward. They didn't rush them as Raf expected but instead approached slowly, steadily. To his irritation, another few Leeches stepped into the corridor. They were officially backed up against a wall and cut off from any route of escape.

In a now empty corridor.

With no security in sight.

On a high tech space station with drop blast technology that may or may not even work on Leeches.

But would definitely work on him and Clare if security triggered it.

He glanced at the floor, where the shock from the drop blast would initiate. A blast would knock him and Clare unconscious, leaving them unable to defend themselves. If it didn't affect the Leeches, he and Clare were dead.

Shit.

"We're gonna have to switch to kill," he told Clare. "The stun isn't going to be enough." They had to get out of here, fast. Before security did something that made the situation worse.

"How much trouble will that cause?" Clare asked.

"Worth it to get out of here before security activates a drop blast. If it doesn't work on the Leeches, we'll be at their mercy."

"Fair enough."

Even as she spoke, he heard the buzz of her blaster shot and the sound of a sharp screech from the right. He glanced over in time to see one of the Leeches collapsed on the ground. Her shot galvanized the others and the Leeches finally swarmed.

With their backs to the closed shop, Raf and Clare fired a steady stream of blaster shots, but the mutants absorbed even the killing blows and kept coming. Bastards were strong.

From the corner of his eye, Raf noticed a single human man enter the corridor, and not run right back out again. Raf was too busy keeping deadly Leech fingers away from his skin to see if the man was a Leech emissary or not, but he'd caught sight of dark skin and ordinary clothes—no sign of the blue and silver jacket that emissaries usually wore.

When Clare squealed, he forgot about the stranger. "You hurt?" He didn't dare look away from the attacking group to check.

"Bastards." Her voice was deeper with pain but she continued to fire and he heard another sharp screech from a wounded Leech.

They were barely keeping a small circle of safety around themselves, and it wasn't going to last long. "We need a better plan," he muttered. "Try to make a hole so we can make a run for it."

Clare shifted a little and then she was firing two blasters, focusing the shots on a narrow area of attack, forcing those approaching Leeches back farther. Unfortunately, they weren't separating enough to give them running room. So Raf started firing at the same spot, stopping only to keep the other Leeches from flanking them.

It still wasn't working and their safety zone was narrowing.

Then blaster fire started from behind the Leeches. The

creatures' attention shifted so that several turned to face the new threat. The divided attention gave Raf and Clare a chance.

"Now!" He focused his shots on the small opening between the distracted attackers until there was room to run.

They tore down the corridor. Raf glanced back and realized the human man who'd entered the fight was following them, but he fired over his shoulder at the Leeches giving chase. Raf had no idea who the guy was, but as long as he was on their side, he didn't care.

When he would have slammed into the nearest lift, the man caught up and shouted, "No, this way. They've got human emissaries nearby."

Which meant the lifts wouldn't keep the Leeches from following them.

Clare hesitated, but Raf grabbed her arm and pulled her along. The young man led them out of the shopping area and into a corridor of closed doors which were likely living quarters for station residents. At one, he slapped the security panel. It sparked and the door opened.

"You know where we are?" Raf asked as he stood at the door, watching their backs for signs of the Leeches and trying to catch his breath.

"Taking a back way," the stranger said. "You're on the *Ebisu*, right?"

Raf gave the man a narrow-eyed look. He was younger than Raf had realized, barely an adult, maybe only in his late teens. His dark brown skin was smooth and unblemished, but his eyes were serious and held more age than his body and face.

"Who are you?" Raf asked.

"We'll have time for introductions later. Right now, you can call me…Ahab."

"As in the captain that followed the white whale?" Clare asked. "That's not reassuring."

"It's not," Raf agreed. "Where are we going?"

"There's a utility tunnel from this room down to the docking bay," the young man said.

"You know this how?" Raf asked.

Ahab glanced past Raf. "They're coming."

Since Raf didn't have a lot of choices here, he followed the kid. Clare hesitated only a moment longer before joining him. When the door to the room closed behind them, Raf noticed they hadn't entered an apartment but a storage unit filled with cleaning implements and janitorial droids. At the rear of the room, Ahab swiped a molecular scanner over a section of wall and a small square of metal moved to one side.

"This way." Ahah climbed through the hole first.

Raf and Clare exchanged a look. But then something started pounding on the door and their options vanished. Raf climbed through the hole first, emerging into a low, narrow corridor. He helped Clare through the hole in the wall before following Ahab's retreating back.

They'd only gone a few meters when they reached a series of ladders. Using the hand holds, Ahab dropped each level in a single, smooth slide, not bothering to use the rungs. Clare and Raf made the descent slower, more carefully. When they reached the docking bay level, Ahab led them toward an exit that brought them out into the bay where the *Ebisu* waited.

"You're gonna have to explain how you knew all this someday, kid," Raf said.

Ahab looked toward the bay doors as yet more Leeches moved into the huge room. "Later. Get to the landing ramp. Now."

Raf ran, Clare at his side, firing toward the Leeches without aiming. The small, side ramp was down and Sonia stood at the top, giving them more cover fire.

"Move, move, move!" she shouted. "Get your asses up here. We're gone."

Raf cleared the ramp into the ship with Clare right behind him, then he hit the panel to retract the ramp without waiting for Ahab to fully reach the ship. The kid dove inside, and the door sealed shut.

"Wait!" Clare shouted. "E. We can't leave him."

"We'll come back for him," Raf said.

"No need," E commented from farther down the corridor.

"Son of a bitch," Raf cursed, hanging his head briefly to absorb a fresh shot of adrenaline. He shook it off. He'd have to ask the scary hybrid for details later. Slamming a fist against the comm-panel, he shouted, "Euan get us out of here."

The ship shuddered under them as it started to lift and move. Raf made his way toward the flight deck. Over his shoulder he shouted, "Sonia, take care of our guests."

"Who's this new guy?"

"Ahab. Give him a bunk."

"What the fuck, Captain?"

"Later!" He broke into a run, anxious to get forward.

He only noticed Clare followed when he stepped onto the

flight deck. He ignored her, though, because he had other things to worry about.

"That fight with the Leeches turned public," he said to his third-in-command as he slid into the pilot's chair. "We get clearance?"

"Had it. Getting some hesitance now, though. Like maybe they don't want to accept the code anymore."

"Fuck 'em." Raf maneuvered the ship toward the opened, shielded exit back out into space. But if the station didn't adjust the shields to let them out, they were gonna end up frying the *Ebisu*.

Claxons sounded from outside the ship—"clear the bay" claxons he was relieved to hear. Just as he got too close, moving too fast to change course, the shields dropped and the *Ebisu* launched into space.

He punched up the speed, racing as fast as their engines would take them from the station, toward a safe jump zone, and out of range of any weapons meant to disable the ship. After a few minutes, when FarMore didn't fire on them, he took a relieved breath and handed the ship's flight controls back to Euan.

"Keep a watch for followers," Raf told him as he sent a series of calculations back to the navigation room.

"To Kierna'Rhoan now?" Clare asked.

"Soon. But not directly. Just in case they try to follow."

"We've got two ships leaving the station behind us, Captain," Euan said.

"Yup." Raf took back control of the ship and changed trajectories. "Hurry with those jump coordinates," he shouted toward the nav-room.

"Coming, Captain," the nav chief, Duster, yelled back. "Almost ready."

Raf watched the screens, keeping track of the two ships behind them. To his relief, the *Ebisu* was faster. The distance between them and the other ships increased. Finally, word came back from the nav-room that the jump engines and coordinates were ready.

"Hold on to something," he told Clare, then took the ship into its first jump.

CHAPTER FOURTEEN

Clare started to breathe normally after they'd cleared their third jump with no signs of pursuit. She left the flight deck to the capable hands of the captain and Euan and made her way on shaky legs to the canteen. She needed a drink.

She found Sonia standing over Ahab where he'd sprawled on a couch, his blaster settled comfortably across his lap. Clare finally took a moment to study the man and realized he was barely out of his teens, maybe not even that old. Though, as she studied him, she thought his dark eyes looked significantly older than the rest of him—haunted eyes with a hardness to them that made Clare's heart hurt for reasons she couldn't fully understand.

"So, Ahab," she said as she crossed to the cabinets to retrieve Raf's hidden bottle of whiskey. "Thanks for the help and all, but who the hell are you?"

"Just asking the same question?" Sonia grunted. She had

her own blaster in hand, resting against her thigh, not aimed but at the ready.

While Clare poured her drink and Ahab remained silent, E came into the room and stood silently off to one side.

Since Ahab wasn't talking yet, Clare turned to E. "What happened to you? How did you get back?"

"Once the Leeches and humans in that room were dead, I returned to the ship," he answered simply.

She took a long gulp, letting the amber liquid burn down her throat as she absorbed his matter-of-fact explanation. "Did you shift more? Did anyone see you?"

"No."

"Well, that's something at least." And the Leeches and human emissaries who'd seen his laser cannon hand were all dead. Clare found it hard to feel bad about those deaths. Especially after one of the Leeches had hit her while they'd been cornered in the shopping corridor.

Remembering the hit, she sat at the table and slipped off her jacket to look at her shoulder. Unfortunately, the spot the Leech had reached was on a patch of muscle near the back of her neck where it met her shoulder, one of the few places her skin had been exposed. She gently touched the area around the wound. It didn't feel as numb as she'd expected. In fact, it stung quite a bit when her fingers got too close to the actual injury. She'd always heard Leech wounds were relatively painless despite being ugly to look at.

She rose again and hunted through the canteen cabinets for something that would serve as a mirror. To her surprise, she found an actual compact mirror hidden behind some coffee mugs—and couldn't help but wonder who had put it there and why. Something she'd have to look into, even if just for her own interest.

She anticipated seeing a blackened patch of dead skin, maybe a little sunken because of the muscle loss beneath, a typical Leech wound she'd have to have the ship's medic look at. Instead, she saw a small circle of red dots, like something from a pressure syringe. She pulled her skin tight, ignoring the sting, hoping she was imagining things. But no, the distinct red dots remained. No dead skin. Another kind of wound all together.

Her heartbeat tripled. "Shit."

"What's wrong?" Ahab asked, rising suddenly.

"This is no Leech wound." She pulled at her skin again, angling the mirror as she tried to get a better look. "Son of a bitch. I think the bastards injected me with something." She showed the wound to Sonia then to Ahab as they approached.

Somewhat to her relief, E remained standing several meters away near the entrance to the canteen.

Ahab motioned her to the table bench. He gestured to her neck as he sat next to her. "May I?"

She nodded, angling her head and sweeping her hair to one side to let him examine the wound. His smooth forehead crinkled and his mouth turned down.

"This isn't good, is it?" she muttered as her stomach rolled. What the hell would Leeches inject her with? And how could they use a pressure syringe? Shouldn't it have malfunctioned when they touched it?

Ahab let out a long breath. "I need to speak with Captain Tygran." He looked up at Sonia. "Quickly. She doesn't have a lot of time."

"What?" Clare squeaked. "What the hell does that mean?

I'm gonna die?" Clare's breath started coming in and out too quickly. Spots darkened her vision. "Shit." She bent over and put her head between her knees, concentrating on breathing so she didn't hyperventilate and pass out. For all she knew, breathing too heavily could speed up whatever had been done to her.

Ahab remained silent while she tried to calm her pulse.

"Not die," he said when she glanced up while still bent forward. "You'd be luckier if this did kill you. But they would have scanned you to make sure before injecting you."

"Scanned me?" She scowled. "Yeah, the lead one talking with Raf, he got one of his human emissaries to scan me. But he didn't say anything about it. And he wasn't the one who hit me with the syringe. E killed the Leech who had me scanned." Clare's heart started to pound again as she watched the young man's frown deepen.

"Get the captain," Ahab said to Sonia. "I'll explain every-thing once he's here."

RAF HAD RARELY HEARD Sonia so worried. They'd been through a lot together over the years. He'd seen her in the best and worst of circumstances, times when they were close to being killed, or caught by some planetary authority. Times when she'd been angry and hard. Or worse. Times when she'd been soft and hurting.

But her voice, when she'd called him down to the canteen over the internal comm-link, had carried a quiet intensity that worried Raf. A lot.

He stormed into the open room and took in the gathering

at a glance. Clare sat at the table looking pale, her fists clenched against her thighs. Sonia stood to one side of the kitchen prep area, frowning, her arms crossed over her chest, but her shoulders lowered and hunched, not looking at anyone else. E had his head tilted forward and down, a position Raf now associated with him thinking deeply.

And Ahab. He sat next to Clare, his expression serious and unreadable. He looked very young if you just looked at his face. All his age was in his dark eyes.

"What's happening?" Raf said into the tense silence.

"Captain," Ahab greeted. "We have a problem. A serious one."

"Does this serious problem endanger my crew?"

"One of them." Ahab nodded to Clare.

Raf didn't bother to correct his assumption that Clare was crew. "Explain."

"The short explanation—she's been infected with the same elements from Gy'lee that mutate humans into Leeches."

Raf stopped breathing. For a full heartbeat, he simply couldn't breathe. He blinked and looked around when he heard Sonia curse. Then Clare folded forward, her head between her knees.

"Shit. Shit shit shit shit. Fuck," she cursed, her voice muffled. "I'm gonna die." Suddenly she stood and darted to the sink, reaching it just in time to throw up.

Without thinking, he found himself behind her, holding her hair back as she continued to wrench. He was breathing again, but raggedly, too stunned to even speak.

"Sorry," Clare muttered, still bent over.

Her sad little apology brought him out of his shock.

"Don't worry about it. Someone on the crew is bound to need a punishment. I'll get them to clean and sterilize the sink."

She snorted an almost laugh and turned on the facet, rinsing her mouth.

He stroked his hand along her spine in soothing circles and looked back at Ahab. "It's not possible, what you're saying. They've never been able to isolate the elements in the atmosphere that cause the mutation. That's been the one saving grace of letting the Leeches run around the galaxy."

"They've made a few advances recently," Ahab said quietly.

"So." Raf swallowed, not actually wanting to say this next out loud. "So she's going to die?" It was an awful death. He couldn't even comprehend the vibrant woman next to him going through that.

"No. Unfortunately." Ahab sounded very sorry about the fact that she wouldn't die.

Which made Raf frown. "Women always die."

Clare straightened and faced Ahab. Raf let go of her hair but kept his hand on her back, pulling her close as if he could keep her safe from all this with just the strength of his arms. His heart broke a little when she leaned into him, her vulnerability palpable.

"You said something about them scanning me," she said. "For what?"

"Very few outside of the Leeches know this," Ahab said. "And the genetics is a little complicated to explain."

"Keep it simple," Raf said. He wasn't sure Clare could take a science lecture just then.

Ahab paused as if considering his words. "The genetic component that causes mutation is a DNA sequence inside a gene only found on the Y chromosome. Without this specific variant inside the gene, a human dies when exposed to Gy'lee's atmosphere. Since this gene isn't present on the X chromosome, a human without a Y chromosome can't mutate. Or so we thought."

"So then how am I not dying?" Clare asked, her voice sounding scratchy and harsh.

"Turns out a variation on this sequence can be present on the X chromosome," Ahab said. "Rarely. But it does turn up inside a very specific intergenetic region."

"Intergenetic region?" Sonia asked.

"Sequences of DNA between genes that don't encode proteins," Ahab said.

"Cut to the chase," Raf said, interrupting what he was afraid could turn into a full blown genetics discussion.

Ahab held Clare's gaze. "A human with this rare sequence at this very specific location on the X chromosome can mutate. They survive. They become Leeches."

Clare closed her eyes. "Not much of a fucking improvement," she muttered. "I'd rather die."

But Raf felt her trembling and knew full well she wasn't ready to die yet either. "How do you know about this?"

"Long story." Ahab shrugged. "Maybe later when there's time. Right now, we need to get her the cure. Soon. Before the mutation progresses too far."

"Cure?" Raf said.

"Cure?" Clare echoed, opening her eyes.

"There's never been even a hint that there's a cure," Raf added.

"Why would the Leeches develop one?" Sonia put in. "They want female Leeches."

"They didn't develop it," Ahab said. "I did. It only works with this X chromosome variant. I haven't found a way to prevent mutation in those with the Y chromosome sequence —it being inside an active gene complicates things. I was able to isolate and reverse the damage caused with the X sequence, though." He met Clare's gaze again. "But only if I apply the cure in time."

"Why should we trust you?" Raf asked. "We have no idea who you are."

"You don't have to trust me," Ahab said. "You can wait for her eyes to turn yellow to know I'm telling the truth. But not long after that, she'll be too far gone to save. And it'll be too late to get where we need to go for the cure."

"You don't have it on you?" Raf wasn't sure he liked any of this. But could he risk Clare's life by waiting?

"It's not a pill," Ahab said with a surprising amount of patience. "It requires some specialized equipment."

"What if the Leeches find us?" Sonia put in. "You know so much about them? Bet they know about you."

Ahab dipped his head in a single nod of acknowledgement. "But they don't know where my lab is. I've been very careful. Believe me, I don't want them to find it either. It'll take me years to duplicate what I've got there and a lot of people will die before I can."

"Who the hell are you?" Raf asked, pulling Clare even closer.

"As I said, it's a long story." He met Raf's gaze when he said, "But I was on the *Venture*."

Raf straightened. Only two people had survived the fate that befell the *Venture*. That incident was the reason Raf refused to transport Leeches. What had happened to the

Venture crew was… Legend seemed the wrong word. Notorious, maybe? But definitely a cautionary tale few captains ignored if they wanted to keep their crew alive.

If Ahab was telling the truth, he'd seen hell firsthand.

Raf held the young man's gaze as he asked Clare, "Do you want to take the chance? This is your life."

"Hell yeah," she said. "I do *not* want to be a Leech. I really would rather be dead."

Ahab turned to her and for a moment Raf swore he saw tears in the young man's eyes.

"You're not the only one who'd make that choice," Ahab whispered. "But you don't have to. I can save you." He faced Raf again. "We don't have a lot of time."

CHAPTER FIFTEEN

RAF SQUEEZED CLARE IN A ONE-ARMED HUG. "WILL YOU BE okay for a bit while I get us on the new heading?"

She nodded without looking up at him. But very quietly, under her breath, she whispered, "Thanks."

He let go reluctantly. There was something devastating about seeing this bold and vivacious woman so scared. She'd walked into that room earlier with the Leeches and never balked. She'd fought her way through the Binnean bar brawl with a sense of humor and a hell of a shot. Seeing Clare O'Malley this terrified was just…wrong. It made him angry. And it made him ache.

"I'll be back soon and we'll talk more, okay?" he said.

"Sure." She pretended at a smile and eased away from him, returning to the table.

"You." Raf pointed at Ahab. "Come with me."

The young man followed without comment.

On the way, once they were out of earshot of the others, Raf said, "You're Mouse, aren't you?"

Ahab raised a brow. "You've heard that name?"

"The *Venture* wasn't just an ordinary cautionary tale for me," Raf said. "I knew Cal." The *Venture's* head engineer had once been a colleague, and a friend.

Raf had met Cal on the very first ship Raf served on, the one he'd stowed away on to escape Jenolon. At the time, Cal had only been a few years older than Raf, still working his way up the ranks. But he'd taken Raf in, looked after him while he got his space legs. Outside of Captain Bael, Raf credited his initial acceptance with the crew, his very survival those first few months, to Cal's friendship.

Ahab's mouth tightened. "He was a good man."

"He was," Raf agreed with a nod.

"But I only joined the *Venture* a few months before that last flight," Ahab said. "How would you have heard of me?"

Raf glanced sideways at him. "Cal sent me a last vid-message before taking off. I think he was…worried. Wanted me to find you and look after you if something went wrong."

"You never found me."

Raf snorted. By the time he'd reached the outpost where the *Venture* had turned up after its devastating encounter with the Leeches, Mouse had already disappeared. "You made sure no one could find you, kid," he said. "I think on purpose."

Raf had still spent two years searching. Even now, three years after he'd stopped actively looking, he kept his ears open for news of the kid. The fact that Mouse had found him, rather than the other way around, would have amused the hell out of Cal.

Ahab shrugged. Then almost smiled, the first light

expression he'd shown. "Had some things to do," he said. "Needed to reinvent myself."

"Again." Raf wasn't asking. It was obvious Ahab had traveled under a number of names. "I'm glad to finally meet you, to see you're doing well. Cal would be pleased."

Ahab didn't comment.

After a moment, Raf said, "What brought you to FarMore Station with such great timing?"

"What do you think?"

"You're hunting Leeches now, aren't you? That's how you know so much about them, why you've worked out a cure for this…injection of theirs?"

Ahab gave him a sideways look then nodded. "I owe them. If I can wipe the bastards out, I will."

"That what you planned to do on FarMore?"

Ahab shrugged again but didn't say more as they reached the nav-room and were joined by several more people. Raf let it go. He could question Ahab later. Knowing who he was helped Raf trust him a little more. At least as far as he was willing to trust someone he'd just met. Ahab had saved his and Clare's lives. Cal had liked him. And really, Raf couldn't blame him for wanting to destroy Leeches after what he'd been through.

But most importantly, this man had an antidote to save Clare from turning into a Leech, and that was really all that mattered right then.

As Raf oversaw the recalibration to Ahab's coordinates, he mentally calculated how far off course this would take them. A week. At least, depending on how long Clare's treatment took. Since no one on Kierna'Rhoan was expecting them, that wasn't a worry. But Longfeather was expecting

Clare back on Narava in five weeks, Naravan time. They'd never make that timeline with this delay.

So did Raf warn the mercenary, to save himself grief and the possible loss of his fee? Or did he wait and see how things with Ahab's cure went first? Raf really didn't want to have to tell Longfeather he got Clare infected with the Leech mutation. It would damage his reputation for one. Longfeather would probably demand his money back as well.

But mostly, Raf was afraid telling someone outside of his crew about all this would somehow condemn Clare to becoming a Leech. Make the whole thing inevitable because he'd admitted the possibility out loud to an outsider.

He rolled his eyes. He wasn't nearly as superstitious as most space captains, but damned if he wasn't a little. His only consolation was Sonia was even more superstitious than he was.

Pragmatically, Raf knew if he contacted Longfeather, he risked giving his location away to the Leeches. If Ahab had been able to stay hidden this long, Raf sure as hell didn't want to risk the security of the place they were going. And that was a much better excuse than admitting he didn't want to jinx Clare's recovery.

With that appropriately non-superstitious justification established, he assured the *Ebisu* was on its new course, passed Ahab off to Sonia to settle in one of the guest cabins, and finally returned to Clare. He wanted more answers from Ahab, but he had enough for now.

He found Clare still in the canteen, sitting at the table, staring into space.

"We seem to meet here a lot," he tried to joke.

She tried to smile. "I'd ask for another drink, but I'm afraid anything I do will make this…infection worse."

He hadn't even thought about that. "I'll go get Ahab and ask what you can and can't do."

"Wait." She held up a hand. "Just… Just sit with me for a minute first."

He settled next to her on the bench instead of across the table.

"I've never been this scared of anything in my entire life," she said bluntly. "And I watched a dragon decimate a squadron of soldiers."

His heart broke a little more. He had no idea what to say. He was usually quick with a quip or comment. But looking at her bleak expression, he had nothing that would make any of this better.

"I have a genetic disorder," she said, her lips pursed as she contemplated a spot on the table. "I wonder if that's what made this possible."

"We'll ask Ahab. Is your disorder common?"

She shrugged. "Not super common. But not extraordinarily rare either. I can't remember if the genes for it are on the sex chromosomes, though. I'd have to ask my doctor."

"Mind if I ask what it is?" He didn't want to push, but since she'd brought it up, he hoped she'd tell him more. Something about her that was real, not the story she told everyone else.

"No big deal really," she said with a shrug. "A few generations back, on Earth, members of both sides of my family underwent genetic manipulation. Weight control." She snorted and shook her head. "The idea was that they'd be able to eat whatever they wanted and never gain weight. Vanity."

"And it didn't work," he guessed.

"No. It worked great for that first group experimented on. It wasn't until they started having children that the repercussions of the experiment became clear."

She stayed silent for a few minutes, so he nudged. "What happened to their children?"

"Some of them missed out on getting the manipulated genes and went on to be perfectly healthy. Some got the genes from one parent and were 'carriers' of a potential issue. And then there are those like me, stuck with the genes from both sides. For me, if I overeat, I start to lose weight. The more I eat, the more weight I'll lose. My body goes into a kind of hypermetabolic state and eventually eats itself."

"You could die from getting too skinny?" he asked.

"Exactly. And I get skinny by eating too *many* calories."

"What happens when you eat less?"

"I need a specific, optimum number of calories a day. If I don't eat enough, I start to gain weight."

He shook his head. "So your metabolism works backward. This makes my brain hurt."

With a snort, she finally looked up at him. "Yeah. Imagine living with it. A healthy diet for me means something completely different to other people. If I eat too much, I waste away. If I eat too little, I pack on the pounds—which, by the way, could also potentially kill me because of the speed I gain and the stress it puts on my body. Losing weight is much more dangerous but either direction isn't good."

"So, you have to eat an exact amount…or else," he said.

"Right." She shrugged. "I'm used to it at this stage. One

of my brothers is my doctor, and he keeps me on track. Biggest problem is getting busy and forgetting to eat. I get really tired of having to think about it all the time."

Raf only ever worried about making enough money to feed himself and his crew. When he first left home, he'd worried about getting enough food not to starve to death. But he didn't really think about food and eating all that much now. He got hungry, he ate. He made sure to make enough money that hunger wasn't an issue. And most of his daily worries revolved around making that money and keeping his crew alive. Having to think about a daily calorie count on top of that would definitely be a pain in the ass—especially knowing it could mean death if you didn't do it.

"Anyone else in your family have this?" he asked.

"My mom is a carrier. She didn't know before she started having kids that my dad was also a carrier. Fortunately, I'm the only one who ended up with the full condition. One brother and one sister are carriers, though."

"We'd better check with Ahab to see if this will have any effect on..." He trailed off, immediately sorry he'd brought the topic back to the Leeches when she swallowed visibly and her hand fisted against the table.

He wanted to reach out and take her hand in his, give her some sort of reassurance that everything would be okay. He didn't.

"I'm very sorry this happened, Clare," he murmured. "I would never have diverted to FarMore if I'd know this was even possible."

She waved away his apology. "How could you know? No one does. Except the Leeches and Ahab. Don't worry about it."

"I'll worry until you're healthy again."

She smiled. Small, but genuine. "Thanks." She sucked in a deep breath and straightened her shoulders, a strange expression coming over her face.

"What?" he asked. "You're thinking very hard about something."

She blinked and looked up at him. "Hmm? Oh, nothing. Just... I have this reporter friend. This would make one hell of a story." She made a face. "I'd rather I wasn't living through it *personally*, but still... Bet getting the story out would save some lives."

"Reporter friend, huh?" There was something she wasn't saying, some part of her story that didn't gibe. Back to the lies, then. Raf smiled, comforted by that for reasons he decided not to think about. "All the more reason to survive," he said.

She nodded and a look of calculation narrowed her dark eyes. She looked...determined now. His smile widened. Not so easy to kill this one, not when she had a goal.

She refocused on him. "I'm going to need to eat soon. We'd better talk to Ahab about what I can and can't do so I don't complicate this mess."

He nodded and stood when she did, then led the way to Ahab's cabin, feeling a kind of relief that would only be matched by knowing the Leech virus no longer ran through Clare's blood.

He refused to consider any other outcome.

CHAPTER SIXTEEN

AHAB'S LAB WAS LOCATED ON A REFURBISHED FREIGHTER ship floating at specific coordinates in empty space, well off the main trade routes. Too small to be detected by random sensors sweeps. Impossible to find on accident. The ship wasn't capable of more than impulse flight anymore, so it wasn't going anywhere. But the life support and power still worked so it functioned as a miniature station, home to a single human.

And the equipment that could cure her, Clare thought.

The *Ebisu* docked next to the freighter, extending an access tunnel to an airlock near the rear of the larger vessel. When the tunnel sealed with the airlock, Ahab led the way onto the freighter.

"How do you get here normally?" Clare asked, walking at Ahab's side as they passed through the wide corridors.

"I have a small jump ship," he said.

"Still at FarMore Station? Won't the Leeches try to find

you using it?" She tried to keep the hint of panic out of her voice but the damned tremor was there.

She hated being this scared. She'd been scared before. Her job had put her in some pretty dodgy situations, a few of which she'd only just escaped with her life. But somehow, this was worse. Until now, she'd never really thought she might die. Despite all the close calls, she'd always believed she'd get out somehow. She'd always believed she could *control* her own outcome. Now… If this cure of Ahab's didn't work, she'd be worse than dead. She'd be a Leech.

Dead looked better.

"They won't find anything on the ship to bring them here," Ahab assured. "I always assume my ships could be taken and don't leave evidence behind."

"Smart," she muttered as she looked around the freighter. She knew once this was over and she was well again, she'd want to tell this story. That meant taking in all the details while she could. She also had to talk Ahab into letting her make this public. Or rather letting Reilly make it public.

The ship was actually quite bright and open as freighters went. The wide corridors had been painted a pale shade of grey-blue, the ceiling was high, the internal lighting a soothing imitation of natural light. While the floor was a hard, cold metal grate, there was a long carpet running down the center of the corridor, softening the entire atmosphere.

"This is really nice," she commented. "How did you find it?"

"Auction." Ahab's voice was neutral, no pride in his surroundings evident.

Raf talked about the *Ebisu* like it was his child. Sonia gave it similar looks of pride. Ahab showed none of that for this vessel he called home. She wondered if it *was* home or maybe he viewed it more like a work space, not the place he relaxed and got to be himself. She spent a lot of time living that way—being "on" and not herself. Even her current apartment was "Clare's" apartment not Emma Reilly's. While she could relax and be herself in that apartment, and it was actually starting to feel like home after playing Clare for so long, it wasn't *her* space. Ahab did his research here. Could it ever be home?

"How'd you get the funds?" Raf asked from a few steps behind them.

"Lot of ways," Ahab answered, again neutrally. "People need things done. They're willing to pay for it." He glanced back at Raf. "You know the way."

She looked over her shoulder in time to see Raf raise his brows and give Ahab a nod of agreement.

So, Ahab probably worked as a smuggler or something similar, like Raf. She was so tempted to ask more, but experienced kept her from opening her mouth. People who engaged in less than lawful activities didn't talk about them easily or openly and were quick to shut down if someone showed too keen an interest. She faced forward again and filed the information away. Once Ahab cured her, she'd have time to ask everything she needed to ask.

God, she hoped he could cure her.

Just before coming aboard the freighter, she'd made the mistake of looking in a mirror. It might have been her imagination, but she could swear she saw a slight yellow glow in her usually brown eyes. The sight had made her sick to her stomach all over again. Even now, the image sent bile crawling up her throat. She forced both the sick and the mental picture away to focus on her surroundings again.

But she couldn't help asking out loud, "How long does this cure of yours take to work?"

"If it works, usually within a few hours."

Clare stumbled. "Wait. *If* it works? You said this would work."

"It will if we've caught the infection in time. If your genetic condition doesn't complicate things."

"Shit." She stopped walking as her breath left her lungs. Her brain stopped working, just completely shut down. "Shit," she murmured again.

The feel of a warm hand on her lower back made her jump.

"You'll be fine," Raf said close to her ear.

His strong, steady presence was incredibly reassuring. She pulled in a slow, deep breath and let it out even more slowly through pursed lips. "Thanks," she said. Then to Ahab. "You said my genetic disorder had nothing to do with my susceptibility to the Leech virus."

"It doesn't," he said. "But I'm not sure if the condition you have will inhibit my cure. The previous women I've applied it to haven't had your metabolic issues."

"So it could make things…worse?"

Ahab shrugged and started walking again.

She hurried to catch up.

"You aren't progressing any faster than any of the other women," he said. "In fact, your progress is moving more slowly."

"Oh. Well, that's good, then, right?"

"Depends. I didn't develop the cure with an eye toward additional genetic complications."

"Shit," she muttered. Again. It seemed like the only word she could muster, given the circumstances. She leaned into Raf's touch, into his strength to keep her standing and moving. Later, she'd probably be embarrassed by that. At the moment, nothing had ever felt better or more secure than Raf Tygran.

They cleared two levels, moving down through the freighter, until they reached Ahab's lab.

It was mostly what Clare had been expecting. Clean, shiny, brightly lit, with a lot of contraptions and equipment she couldn't identify, all with panels of flashing lights and the occasional winking hologram. It smelled reassuringly sterile and bland. And the air was comfortable—not too warm, not too chilly.

"So where do we start?" she asked, turning in a slow circle to take in the entire room.

"Sit over there." Ahab gestured to a metal exam table topped with a thin, sheet-covered cushion. Then he disappeared into a small room just off the main lab.

"Okay." She sat on the table, swinging her legs in a restless motion she couldn't stop. Her stomach was tight, the tension of waiting making her queasy.

Raf stood beside her, not touching but a calming presence that helped. He was so steady she even managed to stop swinging her legs, though she couldn't stop bouncing one foot entirely.

Ahab reappeared with a molecular scanner which he ran over her while she tried to sit still. He examined the readings, then ran the scanner over her again.

When he still didn't comment on the results, her stretched patience broke. "So? What's the verdict?"

"No verdict yet," he said, without looking up from the scanner results. "Lie down, please. Make yourself comfortable. This first part will take some time."

"First part?" She swung her legs up onto the table and settled back on the hard cushion, wiggling around in an unsuccessful attempt to get comfortable.

Raf moved to stand by her shoulder and placed a hand on hers. She squeezed his fingers, her gaze on Ahab's movements through the lab.

"What're the steps involved?" Raf asked the question plaguing her.

"First," Ahab said as he moved a large machine on wheels close to the table, "I have to run the counter-mutant through her blood. The process takes a while. It should stop the mutation in its tracks."

He did something with wires and tubes, twisted some dials, examined a screen, seemed to type something into the screen—all of which looked suitably medical if not really comprehensible to Clare.

"Then," he continued, "I inject you with a compound that will destroy the Gy'lee…disease, for lack of a better word."

"Shouldn't you do that first?" she asked, trying to keep the panic out of her voice.

"If we don't stop the current mutations first," he said, meeting her gaze, "they'll continue even if the actual disease is destroyed. The mutation has to be stopped now. Trust me. I've worked on this for four years to get it right."

She let out a breath to calm her rising pulse rate. "Then what? I'm cured?"

"No." He went back to the tubes and wires and screen on his machine. "I'll have to reverse the mutation that's happened already. That also takes time. But the process doesn't require you to be hooked up to any specialized equipment so you'll be able to relax more."

"And *then* I'll be cured." She was starting to think this could go on forever.

"If it all works as it's supposed to," he said, "you'll be cured. The damage will be repaired—mostly—and you won't change."

"Mostly?" A strange mix of panic and a detached sort of curiosity made her voice drop to a deeper tone. "What does mostly mean?"

"There's always some residual cellular damage. But nothing that will kill you. Eventually, those cells will die and regenerate to healthy cells."

"Now that you've taken a scan, any better idea if my genetic makeup will help or hinder this?" she asked.

"No. We'll only know after we go through the process." He looked up and stared into her eyes. "I'm sorry I can't be more definitive. I just won't know until I've applied the treatment. But I'm hopeful based on the scan that you'll be fine. Now, try to relax as much as you can. You'll feel a few stings as I insert the various needles."

Needles. Ugh. She closed her eyes and breathed deeply, releasing each inhale slowly. Because of her condition, she'd been poked and prodded a lot in her life. She was used to needles. But she still didn't like to watch them go in. She concentrated instead on the feel of Raf's hand in hers and focused on keeping her breathing even.

"All done," Ahab announced after several moments.

She opened her eyes but continued to stare up at the ceiling so she wouldn't have to see the needles she could feel inserted in several places along her arms and the tubes that attached her to Ahab's machine.

"So, how long again?" She swallowed to wet her throat.

"This part, it'll take a few hours. Will you need to eat in that time?"

She blinked. Hell, she still had to worry about that while all this was happening. She hadn't been able to eat more than a nutrition bar before boarding the freighter. It was dense with calories but wouldn't get her through a big chunk of the day.

"This is when I really hate my condition," she grunted. "I feel like I'll throw up anything I eat now."

"What do you do if you get a flu or stomach bug?" Raf asked.

She turned to look at him, keeping her gaze carefully away from her arms. She could still feel his hand on hers and she concentrated on that and his genuinely curious expression.

"Fortunately, I don't get sick often. Turns out that's a benefit of my metabolic issues—extremely good health. But I have gotten a few stomach bugs in my life. I have to stay in bed under medical supervision, and they use IVs to keep my calories balanced. It sucks."

"Sounds pretty crappy," he said. "You a good patient?"

She chuckled. "For the first day. Sort of. But I get restless really quickly. I hate being stuck in bed. Well, when I'm sick anyway."

Raf raised his brows and his mouth tipped up at one corner, his expression turning speculative.

God, he was sexy. He made jokes about how handsome he was, but it wasn't a joke. The man was gorgeous. Light brown hair that looked ready made for a woman's fingers. Those arresting blue eyes. He was almost pretty and yet not quite. Really too rugged for pretty. And she was certain that smile of his had felled stronger women than her. Probably stronger men, too.

At that moment, she wasn't feeling particularly strong either. She felt weak and scared and a little too grateful for his support. She was going to develop one hell of a crush on him during this ordeal. She might have been able to avoid that if she wasn't in danger of dying or worse. She could have prevented unwanted feelings if he'd been an ass about all this, or even just disinterested. Instead, he was…there. Supporting. Comforting. Easy and confident. He had her back.

Damn it. How the hell was she supposed to resist him now?

CHAPTER SEVENTEEN

CLARE HOPED RAF WOULD ASSUME ANY VISIBLE vulnerability on her part was just because of the Leech disease running through her body. That was definitely a factor. But she could feel herself falling as she continued to stare into his eyes. And the last thing she needed was for him to see that.

If he knew, would he take advantage?

He squeezed her hand and said, "Just don't give me any grief during this procedure. I've got a terrible bedside manner. Sonia will tell you. I'll just strap you down and walk away if you get too restless."

She snorted. "Right. You wish you could tie me down. I'll kick your ass first."

His grin was part mischief, part comfort, and Clare fell a little more.

"Now you sound like Sonia," he said.

That made her laugh. "I'm not sure she'd be pleased at the comparison."

"Don't fool yourself. She likes you. And if you did kick my ass, she'd adopt you."

Clare's smile softened. "Your relationship reminds me of my relationship with my brothers. Caring and contentious all at once."

His brows shot up. "Huh. Well, I guess you could say Sonia is my family. The ship, the crew, they're what I have for home and family."

"Is that good?" she asked.

"Yeah, it's good. Why?"

She shrugged. "I'm not sure I'd be able to live and work with my family, not all the time, and in such close quarters." The *Ebisu* was a decent sized ship, but it wasn't *that* big.

"I got the impression you got along well with your family," Raf said.

"Oh, we do. We're very close." She paused. How did she explain this so it made sense? "But it's too hard to be… To be fully myself beyond the habit of who I am with them. They love and support me. I love and support them. We do Sunday dinners still. But I couldn't live and work with any of them. I prefer to work alone."

His eyes narrowed slightly. "That why you don't work with a partner?"

"It is," she answered easily. "I find it easier to do my thing when I don't have to compromise or make concessions to a partner."

She blinked when she realized she was telling him the truth—Reilly's truth, not just Clare's. He thought she was talking about her cover job as a bodyguard and security specialist. But as an undercover journalist, she'd always worked alone and preferred it that way. No support or backup. Often her boss didn't know the full extent of her activities until she handed over her story. Since she always delivered great stories, he didn't try to curb her preferences—though once or twice he did try to encourage her to take on a partner for safety reasons. She was a loner in her work. And she'd always liked it that way.

"Sonia will tell you I suck at compromise," he said. "But having her around keeps me honest. So to speak." He grinned. "And having the crew to look after means I can't take ridiculous risks. At least, not ones I haven't carefully calculated." He shrugged and blinked at the wall behind her head. "Huh. Guess I don't like working alone. Who knew?"

"How long have you had the *Ebisu*?" she asked to keep the conversation going. This was keeping her mind off the coldness climbing up her arms and starting to suffuse her body. But she was also genuinely curious.

"Ten years," he said.

"Did you get it at auction, the way Ahab got this freighter?" The cold was spreading, encompassing her arms fully and crawling over her shoulders and neck. She squeezed Raf's hand a little harder. It was getting difficult to feel his touch.

"No," he said. "I actually won the *Ebisu* in a bet."

"A bet? Some game that must have been."

He chuckled.

"What did you have in the pot?" she asked.

He rolled his eyes. "Oh nothing much. Just every credit I had. And a few years of service."

"Like slave labor?"

"Exactly."

"You must have really wanted that ship." Her teeth started to chatter so she tightened her jaw.

Raf's eyes narrowed. "I did. Was the finest thing I'd ever seen. And Stenovich was an ass for even putting it in the pot."

"Why did they do it then?" Clare tightened her grip on Raf's hand again. The cold moved down her chest.

That look of mischief sparkled in his eyes, and she forced her cold lips up into a smile.

"I might have egged him on," Raf said. "He'd been on a losing streak—to me—and thought it was going to break on this particular hand. I might have given him the impression that I was bluffing."

"How?" She kept her teeth clenched to speak around the chattering now.

"I have this tell when I'm bluffing. Or so the other players at the table thought."

She laughed through the chills. "You *use* your tells to trick people?"

"Better than losing, right?" He frowned and looked over her toward where she could hear Ahab still moving around. "Stenovich was always bad at poker, though. He should never have put the *Ebisu* on the table. Even if he was positive he'd win and get me as a slave for a few years."

She followed his gaze to see Ahab looking at them with raised brows. Her teeth were chattering so hard now she couldn't stop them anymore.

Ahab drew closer.

"Is this supposed to be happening?" Raf asked.

She frowned up at him. "What do you see?" The words came out jumpy and indistinct.

"You're shaking, your jaw is tight, and your teeth are chattering."

"I'm freezing," she said as if that should be self-evident.

"And your eyes are more yellow than they were a few minutes ago," Raf said, all the humor gone from his voice now.

Her heartbeat jumped. "Fuck." She turned back to Ahab. "It's not working, is it? Something's wrong."

Ahab looked her over and ran the scanner down her body. He pressed a few buttons, ran it over her again, hit a few more spots on the screen, then shrugged.

"Everything looks good," he said. "Treatment is stopping the mutation."

"Then why are my eyes more yellow?"

"And are her chills normal?" Raf added.

"The cold is normal." Ahab looked at her when he said, "That's going to get worse before it gets better. Sorry. Nothing I can do about that. I'd offer a heating blanket, but to be honest, it doesn't really seem to help."

"And the eye color?" she asked.

Ahab frowned a little. "That doesn't usually happen. It's like your body is fighting back, like it's *trying* to keep the mutation going. But my compound is working at stopping it. Your eyes should return to normal once we've finished the full process and fixed the cellular damage."

She swallowed hard but nodded. "I'm having trouble feeling Raf's hand."

"'Fraid that's normal too," Ahab said. "It's actually good news you're experiencing the cold."

"Doesn't feel like good news," she stuttered. "I think I just bit my tongue."

"Oh yeah, be careful of that," Ahab said with a shrug. "But don't worry, I can fix that when the rest of the procedure is done. Simple work with a dermal scanner and you'll be good."

She nodded, afraid to talk and risk biting her tongue again.

Raf squeezed her hand hard enough that she felt it. She attempted a smile.

"I'll get the heating blanket," Ahab said. "It might help a little."

Since he'd just said it wouldn't, she didn't hold out much hope.

"So back to the *Ebisu*," Raf said.

She turned to stare at him, eager for the distraction of conversation even if she couldn't really talk anymore.

"I pretended to be a little panicked," he continued, "when Stenovich kept raising the stakes. I put in my entire pot— which contained a significant amount of his money…"

Raf rambled on, telling her in amusing detail how he'd managed to swindle Stenovich of his beautiful ship. Then the ensuing mayhem of taking possession from the reluctant former captain.

"And the crew?" she managed to force out.

"Lots of stories there. A bunch of the previous crew stayed on for a short time but eventually most of them were replaced."

"Didn't like serving under a captain who'd won the ship?" She frowned at the sound of her voice, so garbled and shaky she wasn't entirely sure he'd understand what she'd said.

But he answered as if she'd spoken with perfect clarity.

"Nothing like that. In our line of work, you get used to that kind of thing. But people adapt to a certain type of command and can't always make the transition to a new captain. I let go those who wanted to leave. Dumped a few who weren't working out. It happens." He shrugged. "Sonia was the first new person to join after I took command. Eventually the entire crew was new. Mine."

He sounded very possessive and protective of them, and if she hadn't been so cold, she might have wondered what it would be like to hear him talk about her that way.

"I've had the same crew now for…" He paused. "Huh. Seven years."

"Sound sur-surprised."

"I am," he said. "Even the good captains don't keep the same crew for so long. People move on, more lucrative work, get their own ships, go straight and settle down, get arrested or killed. It's rare to have no turn over at all for so long."

"No deaths?"

"Not on my watch. Not if I can help it. One of the many reasons I don't traffic Leeches."

She nodded. "U…under…understand the other r-reason."

His expression tightened. "Is the blanket helping?"

She shook her head. "Barely f-f-feel it."

He leaned down, putting his mouth near her ear. His breath was warm and felt so good against her cold skin she wanted to bury herself in his heat.

"I'm so sorry this is happening to you," he whispered. "I promise, I'll make it up to you. Somehow."

"N-n-no. No need. Not your fault."

"Don't argue with me," he said quietly. "This is non-negotiable."

He straightened and she missed the heat of his breath.

"Now when Sonia joined the crew," he said as if they'd never changed subjects, "that was an interesting period."

He stood beside her, holding her hand, telling her ridiculous stories through the long, freezing hours. And her crush turned into full-fledged adoration.

If she wasn't very careful, she realized, she might actually fall in love with the pirate.

CHAPTER EIGHTEEN

By the time the first part of the process was over, Clare could barely feel her body. Everything was cold and numb, her teeth chattered so hard she was sure she cracked at least one, and in the final half hour, she honestly doubted she'd survive.

Raf stayed with her the entire time. She was pretty sure he held her hand the whole time too, but she wasn't able to feel his touch anymore. When Ahab reappeared and started disconnecting the tubes and needles, she almost cried. She just wanted to be warm again.

Questions crowded behind her cold lips but she was in no shape to speak, so she waited and hoped heat would climb back through her limps soon.

To her surprise, Raf actually asked a few of the questions she had.

"How long until she's a normal temperature again?" he asked.

"Not long," Ahab said. "Depending on your point of

view, the next part could be considered a reprieve. The process of killing the compound will heat her up."

"How hot?"

"She'll run a temperature of around a hundred and three degrees for about a half hour."

"Is that safe?" Raf asked.

"I'll monitor her closely, make sure it doesn't go too high. It needs to rise while the disease is killed, though. But this part doesn't take as long as the previous stage."

"How long exactly?"

"Only two hours. If the disease isn't destroyed by then…"

When Ahab trailed off, her heartbeat jumped. She was getting feeling back into her limps finally, but she still couldn't manage to speak.

"If the disease isn't destroyed, then what?" Raf asked, his tone serious and soft.

"Then I won't be able to get rid of it completely," Ahab said quietly. "She'll continue to mutate. The infection is self-replicating. It'll return, grow, and take over. Like cancer in the days when humans were still mostly on Earth. If you don't get it all, it returns."

"Can it return even if you get it all?" Raf asked.

"No. That's where the cancer analogy breaks down. If we can destroy this completely, she won't have to worry about turning Leech anymore."

"Shit," she whispered. Her first word forced through still numb lips.

Raf squeezed her hand and she felt it like a distant pressure.

"The first part worked, though?" Raf asked Ahab. "The mutation has stopped?"

Ahab grunted. "Looks like. Her eyes aren't getting any more yellow."

Clare caught a glimpse of his molecular scanner as he ran it over her body.

"Yeah, no more mutation at the moment," Ahab said. "We need to destroy the compound before it starts up again."

She closed her eyes as she felt the barest of pricks as more needles went into her arms. She didn't want to see what he was doing.

"My arms are going t-to l-l-look terrible," she muttered.

"Few holes will only make them more beautiful," Raf commented.

She laughed, surprising herself, but the sound was strange and she hoped he realized he'd amused her. When all this was over, she wasn't sure how she'd pay him back for the support. She was still amazed he was sticking with her. She wouldn't have expected that level of caring from him. But after hearing his stories of his crew, she realized he was a lot more protective and tender-hearted than he let on. A strange trait for someone in his profession, she thought.

As Ahab continued to work, she kept her eyes closed and drifted, letting time pass quietly as her body started to warm. When she could feel her limbs again, she squeezed Raf's hand and opened her eyes.

"Thanks," she whispered. "This is…hard."

"You think this is tough?" he said. "You should try outrunning a ship full of Binnean mercenaries who want to set your head on a spike."

She smiled. "Tell me."

Raf kept her entertained as her body passed through a few minutes of feeling normal before the chills set in again as her temperature rose and her skin grew hot and tight. The fever was actually easier to deal with than the extreme cold had been. She sipped at the water Raf offered every few minutes and let her mind drift again, listening to the sounds of his deep voice, the quiet movements of Ahab through the lab. The fever robbed her of the appetite that she barely had anyway. But Ahab promised he was adding enough nutritional calories through an IV to counter her condition.

She wanted to ask how the process was going, was the infection being destroyed? But she was afraid to hear any doubts or negative news.

When Ahab started to remove needles again, she finally gave in and asked, "Did it work?"

She swallowed to wet her dry throat, took another sip of the water Raf offered. When she felt able, she raised her head off the table to look at Ahab.

He pulled out his scanner and ran it up and down her body. Long, agonizing moments passed as he studied the results, scanned her again, then tweaked a few settings and scanned yet again.

"So?" Her voice jumped to a squeak.

"Looks good," he said.

And Clare thought she might pass out from the relief that rushed through her.

Dizzy, she dropped her head back onto the table. "So it's all gone."

"Just about," he said.

"Wait." She lifted her head up again. "You said it had to

be gone by the end of two hours. That we had to get rid of all of it."

"It's still being destroyed," he said. "We have another fifteen minutes while the treatment continues to work. Then I'll get your temperature down."

"Ah. Okay." She settled back on the table and worked on slowing her breathing. "Damn Leeches."

"My feelings exactly," Raf muttered.

"How much do you hate them?" Ahab asked, his voice soft but intense, his curiosity not idle.

"A lot," Raf said. "Probably as much as you. Or close."

Ahab fell silent. Clare couldn't resist looking at him again. He was staring at Raf, his expression too hard to read, but the intensity she'd heard in his voice tightened his features.

She frowned. There was more here, more in Ahab's hate, than the usual dislike of Leeches. And some unspoken knowledge passed between the two men.

Filled with more questions than she had the faculties to ask, she dropped back to the small hard pillow and groaned. When she was better, she intended to get to the bottom of that look between Raf and Ahab. Her instincts were jumping. There was a whole story in that look, she was sure of it.

She almost smiled. There were a lot of stories out here in the wider galaxy. Naravan stories were plentiful and had given her a stellar career. But there were some very inter-esting things happening beyond the Naravan atmosphere, things her curiosity wanted to dig into.

She'd better get well soon. She had too much to do to turn into a Leech. Or die.

The sobering thought brought her back to the moment.

She started counting in her head, calculating how much of the fifteen minutes she had left before they were sure if she would survive this or not. She focused on the numbers so her heartbeat didn't start to race. And when Ahab returned with the scanner, she continued to count so she didn't have to think about the results.

"Clare," Ahab murmured.

She stopped counting. "Tell me."

"It's destroyed," Ahab said. "Entirely. You're going to survive."

To her utter surprise, she burst into tears. She was so shocked by her own reaction she nearly pulled the needles out of her arm when she slapped her hand over her mouth.

She tried to stop the tears but couldn't. They flowed fast, hot, and sloppy. No soft, pretty crying for her, not in this moment.

Her arm was tugged away from her face, gently but insistently. She turned her face away from Raf and sucked in air as Ahab removed the IVs from her arms. A moment after she felt the final needle tug free, she found herself in Raf's embrace. She was still crying uncontrollably, so she buried her face against his neck, held tight, and let go.

"Sorry," she muttered, hiccupping as the sobs finally subsided.

"Don't be," Raf said, his voice very deep and steady. "Relief is supposed to make you cry."

She smiled. "So much relief." She hiccupped again and chuckled. "And so many messy, ugly tears."

She pulled the bottom of her shirt up to wipe her cheeks and eyes, not really carrying that she was showing her midsection to Raf and Ahab. Maybe if they were busy staring at her stomach, they wouldn't notice the red blotchiness she was positive painted her face now. She'd never been a pretty crier, which was why she did it so infrequently in front of other people.

Sniffling, she let her shirt drop and kept her head bowed as she steadied her breathing. "Wow. Probably my worst day ever. And that includes E and the dragon day."

Raf chuckled. "That's what you're calling that, huh? The dragon day?"

She grinned. "Actually, the whole dragon thing was pretty amazing. But only because he was on our side." She peeked up at Raf from under her lashes. "E is terrifying in a lot of ways, but… I had a weapon I could use against him that day—for what it was worth. With this Leech infection." She shook her head. "Not being about to *do* anything…"

"So much worse," Raf said. "I know."

She stared at him for a moment, at his sincerity.

Well, hell. She was absolutely going to fall in love with him. She could see it now. An absolute.

A complete disaster.

But at least she was alive. And she wasn't turning into a Leech. She'd figure out how to deal with her inevitable broken heart later.

She opened her mouth to ask Ahab about the final step when the freighter suddenly rocked hard underneath them. Raf fell forward, bracing himself against the table, his arms on either side of her hips keeping her from falling off. She clung to his shoulders a moment, then leaned back, her eyes wide.

"What the hell was that?" she breathed.

They both looked to Ahab. He rushed to a comm-center and his hands flew over the screen.

"Son of a bitch," he said. "We just took a laser cannon blast to the rear of the ship."

Raf straightened. "That's near the *Ebisu*."

Clare barely blinked before Raf had disappeared down the corridor, racing back toward the airlock. She slipped to the floor and had to take a moment to steady herself. Her knees nearly buckled with a weakness she wasn't used to.

"Fuck." She held the table as she tried to get her body to work. "You have any weapons on this thing?" she asked Ahab, who was still busy at the console.

He didn't answer, just held the sides of the console when the ship rocked again, then continued punching code into the screen. A moment later, Clare heard a whirring noise, and the lights shivered as the ship jumped.

"I only have enough power for two more of those," Ahab said. "Get back to the *Ebisu*."

"Who is it?" she asked.

"Not sure. Guessing Leeches."

"How the hell did they find this place?"

"Fuck if I know," he said. "Get back to your ship."

She stopped wasting time with questions that could be asked later. Her legs still wobbly, she trotted down the corridor, holding the wall to keep from collapsing. The return trip down the lifts and through the levels of the freighter took her significantly longer than getting to the lab had taken. The ship bounced under her feet again from the discharge of its own laser cannon, and it was hit at least twice more from enemy fire by the time she got to the airlock.

To her surprise, Ahab appeared from a different direction moments after she arrived.

"Short cut?" she asked with no little sarcasm.

"The *Ebisu* had to cut free." He ignored her comment, hitching up the small backpack he had over his shoulders. "We need to take my shuttle. The freighter isn't going to stand up to this attack much longer. Wasn't designed to take the hits."

Her stomach bottomed out. The *Ebisu* was gone? Raf had left her behind?

She knew after their conversation that he'd do whatever it took to save his people, his ship, but still… She felt a stab of pain she wasn't expecting, so sharp and hard it took her breath away. Without a word, she followed Ahab back the way he'd come, to a small bay where a shuttle big enough to carry maybe three or four humans, or two Binneans, sat with the landing ramp down.

She followed Ahab as fast as she could, but the ramp was already rising and retracting by the time she hit it. She barely made it aboard when the door sealed and the shuttle lifted off.

"Strap in," Ahab called from the pilot's seat.

She stumbled forward and fell into the seat next to him, frantically trying to latch the safety harness as the shuttle shot forward toward the opening hatch. The shuttle's hull scrapped the hatch as they burst into open space, a loud screeching sound that made her cringe.

Once free of the freighter, Clare called up a holo display on the console in front of her. She blinked at the image of the freighter, and when Ahab brought the shuttle around, she had to blink again at the real thing. Huge chunks of the vessel were breaking apart and floating off into space. There were hull breaches over the entire ship.

"How the hell did we get out of there alive?" she muttered. There was a significant breach not far from where they'd just been, the edges of the hole still glowing red from being melted away.

"I've got good shields," Ahab said. "Or I did. But not against weapons. Just again hull breaches."

She stared at the side of his face.

He shrugged. "Freighter was pretty beat up when I bought it. Never could tell if there was going to be a leak. Didn't want to get sucked out into space in my sleep."

She blew air into her cheeks, puffing them up. "Fair enough," she murmured. That was the type of thing she'd never had to worry about while planet-side. Suddenly working in deep space didn't seem so exciting.

Looking back at the freighter, she spotted the enemy ship finally. It was a little smaller than the *Ebisu* but significantly larger than the shuttle she as in. And it was heading right toward them.

"Does this thing have a jump drive?" she asked, trying to keep the panic from her voice. "Or shields of any kind?"

"Shields are too weak to take a laser cannon hit," he said. "And we can only make short jumps. But we can jump."

"Think we'd better do that now." Without meaning to, she leaned back in her seat, as if the motion would move her farther away from the approaching ship.

"Almost have the nav-coordinates entered. Gonna take a few more minutes."

"Not sure we've got minutes," she shouted when she saw the line of green energy flash from the other ship's cannon.

Then ground her teeth together against the heavy Gs of the shuttle's sudden evasive movement.

The weight pushing her into her seat eased as the gravitational systems caught up with the shuttle's maneuver. She sucked in air as she punched in a few instructions on the console to pull up a new holo image, this one of the attacking ship, now behind them.

"They're getting closer," she muttered in as calm a voice as she could manage. She didn't want to rush Ahab with the nav-calculations because one wrong number and they could jump into a star or worse. But as she watched the approaching enemy, panic made her pulse race.

Just as the ship's laser cannon started to light up with another shot, the *Ebisu* swooped in between the shuttle and the attacking ship. The *Ebisu's* shields lit up with a pale blue glow as they absorbed the cannon's bolt.

A moment later, Raf's voice sounded over the comm-link. "Transmitting jump coordinates for rendezvous. Get the hell out of here. We'll keep them occupied until you're away."

"Roger," Ahab answered sharply.

A blink later, the shuttle whirled into motion and jumped away from the attack.

CHAPTER NINETEEN

Clare sat breathing heavily as the shuttle floated in empty space, the freighter and the *Ebisu* nowhere in sight.

"Where are we?" she whispered because she was still too shaken to speak normally.

"Far enough away to be safe," Ahab said quietly. "But in the middle of nowhere in particular. Just a different nowhere from where the freighter is. Was."

"How did they find you?"

"Best guess? They managed to get a tracking bug onto the *Ebisu* while Raf was still negotiating with Beyvir."

"Raf swept the ship," she insisted. "The crew kept watch to make sure no strangers got near."

"Couldn't have found my freighter any other way," he said matter-of-factly.

Clare frowned and muttered to herself, "Would have had to have used a human. Could they have bugged Raf without him knowing? Or..." Her mouth dropped open. She closed her eyes for a beat, the realization making her head hurt. "Or did they bug me when they injected that Leech crap into me?" She faced Ahab.

"Son of a bitch," he said. "I should have thought of that."

He moved to the rear of the shuttle and opened the backpack he'd brought with him from the freighter, pulling out a medical scanner. He rejoined her, already imputing data into the device.

"Son of a bitch," he said again. "Bastards haven't done this before."

"How many people have they infected before me?" she asked.

"I've been able to save two dozen women. Not sure how many others I've missed. But there are still no Leech females, so if there were others, the infection wasn't successful on them, or they killed themselves rather than turn." Under his breath, so quiet she almost missed it, he whispered, "Seen that before."

"Find anything?" she asked as he moved the scanner over the injection site.

"Nothing. Wait…" He frowned and rescanned a small patch of skin. "Fucking bastards."

"What is it?"

"Tracking chip." He grunted another curse.

"Get it out! They'll be able to follow us."

"Working on it." He jumped to the back of the shuttle again and dug through his backpack, then rejoined her with a small box.

"What's that?" she asked.

He opened it and showed her a very small pin chip, so small it was actually hard to see. Using a delicate micro-tongs, he pulled the chip out and set it against her skin.

"Don't move," he said.

She sat frozen as he pulled a thin, card-sized controller from the bottom of the box and started punching things on its surface. A moment later, he smiled.

"What?" she said. "I didn't feel anything. What happened?"

"This—" he removed the chip with the micro-tongs and placed it back in the box, "—is a very new bit of technology. Essentially, it works like an EMP burst."

"Wait," she said. "I've seen one of those before."

He scowled up at her. "You have? When? How? They're almost impossible to come by."

"Did you get it on Narava?" she asked.

"Where did you see this?" He motioned with the box, ignoring her question.

"Long story," she hedged, realizing she'd said too much. Damn, she usually kept her mouth shut before blurting out information she wasn't sure she should share. The whole almost-dying thing had knocked her off her game. "At any rate, your chip disabled the tracker? You're sure?"

If this was the same chip she'd first encountered at Ti'ann's paleontology camp on Narava, Clare knew it had worked. The damned things were brilliant, working as focused electromagnetic pulses to knock out only the specific electronics the programmer wanted. They could disable something as small as a tracker chip or as large as an entire ship.

E had been responsible for the one she'd seen, but he hadn't known where it came from. It had just been in the arsenal of tools his creators had given him while he was being "tested" at the paleontology site.

The little focused EMP chips were extremely dangerous, cost a fortune, and were almost impossible to acquire—she'd tried to find someone who would sell her one and had failed.

So how did Ahab find one? Where did he get it? And how could he afford it?

There was a lot more to this young man than met the eye. And though he'd saved her life—several times now—she wasn't entirely sure she should trust him.

He confirmed the tracker was disabled and returned the EMP weapon his backpack.

"We'd better make another jump or two before we rendezvous with the *Ebisu*," he said. "Those bastards no doubt have our current location. Don't want them to track us farther."

She nodded and strapped back in for the jumps. He took them to two more spots that were just as isolated. No nearby star systems or space stations, just the empty void of space and the pinpoints of distant suns.

Finally, he decided they were safe to meet the *Ebisu*.

"If they're there," he said as he entered the coordinates into the nav-computer.

"What do you mean?" she asked.

"If they escaped the attack. If they weren't followed or tracked somehow. We won't know until we get there."

She forced air slowly through her pursed lips. A series of harsh words piled up against her tongue but she was too nervous to actually let them out. Gripping the armrests tight, she counted slowly to one hundred as they made the jump.

When they appeared at yet another spot in space surrounded by nothing, Clare searched the surroundings for the *Ebisu*, looking out the view screen as well as checking the holographic display. Her heart beat hard for several very long moments.

Then she spotted the ship, slowly gliding toward them.

She let out sigh and leaned back in her seat. The *Ebisu* had survived at least.

Still too many questions though. Had anyone been hurt? What happened with the other ship? Was the freighter salvageable? What now?

And the one question she was only just facing. She hadn't fully finished Ahab's procedure. All his equipment was on that freighter, now too full of holes to be habitable. Not to mention the Leeches knew where it was.

So, what happened for her now?

Staring at the image of the *Ebisu* in the holo as it neared, she said, "I won't relapse, will I? You didn't have time to finish the process."

"You won't relapse," Ahab confirmed.

"But?"

"But since I haven't fixed the mutation that did take place, you might encounter some problems until I can."

"Your equipment is gone. How can you fix me now?"

"The last part doesn't require the specialized things I needed for the first two parts. I just need some standard medical equipment. We can go to the nearest human settlement and I should be able to finish."

She closed her eyes, realizing they'd stay yellow for a little while longer. But at least they wouldn't get worse. "That's good news," she said.

The silence that followed her statement was thick with something unsaid.

"What?" she asked, her eyes still closed.

The ship shifted a little around her as Ahab moved to dock with the *Ebisu*. The smuggler's ship was only just big enough to take in the shuttle—and that because they weren't carrying any large cargo. *Ebisu* had two emergency shuttles of its own docked against the sides of the ship, but there weren't any secure, spare places to attached Ahab's shuttle outside of the ship for the jumps back to civilization.

Ahab remained silent so she finally turned to look at him.

"What?" she said again, more firmly.

"You still look like you're changing," he said.

"Yeah. I know. My eyes. Why is this an issue?"

"Up to now, the Leeches have kept their ability to change some women secret. And I haven't tried to make it public either. I can only cure so many people. And I can't cure the Y-chromosome mutations at any rate, so I'm no help to anyone with a Y that could change."

"I know all this, Ahab. You're repeating yourself. Why?"

He concentrated on the instruments in front of him, on docking the shuttle in the *Ebisu's* loading bay. But he did answer her.

"We won't be able to hide that there's something different about you when we go into a human settlement," he said. "Nothing else causes the eye changes that you have, except for the Leech disease."

"Yeah. So." She wasn't sure she saw the problem. She figured the galaxy needed to know the Leeches had developed this infection. And not just because she was a reporter and wanted to break the story—though that did play a pretty significant part. If the various human authorities knew about this, they could do something to protect the people who were vulnerable.

"The reason I haven't gone public," Ahab said, "is because there are people who would *want* to change and give birth to Leech babies. None of the human emissaries who've attached themselves to the Leeches are genetically able to mutate. But if word gets out, there *will* be people who want to change and give birth to Leech babies."

She shivered. "I can't imagine anyone wanting to become a Leech on purpose."

"And yet there are people who serve the Leeches *hoping* they'll be exposed to Gy'lee's atmosphere so they can try to mutate, even if their genes indicate they'll die in the attempt. There's a sort of power to it. And there will be humans with viable eggs and wombs who want that as well."

She frowned, still not sure she understood what this had to do with her eyes or letting people know this was possible. "It's weird," she allowed, "but I don't know why that makes silence necessary."

"If there are female Leeches," he said slowly, as if speaking to a child, "the Leeches may be able to start reproducing biologically. Having babies like a real species. More than just monsters created from a mutation."

"And?"

"They can't be allowed to breed."

She faced him fully, turning in her seat to stare hard at him. "Why?"

"They're evil," he growled, meeting her stare with narrowed, angry eyes.

Every ounce of calm he'd shown before evaporated under rage so thick she could practically feel.

"They have to be eliminated," he said, his voice nearly an octave deeper. "Wiped out. Dead. All of them. Exterminated.

They can't be allowed to breed. They can't be allowed to exist."

The heat and venom in his voice made her lean back. She'd rarely encountered so much pure hatred. And she'd seen a whole hell of a lot.

He looked back at the panels in front of him, ignoring the fact that she continued to stare. His face lost the righteous passion of fury and settled into a more neutral expression. He finished landing the shuttle and started to shut down the engines as if nothing had just happened.

"Ahab," she said, her voice quiet, "we need to discuss this more."

But he was already opening the shuttle's landing ramp, and she could hear the sound of voices in the bay.

CHAPTER TWENTY

CONCERN OVER WHAT AHAB HAD JUST REVEALED GOT PUSHED aside as Clare stepped from the shuttle and saw Raf at the head of the small crowd waiting for them. For a while there, she'd been certain he'd abandoned her.

And then he'd saved them.

She caught herself an instant before she started to jog toward him, to throw herself in his arms, but she didn't try to hide her grin.

"You had me worried, Tygran," she said.

"I had your back," he said.

She blinked at the absolute seriousness in his tone. Before she could embarrass herself by saying something more, E stepped from behind Raf and looked her right in the eye.

"You are not healed?" he asked.

There was no emotion that she could detect in E's voice, but she could swear he was worried about her. It was kind of sweet in a weird and vaguely creepy way.

"I'm fine," she said, for everyone to hear. "We got the

most important parts of the procedure finished before the attack. There's just some repair work that still needs doing." She grinned and winked.

E tipped his head down and forward. She smiled wider.

"We need a medical facility, though," Ahab said from just behind her.

Raf looked between Clare, Ahab and Sonia. He raised his brows at Sonia. "Kira and her crew took a lot of medical equipment with them," he said. "They should have what he needs."

"You think they'll appreciate us bringing an unexpected guest along?" Sonia nodded at Ahab. "They're gonna freak out enough when they see E."

"They don't know he's not part of the crew," Raf pointed out.

Sonia pursed her lips. "Your decision, Captain. Just saying. We might be better off going somewhere else and returning Ahab to his whale hunt."

"He saved my life, Sonia," Clare said, even though she thought Sonia might just be right about this. "A few times. I doubt they'll mind him coming along." She glanced at Ahab. "And it solves a problem if we go directly there. Ahab would prefer word of this didn't get out."

Everyone looked to Ahab.

In a much calmer voice, without the edge of hatred or the declarations that all Leeches had to be exterminated, he explained why he preferred to keep things quiet. The mere threat of reproductively able humans wanting to turn Leech seemed to be enough for everyone else. It surprised her that no one questioned Ahab further. They all just accepted his reasoning and agreed with him.

Maybe it was her—her training and curiosity. She needed to know more, to know why, to understand Ahab's motives. She forgot sometimes that others didn't have that drive to dig into people's lives and thoughts. Or maybe it was her intrinsic fear of fanaticism. The hint of it she'd seen in Ahab's expression scared her, and maybe that was driving her thinking.

Even beyond her curiosity and her fear, though, she was still…uncomfortable with Ahab's goal of exterminating the Leeches. She couldn't stand the mutants, they terrified her—now more than ever. She'd rather die than be one, and she'd yet to encounter anyone who had anything redeeming to say about them. But at one point, most Naravans felt the same way about Shifters. What made Leeches any less worthy of life?

Granted, Shifters didn't go around killing or kidnapping people to mutate them against their will. Shifters were generally quite passive and gentle. But did the Leeches' abhorrent behavior—and she wasn't even sure it extended to all of them—merit extinction?

It was a moral question she'd have to consider more, maybe one she'd put to the public when she eventually broke this story.

"Okay," Raf said, calling Clare back to their more immediate problems. "We go directly to Kierna'Rhoan. If they don't have what Ahab needs, we can always go somewhere else. The mutations won't get worse now, right?"

"No," Ahab said. "She won't get any worse. But the mutations that have taken place might cause some unforeseen medical issues."

"Like what?" Raf frowned.

Ahab shrugged. "Don't know. Never had to put off fixing the damage before."

"Can you use what we have aboard?" Raf asked. "It's not as extensive as a full medical facility, but you might be able to fix some of the damage."

Ahab looked to Sonia. "Show me what you've got."

She snorted. "You wish, kid." Then she turned, the bells in her intricately braided hair tinkling with the movement, and motioned for Ahab to follow as she stalked off on her five inch heels.

Ahab raised his brows, looking a little bemused as he left the bay. He seemed both younger and just a little lighter in that moment, showing hints of a less haunted man. Clare couldn't help but wonder what he'd been through to age him so quickly. To leave him so bitter.

She refocused on Raf and a thrill of giddy tingles tightened her stomach. He hadn't abandoned her. Not during the entire procedure. Not even when his ship was in danger. He'd come back for her.

And she was in serious trouble. Full blown, head over heels trouble. Emotionally and personally invested in the story now kind of trouble.

Her boss would take her to task for this.

Visceral memories of kissing Raf that night in the Docks danced over her lips, in a shiver of awareness. She licked her lips, imagining his taste there, and trying not to let her real feelings show since she was standing in the middle of the cargo bay with most of Raf's crew. She'd have to mull over this change in her feelings from flirty lust to this giddy something more later, when she had privacy and time. At the moment, they had bigger things to worry about.

Raf reinforced this with his next statement.

"We scanned the ship and didn't find any tracking chips," he said. "Not sure how the bastards found us."

"I know." She sighed.

Raf held her gaze a moment, then sent the rest of the crew back to their duties—they had jumps to Kierna'Rhoan to calculate and repairs from the fight to make. To Clare's surprise, every one of them expressed some level of relief and pleasure that she was healed before they left the bay. Delilah even gave her a one armed hug around her shoulders that made tears prickle in Clare's eyes. Talk about emotionally invested. She promised Delilah a chat later, and waited until it was just her and Raf left in the bay before she rubbed at her eyes. At Raf's concerned frown, she made an excuse about being tired to cover her rush of feelings.

"I could probably use a drink, too," she said.

"Come on. You can explain how the Leeches found us on the way to the canteen."

They headed back into the main part of the ship, and she told him about the tracking chip that had been inserted with the Leech infection, and how Ahab had disabled it.

"Bastards," Raf hissed. "Guess they've learned a lesson. If they want to recover the ones they infect, they need to be able to find them. And now they've destroyed Ahab's lab."

"Nothing salvageable?" she asked without hope.

"Complete loss. So many holes it looked like cheese. And the area where the lab was located was completely decimated. Not sure if that was by chance or calculated. Either way, it's gone."

"So if they find someone who fits the genetic requirements before Ahab can rebuild—"

"Which is going to cost," Raf pointed out.

"Basically, they're fucked," she said with a snarl.

"Basically."

"Shit."

"Exactly."

She missed a step when she realized she could have been the one fucked. If the Leeches had arrived a few hours earlier, she could still have the compound in her blood. She could still be mutating.

She shivered and had to pause to catch her breath.

Raf took a few steps before noticing she'd stopped, then backtracked. "You okay?"

She shook her head. "Could have been me."

"It wasn't."

"Could have been. A few hours. Just a few hours earlier."

Raf took her shoulders and she met his gaze.

"But it wasn't you," he said. "You will recover. You'll survive."

"And all the others? What about the ones who won't?"

"They aren't your responsibility, Clare."

For the first time in years, she startled when someone used her cover name—when *he* used her cover name. She'd forgotten. She'd actually forgotten he didn't know who she really was. He didn't know her real name.

"And according to Ahab," Raf continued, not seeming to notice her reaction, "people affected by this version of the Leech disease are rare. Chances are good he'll rebuild before they even find another eligible victim."

She swallowed and nodded, still reeling from her reaction to hearing him call her Clare.

"Hey," he said, all serious and intent.

She met his gaze again.

"It'll be fine," he said. "Focus on what you can control."

What she could control… She could do that. He was right, some things were beyond her control. But how she treated each passing moment wasn't. She stared at him, making her decision.

Then she took his face in her hands and kissed him.

CHAPTER TWENTY-ONE

Raf slid into her kiss as if they did this all the time, had been kissing each other for years. He couldn't help himself. His body reacted well before his mind caught up. He'd wanted to kiss her for hours now. For days. But the need had somehow gone beyond fun and entertaining into something more serious. Something just a little desperate.

When his brain finally did catch up with the situation, he realized they were out in the open. And while he didn't give a fuck if his crew saw them kissing, he wasn't sure Clare would appreciate the audience.

He leaned back just a little, his pulse pounding hard as need raced through his blood. She looked intent, not backing down or regretting her move. Good. Because he had no intention of ending things like this. He took her hand and led her to his cabin. She didn't resist, thank all the gods in the universe.

She still didn't resist when he opened his door and led her

inside. She didn't resist when he pulled her into his arms. And she didn't hesitate when he kissed her again.

She relaxed into him, all lush curves and delicious softness. Desperation gnawed at him, but he didn't want to rush either. He wanted to savor. Her taste, her textures. Every soft inch. Gliding his hand down her spine, he marveled at the combination of strength and pliability. She shivered, and the reaction made his head spin.

Taking her face in his hands, he deepened the kiss, even as he edged her against the wall so he could absorb the feel of her. She rubbed against him, her arms clutching at his back, just under his jacket, and suddenly there were too many layers of material between them.

He dropped the jacket, let her lift his shirt off over his head, then dove back in for another kiss. Another moment passed before he realized he hadn't gotten her out of anything yet. With the care born of years of handling weapons, he unbuckled her blaster belt and set it and the weapons gently on the floor to one side. He did the same with his own holster, ensuring the various weapons would be both safe and easy to retrieve if, for some reason, they needed them. Then he turned his attention to getting Clare naked.

Tugging her shirt out from her pants, he lifted it over her head as gently as he could manage given how desperately he wanted to tear the material off her. Her arms were covered in a series of pinholes from the needles inserted during her procedure. She didn't seem to notice, or feel any pain from all those little wounds, but he felt a gut punch looking at them, at the faint bruising around each prick, at the evidence of what she'd just been through, what could have happened…

More tenderly than he thought himself capable, he raised one of her arms to examine the punctures, kissing the skin gently round each one. She sucked in a breath, and he glanced up to meet her gaze.

"Did I hurt you?" he asked.

"No." She swallowed visibly. "That feels good."

He returned to his exploration, easing up the length of her arm to her shoulder, pausing at sensitive places that made her shiver or gasp. He eased her bra strap to one side, tasting her skin where her neck and shoulder met, where her scent was strongest. Breathing deeply, he pulled in that combination of musk and very faint vanilla. Delicious. Her hair tickled his cheek, so he took the wild curls in one hand and moved the silky mass aside. He couldn't remember the last time he'd been so desperate for someone and yet so happy to just slowly explore.

His muscles tensed when she ran her fingernails up his abdomen, the delicate scratches sending shocks of desire through him. She scrapped her nails in gentle circles back down his stomach, nearing the top of his pants before she moved around to his back. He groaned, resting his head on her shoulder. His hand clenched in her hair when she dipped her fingers just under the edge of his pants, and his desperation jumped to a higher level.

Reclaiming her mouth in a hot, needy kiss, he wrapped his arms around her and backed her toward his bunk. He was the captain. He had a decent sized bed. And he'd never been so grateful for all that space.

Somewhere along the way, he removed her bra and she dropped it to the floor. Her full breasts squeezing tight against his bare chest left him shaky, hungry for a taste of her. He managed to toe out of his boots, awkwardly because he didn't want to release her, and her small laugh vibrated through him. Gods he could listen to that, feel that for the rest of his days and die a happy man.

By the time they'd made it across the room and tumbled onto the bed, he'd lost all track of the world beyond this moment, this woman. The rest of their clothes came off in a burst of tugging and pulling, until finally he could take in the full glory of her naked body. And glorious it was. As lush and soft as he'd known she'd be. Every inch a challenge to see just how much sensation he could draw out of her.

He explored with his hands first, then his mouth. Tasting the length of her, the faint saltiness of her skin. He moved down her body, delighted when he discovered just how sensitive she was. She jumped when he kissed her waist and dug her fingers into his hair, keeping him close. She writhed under him when he licked across her hip and low on her stomach. She cursed through clenched teeth when he settled between her thighs. And she groaned when he licked into her heat. He dragged his tongue across her clit, and she gasped his name.

Her moans, her clutching grasps, the ragged sound of her breathing, all of it for him and what he was doing to her. He wasn't sure he'd ever *needed* to please a partner this much, been so overwhelmed by *knowing* how much she wanted him. Sex had always been a game. An orgasm. A bit of fun. And sometimes a useful tool.

This was more. Better. Stronger. The heat of it, the power of it filling him up. No game, this. He couldn't have described why it was different, what had changed, how he'd feel about it later. But he knew it was all because of her, and the rest just didn't seem to matter.

He licked and sucked and kissed her tender skin, pulling out every bit of sensation he could from her, pushing her higher…and then over the edge. She jerked against his mouth, crying out in the quiet cabin as her orgasm took her. He watched the flush turning her pale skin pink and delighted in her raggedly gasped, "Fuck," as she came back down from her climax.

Then he was over her, moving into her, his cock so hard he ached. Her heat encompassing him, welcoming him in, was as close to a perfect moment as he thought the universe contained. She wrapped around him, her legs around his hips, her arms around his shoulders. Taking him this time.

She nipped at his neck, just beneath his ear, and whispered, "You feel so good. So right."

"Perfect," he agreed through clenched teeth.

They rocked together, gentle at first, then harder and harder still, until he stopped thinking, until his existence was the sensation of her heat and friction gripping his cock, the jolt of building orgasm tightening through him, the sound of her harsh breathing, the slap of skin against skin…

His orgasm hit him with a power that stole his breath, taking him away from everything but that one perfect moment. When he returned to himself, to his surroundings, she was there, smiling up at him, pulling him close.

Calling him home.

CHAPTER TWENTY-TWO

"Well, that was fun," Clare said into the quiet, as they lay in a tangle of sheets and sweat and limbs.

Raf hugged her closer and laughed. "Yes. Yes it was."

More than just fun, she thought. But she didn't want to scare him by admitting that out loud. The thought scared her enough as it was. She'd had more than enough sex in the past to know that something about this time was different. She just wasn't ready to face what that difference was. For the first time in her life, she didn't want to ask the questions.

She just wanted to savor the moment.

She snuggled up against Raf, surprised she *wanted* to. She wasn't usually a snuggler. She usually had too many things to do to linger in bed after sex. Though, she supposed since they were mid-flight, with nowhere to go and nothing in particular to do, staying in bed was reasonable. It was as good an excuse as any.

Raf ran his hand along her back, firm and soothing. The roughened tips of his fingers sent little jolts of sensation through her. Her skin was tender, her nerves still jumping from her second orgasm, but the drag of his fingers along her spine felt so good she couldn't bring herself to make him stop.

Instead, she let her gaze wander around the room. She hadn't bothered to study the place earlier, but now, as usual, her curiosity peaked. His room was a little larger than the others she'd seen so far—including the narrow little space she'd been given. Since he was the captain, that wasn't really surprising. There was enough room for a decent sized bed, a mid-sized desk against the hull, and a set of chairs opposite the bed. The walls were a soft gray-blue color, simple and soothing, the floor covered in a multi-colored rug. The air was comfortably warm, which was nice since she was still naked, and the room smelled like Raf, musk and a faint hint of his secret whiskey. A series of lines in one wall gave the impression of storage cabinets—she'd have a hard time resisting snooping into those if she was alone. And there was a door not far from the bed that she assumed led to a private bathroom.

At least she hoped so because she was going to need that soon and she didn't want to get dressed and leave just to use the facilities. Mostly because it would put an end to the peaceful lull and bring real life back a little too soon.

Though, the longer they lay there, the more she expected him to lift up and get back to the business of running his ship. But he didn't seem to be in any more of a hurry than she was to return to the real world.

"Thanks," she murmured aloud. Then felt stupid. He probably thought she was thanking him for the sex.

He surprised her by not making a snarky comment. "I

need this too," he murmured. He lifted her chin. "It's so odd to see yellow in your eyes."

"I bet." She shook her head and looked away. She'd completely forgotten about that lingering side-effect. "Not sure I want to look in a mirror yet."

"You're still beautiful," he said. "You just have yellow eyes."

"Bet they go real well with all the red hair." She snorted and shook her head.

"Not as well as the brown," he agreed.

"So honest. Most women would be insulted."

"But you're not." A statement, not a question.

"True." Still, she couldn't help wondering if he was just saying that to be kind. Despite his cocky exterior, he was a very kind man. Which surprised the hell out of her.

"You're not as pale now," he continued. "That's a good thing."

She laughed. "We did get the blood flowing just now."

"Your freckles aren't so prominent."

"Argh." She covered her nose. "I hate those freckles."

"Why?" He pulled her hand away from her face and ran a finger over the bridge of her nose.

She made a face. "They're ridiculous. Childish."

"They're perfect." He moved his hand to her cheek and rubbed his thumb over her cheekbone. "Perfect," he murmured again.

Saying that while her eyes were still yellow from almost turning Leech earned him bonus points. She kissed him lightly, then settled at his side again.

"How long until we reach Kierna'Rhoan?" she asked.

"We have to get back to the initial jump spot. Then it will take the same two weeks it was originally going to take."

She frowned. "Won't someone track us or… I mean going back seems dangerous."

"You'll have to go back to Narava eventually, right?"

"Eventually, yes. But I don't want to have yellow eyes when I do."

"You won't," he said.

Sounding more confident of that than she felt.

"We're not going all the way back to Narava now, though," he said. "We just need to get back to the right jump point."

"Still. Won't the Leeches be waiting?" She tucked her head under his chin so he wouldn't be able to see her eyes anymore.

"No reason for them to." He returned to stroking his fingers along her spine. "No one outside my crew knows where we're at right now and where we're going. I didn't advertise to the Leeches that I had other business after my meeting with them. Now that the tracking chip they had in you is destroyed, we should be good."

"I hope so." She couldn't suppress a shudder of unease, then felt weak for the reaction.

"I'll take care of you, Clare," he murmured. "I promise."

Her throat tightened, not at his promise, but at the use of her undercover name.

She'd forgotten who she was supposed to be again. She'd been herself with him during the sex, this entire time after. She hadn't been playing a part or pretending to be this other woman. And realizing he still thought of her as someone else was like cold water to her contentment.

He misunderstood her silence. "You don't believe I can take care of you."

"Not that. You don't need to, by the way. I don't expect you to. But…" She swallowed. Telling him the truth of who she was, why she was here, it would end everything. It would mean the death of Clare O'Malley. She would never be able to use this persona again. She'd have to leave the Shifter support group. She wouldn't be able to stay friends with Ti'ann or any of the Shifter supporters.

She'd have to become someone else. Again.

Before this trip, she'd planned on doing just that once she got the interview with Kira Farseaker and David Cario. Putting an end to Clare O'Malley finally and moving on. It was time. Yet now, faced with the reality of doing it before she was completely ready, she balked. She wanted to come clean with Raf. She wanted him to know who she really was, to see her for herself and not this character she'd created. She sure as hell didn't want him calling her Clare during sex. But…

To admit the truth to a smuggler, even a very kind smuggler? He had no reason to keep her secret and a lot of reasons to use it against her. There were those who would pay well to know who she really was.

Yet, he'd stayed with her while she faced death. He'd saved her life more than once. And just now, he'd helped her feel human again, whole. Could she deny him her real identity? Was that fair to either of them?

"What?" He broke the extended silence, urging her to continue.

She stared at the wall across from the bunk, still hesitating.

"Is this because I called you Clare and that's not your real name?" he asked.

She sat up and faced him, eyes wide, so startled her mouth actually fell open. "What did you just say?"

"I know you're lying about your name." He smiled. "I've known from the beginning."

"And you didn't call me on it?" She wasn't sure whether to be impressed or angry.

He shrugged. "Why should I? Your life. I'm sure you have your reasons. Most people do when they use a fake name. And a lot of people use fake names."

"But… It didn't bother you? Me lying that way?"

He laughed, a deep belly laugh that shocked her silent again.

"I adore liars," he said, pulling her close and kissing her soundly. "They are the best people. I wouldn't have been able to do business with you if you were too honest. How could I trust too much honesty?"

The answer was so absurd, so perfectly Raf, she laughed too. Hard. Until tears leaked out of the sides of her eyes.

"I can't believe you've known all along," she said when she could speak. "No one else has figured it out! Not even Longfeather, and he's used to spotting liars."

"I never said you weren't a *good* liar." He pushed her hair behind her ear and cupped her cheek. "So, do you want to tell me your real name? Do you want me to use it? Or do you want to stay Clare?"

She couldn't believe he was giving her the option. After everything, he just kept confounding her expectations.

She held his gaze for a long, quiet moment. Considering all the pros and cons. But he'd already known she was someone else. All of the things he'd done for her, everything they'd been through, he'd know that whole time Clare wasn't truly *her*.

"My real name is Mary Margaret Reilly," she said, giving in to something she wanted to do. "Everyone in my family calls me Emma. My colleagues call me Reilly."

"Who calls you Mary Margaret?"

"No one," she said firmly, dropping her chin to give him a look.

The sparkle in his blue eyes made her stomach dance with both anticipation and suspicion.

"I like Mary Margaret," he said. "It's very…prim."

"Ha! Well, I'm not. And no one calls me that. No. One. I will not answer to it."

He grinned. "How did you get to be Emma with your family?"

"When my youngest sister was two, she couldn't say my full name—which she thought was my only name because I was always in trouble, and my mother was always calling me by my full name when she scolded me."

"Why does that not surprise me?" He chuckled.

"Anyway," she said. "My sister kept trying to say Mary Margaret but it came out sounding more like Em Em. All my siblings thought it was funny and started calling me Em Em. Over time, that morphed into Emma and I've been Emma ever since."

"Bet your mother doesn't call you Emma."

She scowled. "How would you know that?" Then she realized he was just fishing, and she'd as much as admitted it. "Fine. My mother calls me Mary. Or Mary Margaret when I'm in trouble. But she is absolutely the only person on any planet in any universe allowed to call me that. Even my father calls me Emma."

He studied her, pushing a strand of hair off her forehead. "Why not just change your name legally?"

"Wouldn't change anything. My mother would still call me Mary. Everyone else would still call me Emma. Why bother with the bureaucracy?"

"I like Mary Margaret," he murmured, running his finger across her temple and down her cheek. "Makes me think of…"

"Of?" she said, her heart pumping harder again.

"A tight-laced librarian," he said, "hair all up in a bun, little glasses, ugly cardigan over a white shirt and black skirt. And sleek high-heeled shoes she doesn't think anyone will notice."

The way his gaze danced over her face and down across her body, mostly hidden under the sheet, made her pulse thump. His lids were heavy, his smile secretive and wicked. He was painting a picture she would never have thought remotely sexy, and yet the way he was looking at her made her want to put her hair into a bun and find a pair of glasses, just to see what he'd do. She must have an ugly cardigan somewhere in her wardrobe.

His slight smile rose and she realized her cheeks were hot and flushed, her breathing a little deeper and more erratic. He cupped her cheek in one hand, then caressed down her neck and across her shoulder, his fingers moving in soft strokes down her arm until he reached her wrist. There he drew small circles over her pulse which sent her nerves jumping.

"One day," he promised. "One day, Mary Margaret."

God, when he said her real name that way, it sent a bolt of

heat between her legs and her whole body started to throb. She leaned into him, not even sure what he'd been promising her with his statement, only knowing she wanted him again and had no intention of denying that impulse.

He brought his hand back to her hair, burying his fingers in her tangled curls. His smile dropped away, leaving behind serious, intent heat.

"Don't you dare call me Mary Margaret in public," she said, the threat sounding hollow and breathy. She was too caught up in the growing need to kiss him again to focus on threatening him.

"Clare or Emma in public?" he asked.

"Clare for now."

"In private, Mary Margaret," he stated.

She shook her head, but the gesture turned into her rubbing her head against his hand. "Emma," she said as firmly as she could.

"Mary Margaret," he repeated. Then leaned in and kissed her to end any further comment.

She forgot instantly what they'd been discussing and opened to him. She wrapped her leg around him, rubbing the back of his thigh with her foot as she fitted her hips to his, pressing as close as she could get to his growing erection. He shoved the sheet aside so there was no barrier between them and then rolled her beneath him, his kiss growing harder.

She took her time, savoring each caress, exploring every hard inch of him. He was all lean muscle and more than one scar. The scars surprised her, not because she didn't think his work was dangerous enough to have earned him a few, but because he hadn't bothered to fix them. She was fascinated and yet didn't want to stop what she was doing long enough to ask questions.

Instead, she kissed each one, running her hands and lips along the three slashes in his bicep, the puckered remnants of a blaster shot over his right pectoral muscle, another blaster scar on his right hip. The jagged white welts of a blade slice on the side of his lean waist. Four small dents on his thigh. The evidence of a Leech wound on the back of his right shoulder.

So many scars. Each one a story she intended to know. Some stark white against his tanner skin. One or two still red as if only just healed. Looking at him, watching his casual arrogance, a person could miss all this—the dangers he'd faced, the life-threatening injuries he'd taken.

She was most fascinated by the thin white lines lying perpendicular across his lower back. Six lines stretched the full width of his lower back, in perfectly spaced order. Almost like an odd sort of brand. Those were marks she'd have to ask about. But now, she kissed them, letting her lips travel across his warm skin, enjoying his sharp breath and the tightening of his muscles.

She continued to explore, rolling him so she could finally take his hard cock into her mouth. She loved the taste and feel of him, knowing by his groans she had him at her mercy. She sucked until she felt him quiver, then she crawled up his body and settled over him, letting her wet heat tease the very tip of him. His hands shaped her hips as he stared up at her, his blue eyes dark and full of heat. She held his gaze as she took his cock in her hand and guided him inside.

When she settled completely onto him, she closed her eyes and took a deep breath. She didn't remember sex feeling quite this perfect, or any other man fitting so exactly right. As she moved, the friction sizzled through her, tightening her muscles and drawing out a low groan. His hands on her hips flexed. She opened her eyes to see him watching her, his jaw clenched, his arm muscles flexing.

She couldn't resist him in that moment. She leaned forward and kissed him, pressing her breasts against his chest as she pumped her hips. His hands moved from her hips to her face, holding her head close while he kissed her hard. She moaned in response. Then gasp in surprise when he flipped her onto her back. The movement pulled him from her, but she barely had time to notice the absence before he pushed hard into her again. She rolled her head back and groaned, arching under him.

His rhythm took her racing to the edge of orgasm with shocking speed. After the earlier two, she hadn't actually expected another. But her body had other ideas. He reached between them, fingering her clit as he thrust and that was all it took to snap the impossibly tight pressure. She bit down on his shoulder and let go, her hips bucking against him, every part of her high and free in those moments of release.

She was still soaring when she felt him come, so she was able to drop back with him. Their breathing and heartbeats echoed each other in the quiet cabin.

CHAPTER TWENTY-THREE

<hr>

After Raf went back to commanding his ship, she went in search of Ahab. She'd made the mistake of looking in the mirror when she was cleaning up, and the color of her eyes had so surprised her it was like a slap. She'd spent a long time blinking at herself.

She was used to seeing someone not exactly her in the mirror, she was used to wearing hair colors, eye colors, even undertones and textures in her skin that weren't hers. But the way she looked now…

Raf was right, she was paler than usual. Her freckles stood out sharply, like someone had taken a brown marker to her face. Her skin was almost translucent, with an unhealthy cast to it. Against that color, her hair looked like blood. And then those yellow eyes.

God, how could Raf look at her and still make love to her? She shivered, repelled by her own appearance, glad she hadn't realized earlier.

And he'd said she was looking better. She didn't want to know what she'd looked like on Ahab's ship.

She cleaned and dressed quickly then went to find Ahab. If her outer appearance showed the change so starkly, what had happened to her insides? She thought having the mutations stopped and the infection destroyed would be enough. She was going to survive now and not become a Leech. But seeing herself like this, it was hard to believe she wouldn't continue to change, that she really would recover. And, frankly, she really hoped she didn't have to face this particular look in the mirror much longer. Outside of everything else, it wasn't something she could easily disguise. She wouldn't be able to blend in anywhere and do her job like this.

When she found Ahab finally, he was in the canteen talking with E. Seeing the two of them together made her pause. She'd been so caught up in all that had happened, she'd forgotten to worry about E. For some reason, watching him and Ahab quietly talking raised her warning claxon and her innate curiosity. What did they have to talk about? And could it mean trouble?

She moved into the room without making an effort to call attention to herself and got close enough to catch a few words from Ahab before they noticed her.

"I'd love to see that."

Those words could mean anything. When it came to E, that was literally true. Given that Ahab worked with genetics, though, her instincts jumped to him wanting a look at E's genetic makeup. For some reason, that made her stomach tighten in unease.

She smiled at them but didn't try to hide her anxiety.

Instead, she gave them a reason to think that anxiety was about something else—a not untrue assumption.

"I finally got a look in a mirror," she said. "Scary. Very scary."

Ahab shrugged. "Could've been a lot worse. I've seen more advanced damage before the cure was initiated." He tilted his head and narrowed his eyes, as if trying to see more in her face than was there. "Actually, I think your disorder might have helped you. You haven't lost any fat. A few of the women I've helped have ended up looking almost as skeletal as a Leech. And that was damage that only time could fix."

She sighed. "I probably put on weight if I didn't get enough calories to counter the energy output."

"I did try to keep your intake steady, but…" He shrugged. "Healing takes a lot out of a body."

She gestured to her face. "Speaking of healing, do you think you can do anything with the medical equipment onboard? To fix some of the damage?" She shivered reflexively.

"What is the problem?" E asked, his first contribution to the conversation.

She stared at him. He stared back without blinking. And she realized he really didn't understand.

"The pale skin and yellow eyes remind me too much of a Leech," she told him. "Seeing myself like this, I feel like I'm still changing."

"But you are not," he said and asked at the same time.

"No. Ahab says I'm fine."

"Then why is this a problem?"

She lifted her hands, not sure how to explain. "I don't change my appearance the way you do, E." Not technically a lie, since she couldn't change her appearance by shape shifting the way he did. "Looking at myself as something else is disturbing."

He tilted his head down and frowned. "Would you like to be able to shift shapes? The way I can."

She raised her brows at the unexpected question which echoed her thoughts. That made her a little nervous. E was telepathic like other Shifters. She'd learned after she'd joined the Shifter support group that Shifters could read minds but didn't without permission. She didn't know if E's telepathy was strong enough for him to read minds, but she hoped it wasn't. She didn't think he'd have the same moral stance on mental privacy that ordinary Shifters had.

"I've never thought about it," she answered honestly.

Then she paused to really consider his question and realized being able to shape shift would be a great boon to her career. She wouldn't have to be so careful about her persona and hiding her true identity. She could *really* take on completely new looks for each assignment, adopt any gender, any size, any shape, and no one would know what she really looked like.

Then she considered how long she'd been Clare O'Malley. Would she risk losing her real face as well as her real name for the sake of her work?

"It would be useful," she finally said to E. "In some ways it would be great. But I'd be afraid of losing myself to the different shapes."

His frown deepened.

She tried to explain. "I'd worry about forgetting what I really looked like. Who I really was."

"I don't understand your reasoning," he said.

"Because shapeshifting is normal for you. You trust you'll return to who you are."

Silence followed this comment and he continued to frown, his head tilted forward in his thinking pose.

Though she wanted to delve deeper into this conversation with E, she wanted to stop looking like a Leech more.

"So," she urged Ahab. "Is there anything that can be done before we reach our destination?"

"I can do a little with the epidermal scanners they have aboard," he said, considering her face in a detached, clinical appraisal. "But I can't fix everything. I might be able to correct some of the skin damage, get your color closer to normal."

"And my eyes?" she asked hopefully.

"Will take more than what we have access to on the ship."

She dropped her shoulders, a little deflated. "Okay. At least if my skin isn't so pale, I might not scare myself so much." She tried to smile but was pretty sure she failed to look amused.

Ahab rose. "The infirmary is this way."

She followed, only a little surprised when E joined them.

RAF FOUND them in the infirmary an hour or so later.

"How's it going?" he asked.

He crossed to her where she sat in an exam chair as Ahab ran an epidermal scanner over her. Raf looked over her face and body, then met her gaze, his brows raised in question.

She forced a smile. "Okay, I guess. How do I look? Wait!

Don't answer that." She winced. "I finally got a look at myself in the mirror. Not sure how you can look at me without seeing a Leech."

His frown deepened. Despite Ahab's presence, he cupped her cheek and made her look at him when she tried to look away. "I still see the woman beneath the changes. The rest is just…cosmetic."

"Thanks," she said, relieved. Given the way he felt about Leeches, she still wasn't sure how he could look at her like this and not be bothered.

E emerged from his silent vigil on the opposite side of the room. Raf blinked, the only sign that E's appearance startled him.

"She does not like taking a different appearance," E said.

"I never said that," she said. "Exactly. I just don't like this particular one."

E's head tilted down. "You said you did not want to be able to shape shift the way I can."

She groaned. "E, that's a more complicated question than whether I can tolerate this particular look or not."

"Explain."

She shook her head. "Later. I don't have the energy right now." And she didn't. The toll this entire process was taking on her body was exhausting. She dropped her head back against the chair and looked up at Raf. "How many hours has it been since I've slept? I've lost complete track of the cycles."

"It's been a while," he said. "You should sleep when Ahab is done."

"Rest will help," Ahab confirmed. "I'll be finished with this treatment in another hour."

"What have you been able to fix?" Raf asked.

Which meant her skin and eyes hadn't visibly changed yet. Damn.

"I can repair some of the worst internal damage. She'll need more work there, but the things likely to cause complications with her own condition can be minimized. And she'll end up with a bit more color in her complexion."

"That's good." Raf smiled his real, comforting grin at her. "And the rest we'll sort out when we reach our destination. So you're good."

"If you say so." She snorted.

"Oh, I think you're very good." His smile turned wicked.

She couldn't resist that expression. Her stomach tightened and she found herself grinning back. How could he do that to her? Make her forget everything that was wrong, make her feel feminine and beautiful, despite knowing that she'd currently looked like his most hated enemies.

The man was magic. And she could definitely love him for it.

He stayed with her while Ahab finished fixing what he could, chatting mostly about nonsense.

Her reporter instincts perked up when he mentioned the possibility of a clan war on Binnea, the same rumors she'd heard on FarMore Station. Apparently, his three Binnean crew members had a lot more to say about the possibility. She filed away the information so she could subtly question them. She was going to need her next story lined up after she finished with this one. A war on Binnea would affect all the trade-linked settlements in the galaxy, particularly Narava since the two planets had very tight trade ties.

Knowing she had something else to investigate after this

current story gave her a charge. She loved her job. She might get tired of pretending to be someone else all the time, of never having anyone outside of her family and a few of her colleagues actually know who she really was. But she wouldn't give up her work for anything. Hell, she wasn't sure she could. She was addicted to it. And she couldn't imagine *not* doing what she did.

As she continued talking with Raf, though, her heart sank. She was going to be heartbroken saying goodbye to him when the time came. She studied his sharp blue eyes and crooked smile and knew this wasn't like any other affair. There was more here, from her side anyway. It was going to hurt when he flew out of her life.

But she had him now. She was going to enjoy that, and him, for whatever time he'd give her. Without a single regret.

When Ahab was finished, Raf helped her out of the exam chair.

"Time for you to sleep," he said, tugging her by the hand into the ship's corridor.

She expected him to take her to her own tiny cabin, but he passed it and went to his. When he opened the door, she raised her brows at him.

"I thought you wanted me to sleep?" she said. "I'm not going to if we go into your room." Though the thought of getting him naked again was quite appealing. Sleep could wait a little longer.

His eyes sparkled with mischief. "No fun stuff until after you've slept," he said. "And eaten. How has your calorie balance been today?"

"I've lost complete track." Which was not normal. She could usually calculate her intake automatically, without actually having to think about it too closely. But she'd lost all sense of time and with that everything else was chaotic.

"Then we'll feed you before you sleep. And you can start fresh when you wake up."

"What time is it anyway? Ship's time."

"Evening."

"Guess I do need to eat then. Should we go to the canteen first?"

He shook his head. "I've got a small auto-cooker. You'll eat here then go right to bed. I don't want you getting any more worn out."

"I think you're enjoying taking care of me a little too much," she said. "You do realize this is a rare occurrence, right? I'm not normally so off my game that I need looking after."

He gave her a gentle shove into his cabin. "What can I say? I have a soft spot for women in trouble."

"That I believe." She snorted, none too lady-like. "Do this a lot, do you?"

"Na. Sonia won't let me."

She laughed.

"What can you eat?" he asked. "Did Ahab give you any restrictions?"

"No. Anything. But I'm not really hungry. What do you have?"

He crossed to the series of panels she'd spotted earlier, opening one with a press of his hand to reveal the auto-cooker.

"I've got soup in here, I think," he said. "There's definitely bread and sandwiches."

"What kind of sandwiches?"

"Meat." He glanced over his shoulder. "Anything sound interesting?"

"Soup," she said. "And bread. That should do for calories and still settle okay. Not sure I can handle anything else right now."

He programmed in her meal, then made her sit in one of the room's two chairs. With a voice command, he opened a view screen over his desk and requested a deep space visual. Since they were in the middle of a long jump, there was no "space" to view at the moment. The artificial space-scape, however, was beautiful.

Once she'd finished eating—on a table that also came out of one of the panels on the wall—Raf literally tucked her into bed. She got the giggles when he pulled the blanket up around her shoulders and patted it into place.

He raised his brows at her laughter.

"Just not what I would have expected from you," she said. "You keep surprising me."

"Good. I like to keep a woman on her toes."

"No problem there." She let her gaze wander over his face. "Food gave me a second wind. Don't suppose you'll join me?"

His quiet groan made her stomach dance.

"I would like nothing better," he said. "But you need sleep. You'll be no good to me for the next two weeks if you're exhausted."

The promise implied in his words started her body tingling. "Guess I'd better get some rest then," she murmured.

He leaned down, bringing his mouth close to hers, his gaze holding hers. She hummed a little as she pulled in the lovely scent of him and savored his heat. Then he kissed her. She arched her head up to better the contact and returned his gentle exploration, losing herself in the sweet, oh-so-welcome desire.

"Later," he promised against her lips. "Now sleep." He kissed her forehead and left the cabin without looking back.

She smiled and snuggled deeper into the bed, letting exhaustion take her. She was almost asleep when she realized she'd forgotten about her ravaged complexion and eye color. Again. That he hadn't hesitated to touch her, had treated her as completely desirable. Again.

Raf Tygran was stealing her heart. Probably already had. Just like a pirate, she thought with a faint sigh.

Ah well. She was long overdue for a broken heart.

CHAPTER TWENTY-FOUR

The next two weeks felt like a holiday. Clare spent the travel time either in bed with Raf or engaged in very entertaining conversations with his crew. She and Delilah ended up spending a lot of time together. The woman played a mean hand of poker and seemed to have a never-ending supply of dirty jokes. Others joined their poker games, depending on the duty roster, and Clare learned a lot about the crew.

Like the fact that Sonia had a very volatile "thing" with one of the men living on Kierna'Rhoan. The entire crew was looking forward to the fireworks when they arrived. And the story of Euan's first introductory to the *Ebisu*. He'd snuck aboard to steal something for a client—Euan wouldn't admit what the "something" was to her—and Raf had caught him in the act. Instead of killing him or having him arrested— Clare's suggestion that Raf could have had him arrested was met by belly laughs from everyone around the table—Raf hired him. The story about the day the *Ebisu* landed on Kyoto

Three for a little shore leave and ended up smuggling an ambassador's son off-planet so he could marry against his father's wishes was one of Clare's favorites.

While she mainly sat and listened, absorbing the stories, occasionally she did try to steer the conversations. Her attempts to get Gen'Dar, Bin'Til, and Gen'Lou to discuss the tensions on Binnea failed every time. But they were all more than happy to talk about their early courtship, the day they'd married, and the tech developments being made by their clan, t'Gyn. Clare loved the stories of their early romance best, but they were as enthusiastic about the tech discoveries as they were their romantic history. When Clare mentioned Longfeather's t'Clav clan associate, Bin'Ral, they actually knew of him, or more precisely, his brother the inventor, which led them into another discussion of tech research and development.

While she could never get them to discuss clan tensions, from their cordial comments on t'Clav clan, she felt safe in assuming they weren't two of the clans in conflict with each other. Yet. The fight on FarMore had been between t'Kalb, t'Pree, t'Rawn and t'Sol. The bar brawl Clare and Raf had been in was between t'Kalb and t'Pree. A pattern was starting to emerge, one she'd have to look into more closely.

In the meantime, life on the *Ebisu* was more than entertaining enough to keep her occupied. Raf was as charming as she would have expected, but watching him with his people was illuminating. Each meal or poker game with the crew gave Clare a deeper look at their relationships and histories, the easy camaraderie between them all. And everyone aboard respected their captain, even when they teased or tested him. Their loyalty was absolute.

At first, that had surprised her given the entire groups less than lawful occupation, but the more stories they told her, the more she understood it. Raf took care of them, treated everyone fairly, ensure they all made a lot of money, and while his word was final, the crew did have a say in what jobs they took. By the end of their first week, she understood why he'd kept the same crew for so long. None of them wanted to leave.

No one commented on the fact that she and the captain were sleeping together. Not even Sonia. Clare was a little surprised by that but didn't bring it up. She didn't want to answer questions because she didn't want to think too deeply about what was happening between her and Raf. She also wondered if her relationship with him was the reason the crew accepted her so readily, but she enjoyed their company so much, she didn't question that either.

Ahab hung around, answering questions when asked, but mostly staying in the background, listening to the various conversations. E spent most of his time watching as well, but Clare suspected that was for different reasons.

Ahab gave her two more treatments, but the repair was only internal. Her eyes remained yellow, her skin still unnaturally pale. She made an effort to avoid mirrors but couldn't help catching a glimpse of herself every once in a while. No one else on the ship ever commented, though, or treated her as if anything was wrong, so most of the time, she didn't think about the damage.

And when she was in bed with Raf, she felt like herself. Better than herself. Like the real woman she was under all the disguises she wore.

The day before they were due to arrive at Kierna'Rhoan, her nerves started to dance in anticipation. She'd worked for so long to get this far. Now she was going to meet *the* Kira Farseaker and David Cario. She was going to have to convince them to return to Narava, even though Kira was still technically considered a fugitive. But with the discovery of Lost City, added to the revelations about Kira's ex-husband, Kira and David were folk heroes now. She just had to convince them they had support and would be safe.

She paced the canteen, alone because everyone had something else to do, and considered all the things she needed to say to Kira. She was deep in thought when E walked in. He was frowning, showing more actual emotion than normal, though it still wasn't like real human emotion.

She stopped to stare at him. "What's wrong?"

He stared back with his head tilted forward. "We arrive tomorrow."

E was good at stating the obvious. "Are you worried about seeing Kira?" she asked, sitting at the table.

He didn't join her, just stood there frowning. "I don't worry."

"Okay. Then what's the problem?"

"I haven't been programmed to kill her."

"So we've agreed." She urged him to continue with a hand gesture.

"She will not want to see this face."

"That's true."

"I should change my appearance when I see her."

"Are you worried about her feelings?"

"I don't worry," he said.

Clare jerked her hands up in a frustrated gesture. "So

what is it then? Why do you care how she feels about your face if you're not worried?"

His head tilted forward more. "She can help me. It would be better if she didn't shoot me on our first meeting."

That part might be unavoidable. According to everyone Clare had talked to on Narava, Kira really hated her ex. Clare studied E a moment, his frown so difficult to decipher. "You've said that before, that you think she can help you find your purpose. But what if she can't?"

"I was created from her ex-husband and Shifter DNA. She has worked with Shifters a long time and has the ability to speak with them directly. She understands both sides of me, like no one else can. Now that I'm not following my creators, I require a reason for being."

"Well, E…" Clare sighed. "Everyone spends their lives looking for purpose. Some take years to figure it out. Others never do. Some people are lucky and it comes to them early on."

"Like you," he said. "You have always wanted to be a journalist."

She blinked, several times. Then her heart started to hammer. "How did you know?" she whispered, out of shock more than any thought to keep the conversation private.

"I can sometimes hear things. Thoughts. Shifter and human. I don't control it, it just happens. I have overheard your thoughts."

"Well shit." She sat back and stared at the air. She'd worried about that very thing, but having it confirmed was a gut punch. Her cover blown by a strange hybrid who had no idea what he was doing. That sucked. A lot.

"Have you told anyone?" she asked. Had she been going

around this whole time thinking her cover intact when she was the only one who didn't realize everyone knew the truth? And if that were the case, why the hell would Longfeather have trusted her to make this trip?

"I tell no one what I overhear. Except Councilor Sav at Lost City. She is helping me understand my Shifter nature better."

"You haven't told Val?" Val was the Shifter closest to the leaders of the Shifter support group Clare had been working with this entire time. If E had told Val about Clare's true purpose, Val would tell the group.

"I have told no one but Councilor Sav," E said.

If Clare hadn't known better, she'd swear E's tone was exasperated. The thought made her want to laugh but she was still too shocked.

She finally looked back at E. "Do you intend to tell anyone about me?"

"What about you?" Raf asked as he walked into the canteen.

Her heart lurched. Despite telling him her real name, she hadn't talked about her reasons for having a fake name or what her real job was. And to her relief he hadn't asked. He said he liked liars.

How would he feel about having a member of the press on his ship?

"It's nothing," she said. "E was wondering if he should change his appearance for his first meeting with Kira. So she doesn't shoot him immediately."

Raf went to a cabinet and pulled out a drinks container, cracking it open before facing them. He leaned against the counter with his lips pursed.

"Might not be a bad idea," he said before taking a sip of his water. "When it comes to Ennoren, she is likely to shoot first."

"You knew her," Clare said. "She's going to take this badly, no matter what, isn't she?"

"Oh yeah." He laughed. "She's gonna be pissed. Though who will get the brunt of her anger…" He shrugged. "Probably Shifter Research Center. She hates them almost as much as she hates Ennoren."

"It will be better to be shifted when I meet her," E stated.

"You're gonna have to show her your real shape eventually," Raf said. "The other Shifters, won't they know you're not in your natural form?"

E was silent.

"They will," she answered for E. "They have a sense for shape-shifted fellow Shifters. Though…"

"E's different," Raf finished. "He's not entirely Shifter."

"They do not always know," E said. "At least, the Shifters of Lost City do not always recognize me when I am not in my natural form."

"You are so scary," Raf muttered. He finished his drink and put the container in the recycling unit. "You know, it's probably better humans never learn about you, E. Not the general population anyway."

Since Clare wanted to tell that story, she asked, "Why?"

"You think the Naravans are afraid of Shifters now?" Raf said. "They find out about E, that this is even possible, and that he's so much scarier than ordinary Shifters. There's going to be chaos and mayhem." He sat at the table near her in one of the chairs instead of the long bench, but his gaze was on E. "Having the first colonized planet in the galaxy erupt into war would be bad for trade. For everyone."

"You think just the fact of his existence could lead to war?" She'd heard the argument before from those within the Shifter support group. But Raf was outside the issue, not even a Naravan. If he saw war in this, she was going to have to rethink her desire to tell this story.

"I do," Raf said. "I also think your people were right to get him off Narava. He's dangerous on his own. In the wrong hands…" Raf let out a low whistle and shook his head. "Disaster."

E tilted his head down and examined Raf. "You think my creators could control me now? They could not."

"What makes you say that?" Raf leaned back in his seat, his gaze steady on the hybrid.

"I would not want them to," E said. "I will not be given my purpose by another."

"Yet you're on your way to see Kira so she can help you with your purpose," Clare said.

"I want her help to better understand myself," E said. "So that I may decide my own purpose."

"Can't argue with that logic," Raf said and rose from his seat. He looked at Clare. "You got a few minutes?"

"Sure. What do you need?"

He crooked a finger at her. "This way."

Curiosity always got her into trouble. She acknowledged that. She followed him, giving E a goodbye nod. E didn't return the gesture, and they left him staring at a spot on the floor.

CHAPTER TWENTY-FIVE

RAF LED HER TO HIS ROOM, WHICH SHE'D BEEN EXPECTING, and pulled her in for a kiss, which she'd hoped for. By the time he lifted his head, she was feeling soft and pliable and ready to sink into his bed with him.

His gaze roamed her face, and he pushed a strand of hair behind her ear. "I don't usually ask," he started. "A person's past, their reasons for doing what they do… If they aren't telling, there's a reason for it and I respect that."

"Mmm." She had a feeling she knew where this was going. Despite everything, she still hadn't decided if she wanted to tell him the truth about herself yet or not. She'd been counting on him not asking.

"I know there's more to you than you make out," he said. "I know the stripper as cover for bodyguard isn't the only cover. You've made sure your history is convoluted to keep people from seeing beyond the first 'secret' they unearth."

Her eyebrows jumped to her hairline. "How did you figure that out?"

"I'm a smuggler. Some call me a pirate. I have a remarkably good sense of people, or I wouldn't have survived this long so peacefully."

"Meaning?" she asked.

"Meaning this work is dangerous enough," he said. "If I'm not good at judging character, my crew and I end up in a lot of violent situations. As it is, we avoid more than we stumble into, so no one aboard the *Ebisu* has to put their lives in constant danger just to get paid. That's on me and it's the way I like it."

"Because of your past? The first crew you worked with?"

His gaze narrowed. "I was asking the questions. How did you turn this on me?"

She shrugged. "Just following your lead."

He shook his head. "What I'm getting at is… Is I know you haven't told me the truth, still, about what you do, why you're doing all this."

"And you want me to." She pulled back so she was leaning against the closed door, putting some space between them.

"I do. But not before you're ready."

"Oh?" She hadn't anticipated being let off the hook again.

"I want you to know I know. You don't have to pretend you're not hiding things from me. I know you are. You know I know. We're upfront about that. The rest will happen when it happens."

"If it happens," she said.

His mouth flattened but he nodded. "If it happens."

For some reason her heartbeat hammered and her breathing picked up. And not for good reasons. Yet she couldn't quite explain the feeling of anxiety clawing at her chest.

"Can I ask you something?" She held his gaze. "About your past? You just said you'd let me keep my secrets, for as long as I want to, so I understand if you don't want to divulge yours. I won't press. I just… I am curious."

"You offering a trade?" he asked. "My secrets for yours?"

She hadn't thought about it quite like that, but as soon as he said it, she realized that's what she wanted. If she was going to admit her real job to him, if she was going to take that chance, she wanted something in return, to know the risk and vulnerability went both ways.

"I've told you some of my secrets already," she said. "My real name. Things about my family."

He smiled. "I *knew* the family stories were true. Too much emotion there." He considered her. "And you're right, you did admit your real name. Mary Margaret."

She narrowed her eyes and scowled. She still hadn't gotten used to him calling her that. Somehow, from Raf, it always sounded a little naughty and sexy. And that was just weird.

"But I've told you were I'm from," he countered. "The truth. So we're even there."

"I don't have any family stories from you."

He snorted. "Not sure you want to hear those."

"One," she bargained. "One story."

Pulling in a deep breath, he nodded. He stepped back and motioned her to the softly cushioned chairs. As she settled in, he went to the auto-cooker and ordered up two cups of hot tea. The tea always made her smile. She kept expected something more…piratey, like the whiskey he kept hidden in the canteen. Or at least some Binnean brandy. But the tea seemed to be some sort of nightly ritual with him.

He lifted the steaming mugs as he brought them over. "This habit comes from my younger years, before I got off Jenolon."

"I was just wondering about that," she said with a smile.

He handed her a mug then sat down, sipping and staring at the rug spreading out beneath the chairs. "Jenolon had very few redeeming characteristics. The tea was one of them. The soil on the settled continent, when added to the hydroponics farms, gave the tea this really different and delicious flavor. Can't find anything like it anywhere else." He glanced at her from the corner of his eye. "Might even be addictive."

He grinned when she scowled down at the mug.

"Don't worry," he said, "there don't seem to be any side-effects of going without, even if it is addictive. I went for years without being able to get my hands on any. They don't export it, even though it would make them a fortune."

"Why not?"

"It's considered sacred. Like every other bloody thing." He rolled his eyes and set the mug down on the small table between their seats. "You've heard about Jenolon. You know they're religious fanatics, isolationists, hypocritically dismissive of technology."

"Why hypocritically?"

"They use it," he said with a snort. "Hell, they wouldn't be *on* Jenolon without technology. You can't call it evil on the one hand and have it be the source of finding your 'holy home' on the other. I hate hypocrisy."

"I'm getting that," she said.

"Anyway..." He let out a long breath. "Everything

produced on the planet is considered sacred, even when they use technology to engineer it."

"Like their food," she said.

He tipped his head in affirmation. "They need the same fixes every settled planet needs to make what's grown there edible for humans. They *can* use a lot of what's found naturally on Jenolon. In fact, it's as good for supporting human life as Narava. But they can't just grow crops in the local soil and eat what exists on the planet without some tweaking."

She nodded. That had been one of the more complicated aspects of settling new planets in the galaxy—well, that and getting off Earth and beyond Earth's solar system in the first place. Growing edible food in environments that were compatible with human life but not designed to support it, places that didn't evolve with the same DNA bases, had been one of the first struggles of the early colonials. Food meant for humans to consume had to be engineered.

"All of this is to say," Raf continued, "there are holes in the Jenolon dogma. Contradictions they choose to ignore."

"And which you couldn't," she guessed.

"Just because I respect others' privacy, doesn't mean I can abide willful ignorance."

His grumbled comment almost sounded like a pout. She hid her grin behind her mug.

"How did you manage to not think the way everyone else on the planet does?" she asked. "I mean, how could you have learned any different?"

His smile was mischievous. "I hacked through to an off-planet news feed when I was nine."

She chuckled. Not really surprised. "Why, though? What made you go looking for…more?"

"No one would tell me about our history," he said with a shrug. "Our real history. They kept trying to feed me that crap about the One God scooping up the earlier settlers in his cupped hands and dumping them onto Jenolon. I knew it was a load of bullshit from the beginning. I can't even remember how I knew. I just heard the stories and thought, 'how could anyone actually believe that?' I mean, we *had* technology all around us for farming. Denying it got us to this new home just seemed ridiculous. At nine, I got tired of the fiction and went in search of real answers."

"For someone who's so good at letting others keep their secrets now," she said, "you were an awfully nosy little boy."

A fact that made her adore him all the more. It also sounded familiarly like the nosy mischief she'd gotten up to during her own childhood. They had a lot more in common than she might have guessed.

He laughed. "I surely was. And no regrets either. Besides, they weren't lying to me for any good reason that I could see. What was so wrong about just admitting a ship brought us to Jenolon?"

"What did you learn when you hacked into the news feed?" she asked before taking another sip of her possibly-addictive tea.

"That the galaxy was a very exciting place," he said, "with plenty of potential for an enterprising and energetic young man. I decided about a week into listening to feeds that I would get off Jenolon and make something more of myself, something that wasn't a fanatically religious farmer-priest."

"That was your only option?"

"That and marriage with the expectation of having eight

or more kids." He shook his head. "I like kids and all, but I am not the fatherly type."

Thinking of how he looked after his crew, she could argue that point with him. But he was talking about his past and she didn't want to distract him from that. She also didn't want him to think she was sizing him up for possible fatherhood. She had no intentions of settling into family life with kids for years—maybe ever—and was diligent with her birth control. Being an aunt was more than enough for her at the moment. But now wasn't the time to get into that conversation with Raf.

"So you ran away at fourteen," she said. "You said your family wouldn't have wanted to see you again, but did they come after you? Try to bring you back before you were 'ruined' by the outer world?"

"The minute I stowed away on the ship, I would have been considered ruined. I embraced the technology, you see. I violated one of the fundamental tenants of our *faith*." He snarled the word.

She settled her mug in her lap and considered him, the signs of anger and something she couldn't quite place. "You were so young when you left. Did you ever miss your family?"

"My father was strict and mean, and easy with the whip. My mother was one of the most fanatically faithful on the entire planet. My two brothers were…eager to help old dad dispense justice. And my four sisters had no interest in me whatsoever. So no. I don't miss any them. And I can't imagine they miss me either. In fact, I think it was best for all concerned that I left when I did. The only reason anyone might have come looking for me, wasn't to bring me back to the loving arms of my family. It would have been to keep me from discussing the community. That's considered a grave sin, punishable by beating the sinner near to death."

She thought of the scars across his lower back, the very precisely placed lines, his mean father and fanatical mother, and wondered.

"But they didn't try to find you as far as you know?" she asked.

"Nope. Washed their hands of me I'm sure. Probably even went to the trouble of excommunicating me from the order." He smirked. "As if that would actually hurt me."

She was terrified of fanatics, any kind really, but religious fanatics were their own particular brand of scary. She couldn't imagine being raised by them and still managing enough awareness to think beyond the dogma. The fact that he had deepened her admiration for him.

"None of the religion sunk in for you then?" she asked. "No residual beliefs that give you pause?"

"Nope. Now I'm a happy pagan, offering up prayers to whichever deity might bother to listen."

She waited for more but he remained silent after that, staring at the rug. She sipped her tea, as she contemplated what he'd told her. So very different from her own upbringing in a happy, tight-knit family. And yet…

"You and I have a lot more in common than most people would guess at a glance," she murmured.

He looked up, held her gaze. "I had a feeling."

"Thank you. For telling me a bit more."

"Want to know my real name?" he asked.

She sat up straighter. "It's not Raf?"

"Actually, the Raf part is mine. Or at least it's what I

shortened Rafael to when I left Jenolon. My family would never have desecrated the name by shortening it."

"So Tygran isn't yours then."

"My real family name is Bartholomew."

"Rafael Bartholomew?" She pressed her lips together, trying hard not to smile. "Wow, that's a mouthful." And ridiculously ill-suited to the man before her.

"Look who's talking, Mary Margaret Reilly," he said.

She let out her grin and shrugged. "Point taken. So where did Tygran come from? Did you just make it up?"

"Got that from my first captain. Only the crew of that first ship, and later Sonia, know what the name stands for."

"Oh, I've got to hear this," she said. "If you'll tell me, I promise I won't tell a soul."

He paused for a minute, staring at her with a strange expression. She resisted the urge to fidget under his scrutiny because she really really wanted him to tell her this truth.

Finally, he let out a short laugh. "I suppose since you gave me Mary Margaret, I can admit this. Remember, I was very young when I stowed away on Captain Bael's ship. And I was a cocky shit as well, despite not having any call to be so arrogant. Tygran stands for 'troublesome, young, godforsaken, randy, arrogant, and nuts'."

She felt her mouth drop open a little and had to snap it shut.

"Captain got tired of shouting one or the other of those epithets at me," Raf said. "Never as a compliment, mind. So he put them all together in an acronym. Everyone started calling me that. The name stuck."

She laughed. She'd thought Mary Margaret was a bad name to haul around.

"Why did you keep that?" she said through her chuckles.

"It fit. Better than Bartholomew anyway. I was troublesome and very young. According to my family I was officially godforsaken—I never really minded when the captain shouted that at me. Was proud of that one actually. And relieved." He snarled a little before continuing. "I couldn't really help the randy part. I was more than a little arrogant. And pretty much completely nuts. See. Fits."

He flashed his sexy grin at her and wagged his eyebrows.

She shook her head. "You're right. Definitely fits better than Bartholomew. What did Sonia say when you told her that's what your name stands for?"

"She said, 'Of course that's your name, ya shit. What else would you be called?'"

Raf's imitation of his second-in-command was so accurate, Clare laughed again.

"In my defense," Raf said, "I only told her the truth because she got me drunk and telling stories when I was deciding whether I'd hire her or not. I *had* to take her on after that. Only way to keep her from talking."

"I think I need to chat with Sonia more," Clare said, narrowing her eyes.

"Oh, that's not going to be dangerous at all," he said sarcastically. His scowl was only half-serious, though, belied by the crinkles of amusement at the corners of his eyes.

"Well Rafael," she said. "I think we're even now. I'm not sure even Mary Margaret can compete with Bartholomew and the real meaning behind Tygran."

"One of these days, I'll tell you some of the escapades that earned me those pre-acronym nicknames."

He took her now empty cup from her, set it on the table

between them, then leaned close and took her face between his hands. Most of the time, when they were together, he made her forget how she still looked. But for some reason, sitting there under the intensity of his gaze, she remembered her yellow eyes and too pale skin. She wanted to duck her head and hide, but his hands held her in place.

"Very few people in the galaxy know as much about me as you do now," he murmured. "I need you to understand that if you want to tell me any more of your secrets, they're safe with me. I'm trusting you with some mine in turn. But I really don't expect more than you're prepared to give. I mean that, Emma."

When he used her real name, the name only her family ever called her, she caught her breath. What was he doing to her? Why was he doing all this? He was a smuggler, a pirate, and there was no place in his life for anything but a temporary romantic relationship. Hell, there was no place in her life for anything more than a temporary relationship. But he was doing and saying all the things that made her want…more. She didn't understand his motives. He couldn't want anything permanent with her. That didn't make sense.

And yet…

The longer she knew him, the harder it got to think of walking away from him. She was even falling for his crew. She felt more like herself here, her real self not the Clare O'Malley construct, than she had in years. Maybe even more so than with her own family—which was a complete surprise.

She was relaxed and comfortable around Raf's people, around him. He was right. Something about knowing they were all liars or hiding their own secrets made things better.

It took away the low level of guilt that always followed her around every job and through every persona. None of these people cared that she wasn't telling them the truth about her name or her profession. They just didn't care.

She leaned forward and placed her lips gently against his. He'd given her a very unexpected gift on this trip. The gift of freedom. And she wasn't sure how to explain that, or thank him for it. At least not in words. So she showed him the only way she could, opening to him, deepening the kiss, giving up the barriers between them—if only mentally.

He stood, pulled her to her feet and backed her to his bed, never taking his mouth from hers, holding her close and taking everything she gave.

Who would have guessed she'd find so much peace with a pirate.

CHAPTER TWENTY-SIX

THEY SET DOWN ON KIERNA'RHOAN JUST AS THE SUN WAS cresting the mountains surrounding the valley were the landing pad and settlement was located. Raf stood at the bottom of the loading ramp with Sonia beside him, Clare just behind and to his left, and E waiting at the top of the ramp, out of sight.

In the end, they'd decided E should make his first appearance as someone other than Ennoren until they could explain him better to Kira and David. Raf liked Farseaker. He didn't want to give her an unnecessary scare. The mere fact that Raf was here again was going to start enough questions.

They waited for the security party he knew would approach the ship first. He grinned when he saw Pat among the group. The hacker hadn't changed much. His dark brown skin was a little darker from being in the sun so much. But his head was still shaved, and his short frame was still lanky and muscled. Raf narrowed his eyes, thinking Pat might even have thickened out some living on Kierna'Rhoan. Sonia would like that.

The woman in question shifted beside Raf, and he glanced over to see her cocking her hip farther to one side and folding her arms over her chest. Her eyes narrowed to thin slits. Pat's serious, guarded look dissolved immediately into a wide grin. Sonia grunted something under her breath that Raf couldn't hear, but he was sure Pat was in for a very interesting night.

At the head of the group, David Cario approached with a welcoming wave, but a slight frown. The former Naravan Guard had loosened up during his time here, Raf noted. His dark hair was longer and looser, his clothing a little rumpled, his expression less closed off. He didn't have that stiff spine, hard-edged attitude that that he'd once had—a side-effect of being a Guard. Raf smiled. Obviously, Kierna'Rhoan was treating all of them well.

"Tygran," Cario greeted when he was near enough to speak without shouting. "What the hell are you doing here? *How* are you here?"

"I know I wiped your nav computer," Pat said, his gaze darting between Raf and Sonia.

"Don't worry, hacker," Raf said, "your skills have not lapsed. We got the coordinates from another family member. Two actually—Nathan Longfeather and Jasmine Farseaker."

"Jasmine helped again?" David said.

She'd helped David when he'd had to figure out how to get here to reunite with Kira all those many months ago. Years now, Raf thought, a little surprised by the time lapse now that he was here again. The scene had a sense of déjà vu that shrunk the days since they'd last met.

"Guess you're welcome, then," David continued. "But why?" He glanced at Sonia and Clare with his brows raised.

Raf motioned Clare forward. "This is Clare O'Malley. She's part of Monroe's group now."

David nodded. He would know who Kira had left in charge of the Shifter support group. At least, he knew now. Raf was certain he hadn't known that name before leaving Narava. For the safety of the group.

"I have news," Clare said. "For Kira."

"Must be important for the group to send you all this way," David said.

"Very important," Clare said.

Raf was impressed when Clare didn't push to be brought to Kira. She was anxious about this meeting, excited, even though she hadn't said anything out loud. He wasn't entirely sure why she was so excited, but her restraint in the face of all that energy was impressive. He could practically feel her vibrating.

David finally looked at her closely, did a double-take, then took a sudden step backward.

Clare frowned and looked down, her gaze on the black dirt at her feet. And Raf realized David had noticed her eyes. Raf had gotten so used to looking past the yellow, he'd almost forgot about it.

"Why are her eyes Leech yellow?" David hissed. "What the hell, Raf?"

Three of the five people who'd come to the ship with David and Pat fingered the small blasters they held, not quite lifting them but their arms stiffened as if ready to take aim. This was going to get out of hand fast if Raf wasn't careful.

"That is a longer story," he said, holding his hands up, empty palms facing David. "She's not a Leech—"

"How could she be?" Pat put in. "But…"

"But that's all part of the long story," Raf said. "We have a *lot* to tell you all." He glanced at the surrounding guards. "You won't have to stun her. She's not dangerous." He narrowed his eyes at Clare, then shrugged. "Okay, she's dangerous. but not the way a Leech is."

Clare scowled up at him without lifting her head enough for the others to see her eyes again. "You're not helping," she muttered.

He grinned. The tension in the Kierna'Rhoan group eased, though it didn't go away completely. Raf figured he'd better explain some part of the story now if he and his people wanted to stay on-planet long enough to speak to Kira.

Looking over his shoulder, Raf motioned E down the landing ramp. Behind E, Ahab appeared, taking in the clearing before following E.

Raf considered both of them. How to explain either man in a way that wouldn't get him or his crew stunned?

Rather than broach the extremely complicated subject of E first, Raf gestured to Ahab. "This is our expert on Clare's…infection. He'll need access to your medical equipment to finish curing her."

David glanced between Raf and the kid. "Of course."

And to Raf's relief, there was no hesitance or resistance in David's answer. Raf hadn't realized he'd been worried they might not help Clare until the tension in his shoulders loosened. He liked Kira and David. He liked the Kierna'Rhoan crew. But they weren't his people, and there was only so far he trusted others. When it came to Clare, apparently, he was even more jumpy about people's motives than normal.

As that epiphany sank in, David frowned at Clare.

"You *will* be okay?" he asked.

She flinched but nodded. "I'm not mutating. Anymore. But Ahab needs to finish correcting the damage done."

"Your eyes?" David said.

"Among other things," she confirmed.

David faced the young man. "Ahab? Paul will show you to the medical building. He'll get you what you need. Clare, would you like to go there first?"

She flicked a glance at Ahab. "Do I have to or can it wait? I'd like to meet with Kira first, if it's possible."

Ahab shrugged. "You've waited this long. Nothing left to fix that can't wait a few more hours."

"Good," David said. "Because I don't think I could keep Kira away long enough to leave you to your treatment."

Even as he spoke, Raf saw another person leave the surrounding trees and start toward them. Her hair was a little lighter, but still golden, a color that probably still matched her eyes. She was still tall and slender, and moved with confidence over the uneven ground. He grinned. He'd recognize Kira even at a distance. She was within hailing distance, though, before he noticed the bump.

"Farseaker!" Raf said. "You're having a baby!"

Her laughter carried across the intervening space. "It's good to see you again, too, Raf. What the hell are you doing here?"

"All to be revealed soon," he called. To David, he said, "Shall we settle in somewhere?"

David led their small party toward the trees. As they

reached Kira, David put his arm around her waist, keeping her close as they returned to the settlement.

Their "town" had expanded since the last time Raf had been here. He noted some of the newer buildings, constructed in and around the trees to incorporate the environment without disturbing it. David and Kira took turns telling him about all the changes.

Seeing them together, happy and relaxed, ready to start a family, gave Raf a little shot of satisfaction. They deserved it. And he felt like he'd had something to do with getting them here. He'd literally brought them both to the planet, so he didn't think it was being too arrogant to take *some* credit for their happiness.

The comfortable way they were with each other also shot him with a strange sort of longing he'd never felt before. Like he was missing something. Or wanted something he'd never considered he might want. He glanced at Emma, seeing the real woman even in her Clare O'Malley persona, and he knew what the "wanting" was about. Impossible. But there it was, right in front of him.

Kira took them to a small building they called the café. A series of tables sat out under the trees in the temperate, cool morning air. The building opened onto more tables and an open window through which he could see the kitchen area. The delicious scents of coffee and warm pastry drifted out to him.

He grinned when he recognized the young woman who brought out a tray of drinks. "Hey Vettine," he greeted. "Waiting tables now?"

Vettine was Kira's half sister and while their eye and hair colors were distinct enough to make their relationship unclear, they bore a definite familial resemblance in their facial features. Maybe even more now, Raf realized. Vettine had been young the last time he'd seen her, maybe nineteen. Only a couple of years had passed, but she looked more mature now, more confident and settled in herself. Her blond hair was still short but styled softer, her green eyes bright and sparking with amusement. She no longer had a hunted, nervous edge to her, and the changes suited her.

"This is my place," Vettine said with a saucy smirk. "I only work for me now."

Kira snorted. "Truer words," she muttered.

They settled around the tables, Raf taking the seat next to Clare without anyone arguing. Sonia pretended not to notice when Pat snagged the seat next to her, making a very visual effort to ignore the hacker. Kira leaned into David in the seats across from Raf and Clare.

"So…" Kira said. "There must be something really significant to bring you out here again." She glanced at David, then back at Raf. "Am I going to like the news or hate it?"

"Some of it you're going to love," Raf said.

"Some?" Kira said.

Raf glanced around and saw E hovering on the path, watching a group of Shifters approaching the café. E had done that thing where he'd altered his face just enough to not look like Ennoren. But the fact that the Shifter-human hybrid didn't show much facial expression still marked him as… unique among Raf's crew.

"There's a lot to report," Raf hedged. To Clare, he said, "You want to start?"

She nodded. "First, sorry about the yellow eyes. I'll explain that soon."

Kira startled, and Raf realized she hadn't noticed Clare's eyes before that moment. Her observational skills had fallen off. She didn't have to be on guard all the time anymore.

"The reason Monroe sent me," Clare continued, "with the help of your cousins Nathan and Jasmine, was because of the discovery of a Shifter city about a year ago Naravan time. The city of the lost lines. They're actually calling it Lost City now."

Kira's eyes widened with each word and her lips parted on a soft gasp. "A city?"

She took on a faraway look, something Raf had seen her do before. She was one of the very few humans he'd ever met who could speak telepathically to Shifters, and while he could never be certain, he had a feeling there was a conversation going on just then.

A few moments later a huge bird came swooping down from the trees to land at the edge of the café's seating area. In the next blink, a Shifter with purplish blue-green eyes stood blinking at them.

The Shifters in their natural form were a thing to behold. Long limbs, golden skin, multi-faceted eyes. They were one of the truly extraordinary things about Narava. Humans hadn't encountered anything else like them in the known galaxy.

Unfortunately for the Shifters, they'd scared the shit out of humans when they'd first met them. Humans had never fully gotten over that fear—it drove much of the political climate on Narava. Raf didn't get involved in local planetary politics if he could help it, but even he had to admit, the legal efforts to exterminate an entire species because of fear were repugnant. He'd been happy to help Shifter supporters, despite his insistence that the *Ebisu* didn't get directly involved in the fight.

The newly arrived Shifter stared at Kira for a few silent minutes. E adjusted his stance so he was focused on the new Shifter, his head tilted down, a slight frown his only expression.

Finally, a mouth formed in the Shifter's face and it looked at Clare. Its eyes whirled in what Raf had come to recognize as excitement. He was pretty sure he knew this particular Shifter too—one of Kira's closest friends and confidants, Xep.

"Tell us," Xep said, its quiet voice quivering with intensity.

Clare told them everything in great detail. The story of the discovery, the genetic changes to the Shifters of Lost City, changes that meant they were also capable of violence in a way ordinary Shifters weren't, the attack and subsequent revelation of the city to the planet, everything except the role E played in things.

Raf listened with as much rapt attention as the others. This was the first time he'd heard the story in its entirety from someone who'd actually been there. And he was as awed as Kira and David.

By the time Clare had finished a crowd had gathered around them. Vettine and at least ten other humans, as well as seven Shifters in their natural forms and any number in various other forms. E remained at the edge of the group, silent and watchful. His stillness made Raf a little nervous, so Raf did keep E in his peripheral vision. Just in case.

When Clare finally finished, silence held the crowd as they looked at each other. Raf couldn't read every expression, but the general awe, wonder, and surprise were obvious.

Finally, Xep spoke, "Val is okay?"

That wasn't the first question Raf had expected. By Clare's slight pause, it wasn't the one she'd expected either.

"Val is just fine," she said, referring to the Shifter who'd been with Monroe's group when the city was discovered.

According to Clare's story, Val had been the group's translator with the evolved Shifters. From the intensity in Xep's body language, Raf had a feeling Val was more than an ordinary Shifter, too.

"Spending a lot of time in Lost City," Clare continued, "but not enough to be affected by the parasites that changed the city Shifters."

Xep's whirling gaze moved to Kira, then back to Clare. "My line lost our Keeper of the History to the exterminations, before there was another to take up the place. Val is the oldest Keeper left, the only one with the complete history."

Ah, Raf thought. That explained Xep's concerned for this other Shifter.

Clare nodded. "I understand how valuable Val is to your people. Monroe keeps a close watch and ensures Val's safety."

Xep nodded, its shoulders dropping in what Raf read as relief.

After that, the other questions started, slowly at first, then so fast people were talking over each other and Clare frequently had to make them slow down. By the time most of the questions had been answered, Ahab had rejoined the group.

David noticed him and turned the subject from Lost City to Clare's yellow eyes.

Ahab helped her tell that story—including the fact that his lab had been lost to a Leech attack so his cure wouldn't be available until he could rebuild.

This was met with another long silence.

"The Leeches couldn't have followed you here, could they?" Kira asked into the quiet.

She ran a hand over her thigh, reminding Raf of the attack he'd faced with Kira and David in the Docks two years ago. Kira had been wounded and Raf had never forgiven himself for it. She looked to him when no one answered immediately.

"Ahab found the tracker chip in Clare and destroyed it," Raf said. "And I had the *Ebisu* swept four different times for trackers. They couldn't have followed us here."

"But they might be waiting on Narava for you," David said. "They knew where you were before arranging the meeting on FarMore Station. They might realize you'll return to Narava to finish this mission. There's no telling what information they've dug up on Clare."

Clare shifted beside Raf, subtly, but uncomfortably.

"They probably also know they've destroyed Ahab's lab," David continued without seeming to notice Clare's discomfort. "And his cure. But they don't know if Clare mutated fully or not. They went to all the trouble of using a tracker chip and coming after her. They're going to want her back."

"Can they infect her again?" Kira asked Ahab. "After you've cured her, is she still vulnerable, or does the process give her some immunity?"

Ahab didn't look at Clare when he said, "She can still be re-infected. The others I've helped have gone into hiding, staying as far from Leeches as they can. I don't even know where they are, and it's better that way."

"That must be why the Leeches started to use trackers," Pat muttered.

To Raf's surprise, when Pat leaned closer to Sonia and put an arm around her shoulders, she didn't object. In fact, she leaned in to him. For the first time, Raf realized Sonia was scared of what the Leeches could do now. Her allowing others to see her vulnerability was more disconcerting than the various shape-changes of the Shifters going on around them.

Kira's eyes narrowed. To Clare, she said, "You came all this way to give me the information about the city. What was the plan after? What do you and Monroe expect me to do now?"

Clare glanced at Raf then focused on Kira, holding her gaze steadily. "I'm here to ask you to come home."

CHAPTER TWENTY-SEVEN

Silence descended over the group with that statement. Raf watched Kira's eye narrow and David's shoulders straighten, but beyond that heightening of awareness, he couldn't tell if they liked the idea of returning to Narava or hated it.

Clare continued, "Kira, you and David…you've become folk heroes to the cause. Add your voice to the calls for peace between Shifters and humans. We're sure with you and David supporting the peace movement, the hold outs in the government will have to give in."

David took Kira's hand and squeezed. "We can't," he said. "She's still wanted on Narava. Even a pardon won't keep her safe from the powerful enemies she has there. Powerful enough, I couldn't flush them out."

Clare moved her steady gaze to him. "Senator Johnson. He's the main man—at least in the senate—behind the push for the exterminations. There are others, private powerful people, but he's the top one in the government."

"How did you find him out?" David asked.

Clare shrugged. "We've been looking for him. His aide was the one arrested for ordering the attack on Lost City. He could disavow knowledge of his aide's work all he wanted, but we knew then he was behind…a lot."

Her gaze danced to E, and Raf sat up a little straighter.

David noticed the gestures. He turned his attention to E. "There's something you still haven't told us," he murmured to Clare.

She nodded. "First, you need to know you'll be safe if you return to Narava. Monroe, Longfeather, the Shifters of Lost City, they would all ensure your security. In fact, turns out Longfeather's former partner married a woman whose father is pretty damned influential himself in the private sector. Owns Xanac Corp."

"The R&D company?" Pat asked, then whistled under his breath. "I hear they're doing some really innovative stuff with nano-tech there."

"There are enough people willing to protect you to make your return much safer," Clare continued. "And if you go public, allow yourselves to be interviewed by the press in a live feed, Senator Johnson won't be able to touch you without causing a whole world of chaos."

"You think that will work again?" David asked.

The team that discovered Lost City had gone public as a way to protect the city from more military attacks. It had worked. But given they were talking about the woman David loved, Raf could understand the man being hesitant and suspicious.

"We do," Clare said. "We think getting you both on the record and presented to the public will be the final key to ending the exterminations once and for all. We even have a reporter lined up. A friend of mine—the one who broke the Lost City story. Someone we can trust to report only what you want made public."

As David and Kira exchanged a long, silent look, Raf studied Clare. She was sitting up, her body tense, but her eyes were sparking with excitement—even through the yellow. Her voice had gotten more intense when she'd mentioned the reporter friend. Something there. Something about the reporter…

He didn't want to question her in front of the others. In fact, he probably shouldn't question her at all. But with Clare—Emma—he was finding he didn't like secrets between them. He'd told her the truth last night when he said he wouldn't push her to tell him anything she didn't want to. He respected people's rights to their mysteries. But he still found he wanted her to tell him everything. To give him all those secrets to hold in trust, the way he'd given her some of his. Even more surprising, he wanted to share more, everything he'd kept hidden. It was such a new and odd need, he lashed it down tight until he could examine his reasons more closely.

"We'll have to discuss this," Kira said. Turning back to Clare, she said, "If I weren't pregnant, this would be an easier decision. But I can't take unnecessary risks with our baby. We need to consider our options." She glanced at Xep for a stretch of silence, and the Shifter nodded as if answering a question, or confirming something.

"We have time," Clare said. "I know this is a lot. Too much to process quickly. Just know, we will do everything in our power to ensure your safety." More quietly, she said,

"They need you, though, Kira. Your voice, and David's, will sway more people to the side of the Shifters than any other human voices. You could ensure this whole thing ends quickly and peacefully."

Kira's mouth flattened into a thin line, but she nodded. Taking David's hand, she rose to her feet. "Feel free to explore the village," she said. "And the medical tent is at your disposal when you're ready." She glanced at Ahab, then to Pat. "Make sure they get settled into accommodations in the village." Back to Clare. "We'll talk more later in the day. After lunch?"

Clare nodded and stood too. "Thank you for considering this. I know it's a huge decision. We discussed it for months before I was sent to tell you everything."

"I promise not to take months to decide," Kira said with a slight smile. "But I will need a few days."

Raf rose too. "Don't worry about accommodation. We've got more than enough room aboard the ship." And years of working as a smuggler had ingrained a few eccentricities that had saved his life more than once. One of those was to always sleep on his ship whenever possible. Even someplace safe like Kierna'Rhoan, he still felt odd not staying in his own bunk.

Kira smiled slightly, no doubt remembering his preference from the last two visits. Though the *Ebisu* hadn't stayed long during that first trip, he'd turned the second visit into a short holiday for his crew. And he'd slept on the ship every night. Just in case.

As the group split, Raf motioned Ahab and Clare to the side. "You have what you need here?" he asked Ahab.

Ahab nodded. "She'll be back to normal in a few days.

The reversion process will take time."

"At least I won't look half Leech anymore." She sighed.

Her gaze trailed away and Raf followed to see E standing with a small group of Shifters, including Xep.

"They know," she murmured. "I'd lay money they know about him."

"When are you going to tell Kira and David?" Raf asked.

"I've got a feeling I won't have to." She shook her head. "I meant to discuss him before they left but…"

"You got distracted by the other reason you're here."

She shrugged. "If E admits his real nature to Xep, and Xep tells Kira, do you think it'll come as less of a shock?"

"Maybe. That's *if* E admits to his real nature."

Her mouth pursed as she stared at the group of Shifters. Releasing a long breath, she faced Ahab. "Okay. I'd love to get started on the repair process. Can we do that now?"

Ahab led them to the medical tent. Knowing she was still a little scared and would never admit it, Raf went with them to keep her company. There were other things he could be doing, looking after his ship, settling his crew, tormenting Sonia about her relationship with Pat. But the only thing he wanted to do was stay with Clare. With Emma.

Knowing her real name, using her real name was a delicious little treat for him. He mostly tried not to think of her as Emma so he wouldn't slip up in front of his crew. But when they were alone, and sometimes when he needed to remember their shared connection, he thought of her by her real name. He was possessive and protective of the knowledge. No one else knew the truth. Only him. And it made him feel as if he had a claim on her he probably didn't have any right to.

But for a little while longer, he could pretend. It was just another kind of lie, and he was as good at lying to himself as he was at lying to others.

Ahab worked on her for several hours. During the procedure, Raf talked with her about nonsense to keep her distracted. And when she griped about needing to eat despite not being hungry, he went and got her food. Once Ahab had done as much as was possible for a single session, Raf walked her back through the settlement.

"It's changed a lot since I was last here," he told her.

"I got that impression. How long has it been?"

He squinted up at the trees and calculated. "A year and a half, Naravan time." He looked around. "Never expected them to build things like cafés, though they'd already built a performance hall by the time I brought David here, so I don't know why I'm surprised."

"It looks like a real, proper settlement. A home." Her gaze roamed over the huge trees, the black dirt, and bluish-green grass. "It's so…clean."

He laughed. "City girl."

"You know what it reminds me of? Lost City."

"Really?" He glanced at her. "Thought that was all caves."

"It is. What I mean… There's a feel here. Peaceful and clean and flowing with life." She dipped her head to one side. "It's noisier here. Lost City is eerily silent."

Because Shifters didn't naturally communicate aloud, they used telepathy instead, he supposed a city full of them would be quiet.

"Did you know they have music?" she asked, looking up at him.

"Shifter music? That's new to me."

"They use themselves as instruments," she said, awe clear in her tone. "It's wild."

"Looking forward to seeing that city one of these days," he said.

"If it isn't destroyed in a war."

He nodded. He liked Narava. It was one of his favorite planets. He really hoped they didn't dissolve into war.

He returned Clare to the café and then excused himself. He'd ignored his duties long enough. There were things he needed to do back on the ship. But before he left, he handed her a comm-card.

"Let me know when Kira and David are ready to meet again. I'll come back. Or you can just ping me if you need anything else."

"I'm glad we'll be staying on the ship," she said, surprising him.

"You worried about this place?"

"No. I'm worried that if I stayed here, I'd never get any peace." She nodded to three Shifters hovering nearby. She smiled back at Raf. "I'm as excited to talk to them as they are to talk with me. But Ahab's treatments take a toll. I'm going to have to sleep at some point."

"Don't worry," he said, lowering his voice for her ears only. "I'll get you into bed soon."

His wink made her laugh, crinkling the skin around her eyes. They were browner now and they sparkled with her amusement. That did his heart good, giving him enough peace of mind to get back to the ship.

The Shifters surrounded her the minute he walked away.

CHAPTER TWENTY-EIGHT

THE NEXT FEW DAYS WERE FILLED WITH DISCUSSIONS AND conversation, but to Clare's surprised, the subject of E didn't come up until day three. When it finally did, it was E himself who started things.

He walked right up to Kira Farseaker and said, "It is time we talked."

Kira raised her brows and nodded. They were sitting at the outdoor tables at Vettine's café again, the place everyone seemed to gather daily. Almost as soon as E approached Kira, Xep dropped from the trees, shifted to natural form, and settled at her right shoulder.

Clare knew that pose. Xep had taken up a protective position, at the ready to keep Kira safe from this possible threat without actually getting in her way. Kira frowned at the Shifter, then turned back to E.

"Something I should have known about before now?" she asked both Xep and E.

E tilted his head forward. The face he was currently

sporting was broader than his natural form, his hair a dark brown, his eye color brown too. His body shape was essentially the same, but with the changes to his face, there was nothing that screamed Ennoren about him.

Clare rose when she realized E might just shift suddenly and reveal himself. He'd never been big on subtlety.

"E." She caught his attention. "Remember your reasons for—" she pointed at his face, "—this. Go slowly."

"What the hell is going on?" Kira asked, her tone sharp.

Clare settled back into her seat but remained on the edge of it, ready to leap up and intervene if necessary.

E held still and quiet for a long moment, just staring at Kira. Xep straightened, its lean, long limbs suddenly seeming longer, and larger.

When she couldn't take the quiet tension any longer, Clare broke into the silence, hoping to ease things along as gently as possible. "Kira, E is special. We have kept some things about him disguised so as not to… Well, to startle you or piss you off."

"Piss me off?" Kira asked slowly.

"You should know," Clare said, "Monroe and the others all know about E. They wanted him to come and meet you. So you know he's not dangerous to you."

"Is there a reason he should be?" Kira said.

E took that moment to do exactly what Clare was afraid he would—he shifted back to his natural form. Kira's gasp was echoed by half a dozen humans, and before Clare could get a word out, Kira was pointing a blaster at E. Clare wasn't even sure where the weapon had come from as she hadn't once noticed Kira carrying it.

"Wait!" Clare leapt between E and Kira, raising her hands

toward Kira, palms out. "He's not Ennoren. I know he looks like him, but he's not. Please, let me explain."

"What…?" Kira's breath came in pants and her hand shook but she didn't lower her weapon. "How? How is he here? I killed him!"

"Ennoren is dead," Clare assured. "E is… Different."

"He shifted. You're a Shifter?" Kira asked, finally letting the blaster nose lower, but she kept the weapon in hand.

"He's a…hybrid," Clare said. "Between human and Shifter."

"Not possible." Kira shook her head.

Clare shrugged. "He exists so it has to be possible."

Kira glared at E. "Why are you in Ennoren's shape if you're a Shifter?"

"This is my natural state," E answered.

"Why? How? Impossible."

Kira stood her ground, but Clare could see her hands were still trembling. Xep put a hand on her shoulder and the woman shuddered. Before Clare or E could say more, David came running up to the café.

"What the hell's going on?" He turned, saw E looking like Ennoren, stepped in front of Kira and pulled a blaster. "You're dead! How the hell is he here?"

Clare kept her hands up and stayed between E and the blaster—not because she was worried about David shooting E but because she was afraid of how E would react if David shot him.

"Just calm down. Please." She motioned to Kira's lowered gun. "We were just getting to the full explanation. I promise, he's not a danger to any of you or we wouldn't have brought him. He's *not* Ennoren."

David exchanged a look with Kira and only at her slight nod did he lower his weapon. But like her, he kept his blaster in hand.

"Please, sit." Clare gestured to their abandoned seats. "I can explain—or at least give you the closest thing to an explanation that we have. Some of it is conjecture because we don't know exactly what was done, but scientist friends with a decent understanding of genetics have a basic idea of how E came to be."

"What the hell is he?" David asked, not sitting.

Kira eased back into her chair, though, and remained quietly staring at E. Xep kept a hand on her shoulder.

"He's a hybrid," Clare repeated. From the corner of her eye, she saw Raf approaching, hand on the blaster in his belt holster. "And this is his natural form."

David finally sat down, dropping into a chair like he'd taken a blow to the stomach.

Clare turned to E. "Sit," she said to him. "It will help things."

He frowned slightly but took a seat next to hers. She returned to her own chair once everyone else seemed settled. Raf stepped up to the edge of the area, keeping all the gathered humans and Shifters in sight. The crowd was growing with each passing second, and Clare heard the murmurs about Ennoren running through the group. She took a deep breath and began the explanation, loud enough so that everyone could hear. She told them about the SRC research, the way they'd likely used Ennoren's corpse as a template to form E, growing him from a mixture of human DNA and Shifter. E added that he was the fifth experiment, and the only one to survive successfully. Clare also made it clear that the Lost City Shifters were working with E, helping him to understand his Shifter half.

When she was done, silence filled the clearing. She finally looked around, and realized that the entire settlement had joined them. Shifters and humans alike were staring between Kira and E, waiting for her reaction.

Clare met Raf's gaze and raised her brows. He gave her a small smile but his expression was tense and worry tightened his mouth when he looked away from her.

She faced Kira and David again, waiting. Kira was pale and looked a little sick. David's expression was impossible to read. Clare realized as she looked at him that this was his "cop face," the expression he must have worn frequently when he was still a Guard.

Finally, Kira spoke. Her voice was harsh and quiet. "I can't believe they did that with Eian's body. I hated the man in the end. I wasn't sorry to have killed him. But… But he would be really pissed off at being turned into… Into E."

E tilted his head down but otherwise his expression was empty of reaction or emotion.

"One last thing," Clare said.

"Oh god, what else could there be?" Kira said.

"He can shift to non-organic things. That's how we got him off Narava." Clare looked at the other Shifters in the surrounding crowd. "Whatever Shifter DNA they used to make E must have had the same mutation as Xep's line."

"Son of a bitch," David muttered.

Kira's skin paled further and David leaned in to wrap her in his arms.

A wave of movement went through the Shifters, silent but Clare recognized it as unease.

Xep finally formed a mouth and spoke up. "We hoped that mutation would remain secret. But we did lose members of our line early on, just as the mutation was starting to show up. It is very possible SRC used the DNA of one of those Shifters without realizing what they had." Xep faced E. "Do they realize your ability to shift to non-organic forms has evolved in some Shifters, or do your creators think that's an oddity of your mutation?"

E's expression never changed. "I don't know. I don't believe they know other Shifters have evolved this trait. But I was not told everything. They lied to me about my purpose."

Clare knew first hand that E considered lying to him the worst of offenses. She wasn't sure why that bugged him so much, but she'd never been brave enough to ask—which was unusual for her. One day, she promised herself she'd step up and put the question to him.

"What were you told was your purpose?" Xep asked.

"To kill Shifters," E said. "That I was superior and was to do what my creators told me to do."

"You were created to kill other Shifters," Xep said quietly.

"We also think," Clare put in, "that he might have been intended to hunt down and kill Kira and David."

"What?" David barked.

"I have your faces in my mind," E said without reacting to David's outburst. "I have no association with your faces. I feel nothing about those pictures, and they are not memories. But I have you in my head."

"Our Shifters made sure there was no trigger associated with those images," Clare assured. "Val even took on Kira's face in front of E to prove the point."

"Then… Why?" Kira asked.

"We think when he was sent to the Lost City dig site he was being tested," Clare said, "and they hadn't actually finished programming him yet."

"They sent inferior beings to destroy the city," E said. "They told me to stay out of the way, but also told me I was superior at killing Shifters. Why would they send inferior creatures to do what they told me I was best able to do? They lied to me."

"E doesn't like being lied to," Clare murmured to David and Kira, sort of pointlessly but she couldn't help herself.

"So you defected?" Kira asked.

E dropped his chin in his equivalent of a nod. "The Shifters of Lost City…they are familiar to me." He frowned. "No. They speak to my nature."

"The fact that they're male and female, like he's male, seems to make a difference for him," Clare said.

Most Shifters were asexual, reproduced asexually, and had evolved away from genders centuries ago, when their species first evolved the ability to shift. A parasite in the underground environment of Lost City had driven those lines to re-evolve two-gendered sexual reproduction. No matter how often Ti'ann explained it to her, though, Clare only vaguely understood the science behind it all.

"With other Shifters," Xep said, "you still feel the need to hunt and kill?"

E met Xep's whirring gaze. "I am not compelled to kill Shifters. I am simply very good at it. But I do not do it anymore."

"Why?" Xep asked.

"Because I don't want to," E said. "I do what I want to do now."

Kira and David exchanged a look, then Kira and Xep stared at each other for a long, silent moment. Clare knew from Monroe that Kira could speak telepathically with the Shifters, even better than Monroe could.

"What do you want to do now?" Xep finally asked E.

E was silent. Then, "I no longer know what my purpose is. I hoped this trip would help. That Kira Farseaker and David Cario would be able to help me find my purpose."

"Us?" Kira said. "Why us?"

"Because your faces are in my head," E said. "I am built from your dead husband. We are…tied together."

Kira's golden eyes narrowed. "I don't know what we can do for you. I still can't believe you exist."

E looked at the ground without answering.

Xep stepped into the silence. "We can try, though," the Shifter said. "We can discuss what would be the best ways for you to use your unique nature. What do the Shifters of Lost City say?"

"They thought I should seek out Kira Farseaker and David Cario," E said. "That I would find my purpose in the history of my different ancestries."

Kira sat back in her chair and David finally released his tight hold on her, though he did keep a hand in hers.

Kira raised her brows. "I suppose we should help you then," she murmured. "I'm not sure how, but…" She glanced at Xep then back at E. "But I'm willing to try."

A tension that had held E tight eased. The change was subtle and maybe only Clare noticed it because she'd spent enough time with him. But the exchange seemed to take away any anxiety E might have felt, if that was the right word for what E felt. It also eased the tension in the entire group. A collective sigh of relief seemed to wave through humans and Shifters, and the crowd started to disburse.

Before long, only David, Kira, Xep, Vettine, Raf, Ahab, and E remained with Clare at the café. Vettine moved back inside and reemerged with fresh coffees for everyone. Raf finally took a seat. So did Ahab. He was staring at E more intently than the others. Clare recognized that expression—she looked at things that way when she was on a story. She knew Ahab would be fascinated by the genetics that went into creating E, but she couldn't help wondering if the young man was thinking of other uses for the hybrid.

And for some reason, the thought that Ahab might have a purpose for E made Clare nervous. She wasn't sure why, but the look in Ahab's dark eyes made her jumpy. Without realizing she was doing it, she took hold of Raf's hand and squeezed. They exchanged a look and she nodded subtly to Ahab. Raf's answering nod was so slight, she was sure no one else noticed. But she got the message.

They would talk later.

CHAPTER TWENTY-NINE

When Kira asked Clare to go for a walk after the discussion about E, Clare expected the other woman to grill her more in private about the Shifter-hybrid that looked so much like her ex-husband.

Instead, Kira broached a topic Clare was surprised hadn't come up the first day on Kierna'Rhoan.

"Why you?" Kira asked, her voice quiet, her hands on her stomach as they strolled down a narrow dirt path through the trees.

Clare took a deep breath. She had her story ready. The same story she'd told Raf. "They sent me," she said, "because I didn't know you before and had no direct connection with you."

She repeated the entire excuse—that everyone related to Kira or David in any way was being too closely watched. If one of them disappeared off-planet for any length of time, there would be questions. There would be time for Kira's enemies to prepare for her return and maybe ambush her.

Clare was the precaution against that, the only person James Monroe could trust who hadn't known Kira. No one would think to follow Clare, or wonder why she was missing.

"So, James does trust you?" Kira said. "When did you join his group?"

"I was working as a stripper in the Docks," Clare said. "Actually, working undercover as a bodyguard to one of the strippers. I met Mike Warez—not in the Docks, in the city." She laughed at Kira's raised brows. "And when I mentioned in passing that I did security work, we talked more. Eventually, Mike introduced me to Monroe, and I found out what kind of security they were looking for. And that they were part of a Shifter support group. I doubt I would even have met Monroe if Mike hadn't decided I could be trusted. But Monroe was cautious and it was a while before I was allowed to know much about the group."

"But you know everything now?" Kira asked.

"Most things. I need to in order to keep them all safe."

"You specifically work at protecting the support group?"

"Keeping their meeting places secret, making sure there's no monitoring equipment, trackers or human infiltrators. Whatever I can do to keep the organization from being hurt by the wrong government people."

Clare was actually really proud of the job she did for the support group. It wasn't her main purpose for being there, but she did the job thoroughly—mostly to maintain her cover, but also because, now, she believed in what she was doing. At first, this was just another story. But to gain the group's trust, she couldn't slack on doing her pretend job. After a few weeks, she hadn't wanted to slack on that duty. And because of that, she was in this position now.

"We never had that when I was in charge," Kira said. "We all worked at the security part of things."

"And did a great job of it," Clare said.

"But it's a good idea to have someone dedicated to that kind of work. I'm glad I left James in charge. He's doing good."

"He is. And with the discovery of Lost City, hopefully I won't have a job much longer."

Kira looked at her with raised brows. "You're hoping to be made redundant?"

"It will mean they're no longer in danger just because they're trying to protect the Shifters." Clare smiled. "I think that will be a good thing. And there are always other jobs for someone like me." She liked to skate as close to the truth as possible and this was a truth. Once this story was done, she'd still have plenty of stories to cover.

"I see why he sent you now," Kira said. She was silent for a bit, looking around the trees. "I love this place," she finally murmured. "I haven't felt the peace I feel here since my parents were killed. There are a lot of bad memories on Narava."

"You don't want to go back," Clare said. Not a guess. It was clear in Kira's tone.

Really, Clare couldn't blame her. But the part of Clare, the part of *Reilly* that needed this story had to be ruthlessly silenced in that moment. If she pushed Kira, if she tried too hard to make her return, Clare would only succeed in chasing the other woman way.

Kira patted her tummy. "I want my baby born here. I want my baby to live in peace, not under the constant fear someone will try to take revenge on her for the sins of her mother and father."

"Coming back doesn't mean you'll have to stay," Clare said, keeping her voice calm and reasonable. "In fact, I doubt anyone would expect it."

"No, they will expect it. They'll want me to stay, to be a spokesperson. Hell, they might want one or both of us to run for the senate. The topic has been…mentioned since you brought the news. If my own people think that's a good idea, the supporters on Narava will think of it too. How will I be able to say no?"

"No," Clare said with a shrug. "Easy enough word."

"Not without a great deal of guilt behind it."

"You aren't responsible for saving the entire species," Clare said quietly. "They want you back to add weight to the final weeks of the debate, to ensure things go the way they should. But you don't have to take up the fight again. You've done your part."

Kira laughed. "Thanks. But that won't be how things work out. You know it."

Clare pursed her lips and remained silent.

Unfortunately, everything Kira said was true. Clare could see the others encouraging her to stay, to join the senate, to fight again. And Clare understood exactly why Kira didn't want to do that anymore. But Clare still wanted Kira to take the risk and come back to Narava—for the purely selfish reason that Reilly wanted this interview. She wanted this like she wanted her next night in bed with Raf. And it took a lot of self-control to keep from showing her eagerness that verged on desperation.

"So about this interview," Kira said after they'd walked a bit longer, almost as if she'd read Clare's mind.

Clare suppressed a frown, but glanced sideways at Kira. Monroe had assured Clare that human telepaths couldn't read other human's minds, not with any ease, that he couldn't read hers. Was Kira a stronger telepath who could?

"I guarantee," Clare said after a brief pause, "My reporter friend will look out for you."

"I believe you," Kira said. "But how will it work? You mentioned they won't actually meet us face to face. Why?"

They'd discussed the interview once or twice before, Clare careful never to mention Reilly's name in front of Raf since he knew her real last name now. Each time she discussed the topic with Kira, Clare emphasized that she and David would be protected. This felt like the final discussion, the point at which Kira would decide if she'd risk the interview or not.

"My friend won't meet you in person to protect you, and to protect their identity," Clare said. "My friend works some sensitive stories, which makes anonymity necessary. But if discovered, they won't be able to lead anyone to you, because you've never really met."

"But it'll be a public interview," Kira said. "A live interview. I'll be out of hiding."

"In a protected studio, your interviewer in a separate location, with the weight of the entire network to ensure nothing goes wrong."

"If we won't meet your friend in person anyway, can't we do the interview remotely, even from here?" Kira asked. "Won't a pre-recorded vid work just as well?"

They'd gone through this before, but Clare understood

Kira's continued questioning and patiently explained again. "After the interview goes live," Clare said, "every other reporter on the planet will want to talk with you and David. If you're not available, it'll be very easy to have the interview dismissed as falsified. Vids can be manipulated, a little too easily. The live interview will be impossible to dispute. Especially if you talk with other reporters afterward."

"But if we take those other meetings, we'll be exposed."

"Only *after* you've gone public on your own terms. That will give you a public layer of protection that won't be there before the interview."

"How did this work when your friend revealed Lost City to Narava?" Kira asked. "You mentioned that going live was to prevent the government from making another attempt to destroy the city. A 'public layer of protection' for the city."

Kira glanced at Clare, and Clare tried not to wince.

"It worked, obviously," Kira said, "but was there any trouble during the initial interview?"

Damn. The one question Clare had really really been hoping to avoid. Because things had almost gone very badly. Admitting this out loud might be the nail in the coffin of a live interview with Kira.

Clare considered lying. Or hedging around the truth with more assurances. But if she got Kira back to Narava under false pretenses, if Kira learned the truth, she might leave without going through with the interview. And that breach of trust would definitely get Clare tossed out of the support group, might even risk her cover.

Reluctantly, she admitted, "There was…one issue during that interview. E stopped a small, three man group from silencing the broadcast and killing Nathan and Dr. Jones."

"What?" Kira stopped mid-stride and turned to face her.

Clare did wince this time. But she went on. "We thought the location was secure. Nathan and Ti'ann had just started the interview when the transmission was cut. A few moments later, the transmission came back on and the interview continued without another hitch. We only found out later about the small strike force, and that E had killed the group. But we learned a lot from the incident, and I can promise nothing like that will happen again."

"How?" Kira asked pointedly.

"No one will even know you're on-planet until *after* the interview this time. The elements in the government that wanted to silence the Lost City story knew that interview was going to happen. No one will expect this one. Also the studio has upped their security efforts significantly after the last incident."

Can't have sources killed while they're giving us an exclusive, Reilly's boss had said. Wouldn't be good for business.

Kira frowned. "I'm not sure what bothers me more, that my cousin and his wife were nearly killed trying to make knowledge of the city public, or that E so easily fixed the issue without anyone knowing."

"E is terrifying," Clare admitted. "But so far, he's on our side, so I'm not going to turn away his help."

"I can't get over that he looks like Eian." Kira shuddered, then started walking again.

Clare fell into step beside her, trying not to let her anxiety show. This was so damned important to her. But Kira couldn't know just how much Clare would be affected by her decision.

"Did anyone go after Nathan and Ti'ann after the interview?" Kira asked.

"No. That all worked out exactly as we hoped. A public layer of protection," Clare said with a slight smile at Kira's snort. "The city was safe and no more attempts were made on Nathan and Ti'ann."

"Probably because of E," Kira said.

"Maybe. The same people who wanted to shut us up were likely the same people who created E. They know what he can do."

"I'm sure Nathan has ensured more security too." Kira smiled. "I wish I'd had a chance to know him better. Our families were estranged for a long time. He sounds…entertaining."

"He's a good man," Clare said, meaning it. "You'll like Ti'ann too. She's super smart. And crazy. In a good way."

Kira laughed, but the amusement didn't last long. "I thought I'd left the crusading behind," she muttered, rubbing her belly.

"Nathan never thought he'd be a crusader, but he's joined the fight too. I'm not sure any of us can be neutral anymore. Or silent."

Clare was a little surprised to hear those words come out of her own mouth—she wasn't supposed to be a crusader either. But she sure sounded like one. Somewhere along the lines, she'd really gotten attached to this cause. Clare O'Malley had, anyway.

She wasn't sure if her real self felt the same way or not, and it was one of the stranger disconnects she'd had over the years, between the real her and one of her personas. Did

Reilly care about the Shifters? Or just the legend-making aspects of the story?

Busy shuffling through the layers of her convoluted feelings from duel personalities, she startled when Kira spoke again, bringing Clare sharply back to the issue at hand.

"I've done my part," Kira murmured.

Like she was trying to convince herself of that fact, Clare thought. Aloud, she said, "Yes. You have. Between you and David, you managed to put us on the path toward the end of the exterminations." Very quietly, she added, "Don't you want to see things through to the end?"

Kira sighed loudly. "Unfortunately, I do." She rubbed her belly again. "Sorry baby," she murmured down. "But I need to finish this, once and for all."

Clare carefully concealed her burst of triumph and touched Kira on the arm. "We'll keep you all safe. And get you back to Kierna'Rhoan for the birth of your baby."

Kira pushed out a sound like a half-laugh, half-snort. "We'll see. In the meantime, let's head back. David and I need to talk."

"Is he going to object?"

"Not since he's coming with me. We've been through a lot together. We need to finish this together, too. But he left the final decision up to me."

Clare's heart twisted a little at the love between them. Such trust. She'd never trusted anyone outside her immediate family like that, loved anyone like that. What would it be like to know someone had your back that way?

When they returned to the café, Raf was sitting across from David, his expression serious. Until he looked up and saw her. Then he smiled. A soft, personal smile meant just for her. And her heart did another twist for an entirely different reason.

What would it be like? she wondered again. Looking at Raf, she thought she might just be able to understand, at least a hint of what she saw between David and Kira. Between Nathan and Ti'ann for that matter.

Trust a smuggler? She wanted to laugh. Only she would find the most untrustworthy man in the universe the one man she might just trust beyond all others.

How was she going to explain this to her mother?

CHAPTER THIRTY

WHEN CLARE RETURNED TO THE *EBISU* LATER THAT EVENING, she found Raf in the canteen examining the cupboards.

He looked over his shoulder and smiled at her. "Hungry?"

"Kind of. I need to eat."

He turned to face her, crossing his arms over his chest. "Do you even enjoy food? Do you ever get to simply savor a meal?"

She shrugged. "I suppose I enjoy my dad's cooking. He's really good. My mom's not bad, but my dad's a secret chef. But to be honest, I eat for the calorie balance. What the food tastes like barely matters."

"No way to live, O'Malley."

She grinned. He was so careful about only using her real name in private. Even when it seemed like they were the only people around, if they were in a public space, she was Clare O'Malley. The realization made her think back to her earlier consideration of trust. For a smuggler, he was pretty damned reliable.

"You're one to talk," she said, settling her hip against the counter next to him. "You live on as many nutrition bars and quick food as I do. I've seen the contents of your cabin's auto-cooker, remember?"

"Yes, but I know how to enjoy food. And tonight, I'm going to remind you."

"You're going to do that by…what? Programming up something wonderful?"

"I'm going to cook for you."

"Cook?" she asked, dropping her chin to give him a look. "On your ship?"

"This is a working canteen. Not just reliant on the auto-cookers." He smiled. "I'm old fashioned."

"Why didn't I know you could cook?"

"Because if I show off my kitchen skills in front of my crew, the blackguards will expect me to cook for them. All the time. Can't have that."

"Does Sonia know?"

"I think she suspects." He chuckled. "Every once in a while I surprise them all with food that didn't come from the auto-cooker, but I never admit where it came from."

"That's…sweet." She raised her brows and quirked her mouth. "You just keep surprising me, Tygran."

"Good. It's important to keep a woman on her toes. You learn all my secrets, you'll have no reason to keep seeing me."

He turned back to the cupboards before she could read his expression but his comment made her stomach tighten and dance. Did he want to keep seeing her after this job? And if he did…how would that even work?

"Anything you can't eat?" he asked as he started pulling sealed packages down and lining them up on the counter.

She shook her head. "No allergies."

"Do you need a big or small meal?"

"Probably a big one." She counted up her day. "Yeah. I've done okay, but still need a good feed."

"One good feed coming up."

Before he could move away, she grabbed his lapels and pulled him close, kissing him soundly on the mouth. When she eased back, he cupped her cheek, then ran his hand up through her hair.

"What was that for?" he murmured, his gaze moving over her face.

"I wanted to."

His lips lifted. "Keep that up."

"What?"

"Wanting to kiss me. I like it."

She smiled back and released him. She liked it too. She liked him. Very much. And for the first time in her life, she wasn't in a hurry to get back to the story.

"So," he said as he set about prepping the things he had on the counter, "David and I had an interesting talk after you and Kira went for your walk."

"Kind of thought that might have happened. What did he say?"

"He wanted to know if I trusted you."

She sat down at the table and watched as he opened various packages. "What did you tell him?"

"That you were sent by Kira's former group and her own cousins. If Kira trusted any of those people, then they could trust you."

"That wasn't an answer to his question," she pointed out.

He laughed. "That's what David said. I told him I didn't think you intended any harm for them."

"And when he pointed out you still weren't answering his question?"

"I said you were a liar, so of course I trusted you."

"You told him I was a liar!" She half-rose, then collapsed again. Not sure how much damage Raf had done with that comment, but her heartbeat thundered in her ears as panic set in.

Raf didn't seem to notice her distress. "Oh, he knows how I am with liars. If I told him you were an honest person and I trusted you, he would have thought something was wrong."

She blinked, silent for long enough, Raf looked back at her.

"You okay?" he asked.

She nodded but still didn't know quite what to say.

"David's probably the most honest person I know who I still sort of trust," Raf continued. "And I only trust him because he was lying when we met. He's an excellent liar actually. For such an honest man. Guess that's why he was so good undercover."

She blinked. In her panic, she'd forgotten David had worked undercover too—only as a Guard rather than a member of the press. But essentially, they did the same thing for their respective jobs.

She watched Raf mix something in a bowl for a few moments before she finally found her voice. "What did he say when you told him? Did he... Did he ask what I'd lied about?"

"Na. He knows about secrets. He just said if I trusted you then he could be sure you weren't sent from Kira's enemies in the government. And that's all he really cared about."

"She said she'd go back with us," Clare blurted.

Raf nodded but he kept his focus on the food. "I thought she would. Not in her nature to see a thing unfinished."

"She left Narava, left the fight unfinished to hide here," Clare felt compelled to point out.

"Not because she was leaving the fight," Raf said. "It was the only way to save at least one line. She did her part."

"That's exactly what she said." Clare watched his hands as he worked. He had very nice hands. "So why do you think she's agreed to return?"

"Honestly?" he said. "I think she just wants to see Lost City. I do, and I'm not invested in all this the way she is. I suspect Xep will return with us too."

Clare made a face. "Not sure that's a great idea."

"Xep is protective of Kira, as protective as she is of Xep. And I imagine Xep will want to see Lost City to report back to the line here."

She frowned as Raf added something to the mixing bowl that looked suspiciously like nutmeg. "What the hell are you making?"

"Butternut squash ravioli with a white sauce."

"Why are you adding nutmeg?"

"Because it tastes good," he said, giving her a narrowed-eyed look. "Do you want a cooking lesson?"

"No, no." She held up her hands. "I'm good with the auto-cookers."

"Ever considered what you might do if you landed somewhere where there weren't auto-cookers?" he asked.

"I've never left Narava," she said. "It's never been an issue."

He titled his head to one side and considered her. "Is that on purpose or just lack of opportunity?"

"I suppose I could have left if I wanted to." She shrugged. "But my work has always kept me on-planet."

"Would you consider taking jobs off-planet?" He returned to his mixing, seeming only casually interested in her answer.

Until this trip, she hadn't thought about it. Narava was rife with enough drama to keep her career hopping for years. But now, she was realizing how many fascinating stories she might tell by getting off Narava every now and then.

She raised her brows, the idea more appealing every time she thought about it. "I might consider it. Depending. But… at least for a little bit longer, I'm needed on-planet."

He glanced at her, his expression unreadable, then turned back to his food.

She wasn't sure what to make of his question or his reaction to her answer so she hunted around for another topic of conversation. "Where's the rest of the crew?"

"In the settlement," he said. "We're leaving soon. They all wanted to spend as much time on solid ground as they could. And there's a concert tonight. Good excuse."

"Did you kick them off so they wouldn't catch you cooking?" she asked.

"I might have. But I'll never admit it."

She laughed, glad to hear his normal cocky, easygoing tone. Sometimes, when Raf got serious, she got nervous. She didn't know what to expect from a serious Raf Tygran, and she didn't know where she stood with him when he was like that. Though, truth be told, she didn't know exactly where she stood with cocky, easygoing Raf either.

She knew he liked her in his bed. She liked being there too. And there were these hints that maybe he like her for more than just a good fuck. But for what, exactly, and for how long? She was afraid to ask, afraid to face a conversation she didn't have answers for herself. She didn't know what she wanted from him, from this relationship. Did she want him to fly away at the end of the job and never look back? Would that be easier?

The fact that she'd already tried to figure out how to introduce him to her family didn't bode well.

What did she want from him?

As she watched him cook, folding spoonfuls of his butternut squash mixture into little squares of pasta dough, the only thing she knew for sure was that she wanted him tonight. And she wanted him for the rest of this trip.

Once this job was done…

She'd consider that when the time came. For now, she had him, and his continued surprises.

He proved to be an excellent cook. She literally licked up the extra sauce from her bowl. And later, when they stumbled into his bed, she continued the licking, savoring his body as much as she'd savored his food.

For now, that was enough.

CHAPTER THIRTY-ONE

THEY PACKED UP FOR THE RETURN TO NARAVA THE NEXT DAY. Raf felt a strange sense of reverse déjà vu as he watched Kira and David return to the *Ebisu*. It seemed so recently he'd dropped them each off on Kierna'Rhoan. Now they were leaving. And while he did trust that Clare meant it when she said the Shifter supporters would protect Kira and David, Raf still felt an edge of anxiety. He liked them both. And they weren't going to be safe on Narava, no matter what was done. He didn't want to see them hurt.

He watched Clare hover anxiously around them as everything was loaded onto the ship. She was excited about bringing them back to Narava but worried too, though she did a fair job of disguising her nerves. He'd spent so much time watching her, he picked up the nuances now, so she couldn't hide her emotions from him. Her worry was probably good. If she was ready for trouble, she'd plan for it, be prepared. He was a firm believer in being prepared for trouble at all times.

Probably because he was always getting into trouble.

When they were loaded up and their passengers all aboard, Raf stood at the top of the landing ramp, taking one last look around the planet as his crew said their goodbyes. He grinned at Sonia and Pat's face off. Speaking of trouble. Those two were going to have to accept they were in love one of these days. Sonia hadn't bothered with any other men or women since meeting Pat. From what Raf had seen of the hacker's interactions with the rest of the humans here, he got the impression Pat had been the same.

The thought of losing Sonia to Kierna'Rhoan broke Raf's heart—in more than a mercenary Sonia-was-good-at-her-job sort of way. But as he watched his second dance around her emotions, he accepted that one of these days she was going to retire. And she was going to retire to Kierna'Rhoan.

He chuckled. There were worse ways to leave the smuggling behind.

Glancing back into the ship, he caught sight of Clare moving toward the lifts. She didn't see him before disappearing so he was free to stare and wonder.

Did they have a future?

He'd never expected to want something permanent. But with her, things had changed. He hadn't been looking for her, but turned out she was everything he wanted in a woman. She was brave, sexy, smart, and fun. Loyal, ambitious, and kind. An adrenaline junky who could hold her own in a gun fight. A big softy when it came to those she loved. All the complicated parts of her combined in just the right way to be perfect for him. And she fit with his world.

His crew had taken her in like one of their own, in a way they didn't with clients and passengers. They liked her, not just because he was sleeping with her—that usual worked against a woman—but because she fit. He wasn't sure how else to explain it. Watching her play cards with his people, the friendship she'd developed with Delilah, who was notoriously difficult to befriend… It was like she'd been part of their world for years.

He wasn't going to give up smuggling. Not yet. He was responsible for too many people. And beyond that, he loved what he did, the rush, the risk. The money. But it wasn't a job that lent itself to a permanent relationship. So where did that leave them?

He wasn't prepared to call this love yet. He'd had too little experience with it to recognize the emotion in himself. But he did know he wanted Clare to remain in his life, in whatever way she was willing. And that was a lot more than he'd ever wanted from a woman before.

The question was, what did she want from him?

He shook off the introspection and slapped Sonia on the shoulder when she finally topped the ramp. "You sure you don't want to ask Pat to come along?"

He was only half-teasing. They had enough room since just Kira, David and Xep were coming back to Narava.

"Don't be an ass," Sonia said, with a snort of derision. "Why would I do that?"

"Ah, Sonia." Raf sighed and tugged her close for a quick shoulder hug as the ramp rose and blocked out the view of the planet. "That man couldn't be more in love with you if he tried."

"So." She crossed her arms over her chest, staring at Raf defiantly, as if Pat's feelings meant nothing to her.

Raf laughed and shook his head. "Hey, it's your lonely bed. Go check on Duster, make sure he's got the nav coordinates worked out. I'll meet you on the flight deck for final checks."

She rolled her eyes, but he didn't miss the very real confusion in her frown. He empathized with his co-pilot. He was feeling some very real confusion himself.

They left Kierna'Rhoan behind less than an hour later. Once beyond the edge of the system, they made the first jump back to familiar space. Pat had ensured that once they reached coordinates they could navigate from, the location of Kierna'Rhoan would, once again, be wiped from the computer. Raf had given up trying to override the hacker's efforts. Pat was superior to the *Ebisu's* techs, and no matter what they did, the Kierna'Rhoan coordinates always disappeared without a trace. It was almost funny now, how often Raf ended up on a planet he couldn't find without help.

Once they'd made the second jump securely, he left things to Sonia so he could find Clare. Delilah stopped him in the corridor just outside the flight deck.

"Captain," she said, "this message came through the instant we hit familiar space, before we made the second jump. Looks like it's been broadcasting for days, waiting for us to receive."

He snatched the messaging pad from Delilah and stared down at it. His heart stopped for a split second before starting to thunder painfully fast.

"You read this?" he asked without looking up.

"Yes, sir. Couldn't help it."

"Keep it to yourself," he said, raising his eyes to meet and hold her gaze. "That's an order."

"Aye, sir. Mouth shut. You gonna tell Sonia?"

He nodded, though his thoughts were running ahead of

his conversation. "But I don't want the whole ship knowing about this. Not yet."

"You're not gonna do it, are you?"

Raf gave her a look.

She ducked her head. "Sorry, Captain. It's just…"

"I know," he said. "I understand the question."

The Leeches had been a bane to his existence for a long time. They'd complicated his business and his ability to take certain jobs. Getting them off his back once and for all was a very very tempting carrot. That promise had led him to FarMore Station even though he'd suspected it was a trap. He still wasn't immune to the lure.

But what they wanted in exchange was unacceptable.

"You gonna tell her?" Delilah whispered.

He jerked his head once. This wasn't a secret he intended to keep. The problem was *how* to tell Clare without freaking her out.

The Leeches still wanted her. And they were willing to do a lot to get her back.

"She's not going to be safe from them. Ever." Delilah broke into his thoughts, her rough voice hoarser than usual. "Not on Narava. She's going to have to disappear."

He nodded, still considering what to say to Clare and how to fix this mess.

"She could disappear aboard the *Ebisu*," Delilah said. "We'd all welcome her."

Raf straightened his shoulders. His people would accept her. He could offer her a place here. But…

"I'm still a Leech target," he said. "She'd be safer disappearing somewhere away from the *Ebisu*." Admitting as much made his chest tighten, even if he knew it was the truth.

"But you wouldn't really know she was safe unless she was here," Delilah said. "We're used to avoiding the Leeches."

That was true enough. Still. "Clare has a life on Narava. Has to be her decision how to handle this."

"Offer her a place here, Captain," Delilah said. "At least make the offer."

He held her gaze for a long moment as her words sank in. She stared at him with all that wisdom and history in the depths of her eyes. He wanted to take her advice. More than he might have guessed. But to do so carried more implications than just Clare's safety.

"I'll consider it," he finally said, refusing to commit until he'd thought things through completely. "Back to your station. And remember, not a word of this to anyone."

"Aye, Captain." She gave him a little salute that was only half a joke, then turned and disappeared down a side corridor.

Raf remained where he was for long minutes, considering this newest complication. What to do, what to do? Offering Clare asylum on the *Ebisu* appealed to him on a very primitive level. He could keep her, he could protect her, he could have her as his own.

But…

What happened if things didn't work between them? Or worse, what happened if she said no? What if she didn't want him? Could he still give her the safety of his ship without asking anything else of her?

Yeah. Yeah, he could do that. He'd gotten her into the mess with the Leeches. Whether she wanted him personally for the long term or not, the least he could do was offer her the safety of the *Ebisu*.

Damn that was very self-sacrificing. He wasn't used to self-sacrifice. He was going to ruin his reputation.

With a grunt, he continued his hunt for Clare, still not entirely sure what to say to her. The return to Narava had just got a little more complex.

CHAPTER THIRTY-TWO

RAF FOUND CLARE IN HER CABIN, TALKING WITH KIRA. KIRA
looked up, met his gaze, and excuse herself without asking
any questions. She squeezed his arm on the way out the door,
a show of support he found touching.

Once they were alone, though, Raf still didn't quite know
how to tell Clare about the Leeches' offer. He stood in the
open doorway, staring at her as she stared back, her brows
raised.

The silence gave him a chance to take in the deep chocolate color of her eyes, the beautiful, creamy smoothness of
her skin, those delicious freckles across her nose, the mass of
red curls she'd barely tamed into a bun. She was beautiful.
Her external beauty had been obvious from their first intro-
duction. But when he looked at her now, he saw…more. He
wasn't even sure how to describe it. He still *saw* her features,
recognized they were beautiful, but the woman he stared at
was so much more stunning than the sum of her physical
parts.

He closed the door and took a seat in the cushioned chair Kira had just vacated. Clare remained sitting on her bed—a bed she'd barely used since coming aboard, he realized. She'd spent most of her time in his cabin.

"Something serious," she said.

Didn't ask. Said. "Yes," he confirmed with a nod.

"News from Narava? The Shifters?"

"The Leeches."

She straightened. He watched as fear tightened the skin at the corners of her eyes, then she frowned, her brow creasing and her eyes moved as if she were reading. When she looked up, her eyes were wide.

"They offered you a trade," she said. "For me."

He wanted to laugh. So much for worrying about how to tell her. "Sometimes I think you might be a little too smart. I like that about you."

She smiled, but it was forced. "What did they say? Exactly?"

"They'd stop chasing me and my crew, leave us completely alone, not try to exact any revenge, if I hand you over. They've even designated the spot. Narava."

"They know where we're headed?" she said.

"Doubt it. It's just a convenient location, not far from where they lost you on FarMore—where I doubt they're welcome anymore." He paused. "I'm not likely welcome there either, although that's never stopped me."

Her slight smile was more genuine this time.

"And meeting in the Docks," he continued, "where planetary authority doesn't tend to go officially, would make a handoff easier."

"They can't know I'm from there, right?" she said. "I played like I was part of your crew."

She wrapped her arms around herself, a protective hug, and it was all Raf could do not to go to her and wrap her up in his own protection.

"They don't even know your name," he confirmed. "They just said to bring the Leech female."

She snarled at that epithet, then heaved a heavy sigh and stared at the wall. "Glad they don't know my name. Especially my real name."

He knew she was careful about her identity, but he still had to ask, "You're sure your alter ego is…complete enough?"

She nodded, still not looking at him. "I hide my real name for a lot of reasons. I didn't expect this to be one of them. But at least the Leeches won't be able to track down my family." She glanced at him. "Clare doesn't have any family."

He nodded but remained silent, waiting for her to work through the situation.

"You'd be safe," she said. "Your crew would be safe."

Again a statement. Not a question.

"They offered that same 'release from our debt' to lure me to FarMore Station," he said. "I'm not inclined to trust their assurances."

"They want me badly enough they'd follow through," she said. "Ahab and I have talked a lot about this. The Leeches want to be *recognized* as a separate species by the galaxy at large. They want to reproduce biologically, to have babies born as Leeches, from Leech sperm and Leech eggs. According to Ahab, it's not even about sex for some of them. Artificial insemination would do. They just need Leeches with fertile eggs and healthy wombs. And nothing else matters." She pulled in a deep breath. "They know for sure I can mutate. And Ahab's lab was destroyed, along with his cure. They take me now, there's no way for me to reverse the process. I'm sure they realize that."

He didn't know what to say. She was right. They both knew it.

"I don't want to be a Leech," she murmured.

"I have no intention of turning you over. You know that, right?" He couldn't read her expression, couldn't tell what she was thinking.

"You'd be safe," she said again.

"Not that way. It's not an option and never has been." He stood because sitting no longer felt comfortable. Did she really think he'd betray her like that? After everything that had happened between them?

She reached out and grabbed his arm as he paced past her, halting his restless movements. He didn't look down until she squeezed hard and tugged at him. When he did meet her gaze, he kept his expression as neutral as he was able given the circumstances.

"I didn't honestly think you'd give me to them," she said. "But I had to be up front. I'm not prepared to sacrifice myself for your freedom from them."

That comment left him angrier than he could remember being in a long time. So angry he couldn't speak for a full thirty seconds.

Then, very softly, he said, "What makes you think I want you to 'sacrifice' yourself? What makes you think I'd allow that? I'm no one's charity case. I don't need your *sacrifice* to help me with my problems."

He jerked out of her hold and stalked to the door, too angry to think straight or talk this out. He wasn't even entirely sure why her comment had hit so hard, but he could barely see straight and he needed to leave this room.

"We'll talk more when I calm down. Don't say anything to anyone. No one on the crew but Delilah knows and I intend for it to stay that way until I'm ready to tell them. That's an order."

He left before she could say anything, even argue with him ordering her around. He couldn't actual order her the way he could his crew, but hell if he'd let her know he realized that.

He'd barely made it out of the guest cabins before he slowed and finally stopped. He stood still, breathing hard, staring at the hard metal floor, his fists clenching and unclenching. What the hell was wrong with him? His reaction, his anger didn't make sense. She hadn't said anything that wasn't straightforward and realistic. She'd been honest with him. So why did her honesty piss him off so much?

Focusing on his hands, he flexed and relaxed, flexed and relaxed until the tension left his muscles. Then he dropped he head back to stare up at the ceiling and let loose a long breath. Stupid. He was an idiot.

He headed back toward her cabin, ready to return to the actual important part of this situation. He bumped into her around the first turn in the corridor.

"What the hell?" she said when she saw him. Her eyes were bright and her expression hard.

"Sorry," he said before she could build up any more steam. "I shouldn't have walked out. This is too serious. But just know, if you bring up *sacrificing* yourself again, I will not be a happy man."

She rocked back on her heals and her gaze jumped from the ground to his face to the ground before she settled on his face again. "Fine. Whatever. You just needed to know…how I felt."

"Fine," he echoed. "So do you want asylum or what?"

"What?" She scowled again.

He grunted and dragged a hand through his hair. He was not handling this well. What was wrong with him? He'd never handled himself so piss poorly with a woman before. He *wanted* her to stay. He *wanted* her to want him enough to stay on the *Ebisu*. So why was he working so damned hard at driving her away?

"I meant to say that better," he admitted. "The crew would welcome you. We're used to avoiding Leeches. You'd be safe here. With us." With him. He would keep her safe, too. But he couldn't quite meet her gaze after the offer was made.

She just stared, blinking, no real readable expression on her face. He tipped his head to one side, then the other, letting his neck crack and releasing some of the tension building in his shoulders.

"Well," he snapped, then shook his head. "Sorry. I'm not trying to pressure you. I don't… I don't expect anything personal either. The offer is made in good faith. You could join my crew and be safe."

"And never see my family again?" she asked, her tone carefully neutral.

"I end up on Narava a lot," he said. "Pick up some good jobs in the Docks, jobs I'm not willing to give up. So you could see your family whenever we were on-planet."

"You said you don't expect anything personal. What *do* you expect in exchange for a place aboard ship?"

He glanced around the corridor, where they would be overheard by any passing crew member, and cursed. "Let's talk in my cabin. Or yours. Whatever. But I don't want this public until we've worked things out."

She nodded and motioned for him to lead the way.

Because it was closer, he returned to her cabin. He figured she'd feel less pressure this way. He still wasn't sure what he expected to happen at the end of this conversation. But he was in it now, so he'd see it through.

Once the door was closed, she rounded on him. "What do you mean by 'personal'?"

"I mean us," he said. "I wouldn't expect you to keep sleeping with me just because I gave you a safe place to live."

"Tired of me already, then?"

He scowled. "You know better than that."

"Do I?"

"Yes," he snapped. "And you're being purposefully argumentative."

"You're the one growling," she said. "You're the one that threw the offer of asylum at me like a rock. If you didn't want to offer, you shouldn't have."

"I wanted to offer. I want you to stay. But I can't make you..." He trailed off, still scowling, and started to pace the room again.

She stood where she was and watched him. "I'm not entirely sure what to make of your offer, Raf. You seem very pissed off about the idea that I might be staying. Then you tell me you want me to stay."

"I thought you could read people better than that," he grumbled.

"Guess you're the exception. What the hell do you want?"

He snorted and turned his hands palm up. "I want you to stay with the *Ebisu*." He stopped and looked at her, in the eye so she would understand. "I want you to be safe. I want you to stay with me. I want you. Period. But… But I don't want you feeling obligated to me. I don't want you guilted into sleeping with me because I'm protecting you from something that's my fault to begin with."

"And this offer isn't made out of guilt? You're telling me that if the Leeches weren't a factor, you'd still want me to stay aboard your ship?"

She was quiet and serious as she asked. What she wasn't was accusing, sarcastic, or sharp. Her question was sincere and honest. So he had to answer with as much honesty as his liar's soul could muster.

"I don't know," he admitted. "I don't know how things would have gone with us if the Leeches hadn't…sped the process up."

"Sped things up?" she asked.

He almost laughed. "I wanted you in my bed from the beginning. But I'm not sure the dance we were doing would have taken us there so quickly if not for the Leeches. I'm not sure we would have spent enough time together to really know each other as well as we do now."

"Do we?"

"I know your real name. You know my real background.

My real name. You're one of a small handful of people who know all those things about me. I don't go around telling every woman I sleep with about my past."

She finally sat down in the chair, and again, he couldn't read her expression. Damn. He was slipping. But only with her.

"Raf," she sighed. "Before I..." She stopped, looked up at him, vulnerability plain in her expression. "How do you feel about me? Really. Personally. Not the guilt or the obligation. Not even the lust. How do you feel about me?"

She'd hit the point like a laser. And he was forced to face his future straight on.

"I'm not sure what to call how I feel," he admitted. "I don't have a lot of experience with this."

For the first time since they'd returned to her room, a small smile cracked her expression. "Me neither."

Her admission took a world of tension out of his body and he dropped onto the edge of the bed. "I don't want the situation to force you into anything you don't want. But you're never going to be safe from the Leeches. At least, not on your own. I can keep you safe. The rest... The rest we can deal with as it happens."

She nodded. "Raf, I appreciate the offer. Deeply. You need to know that. And I'm much more tempted than I ever thought I'd be—not just because of the Leeches."

"But," he said. "You don't want to be stuck on a ship."

"It's not that. You travel all over the known galaxy. That's not 'trapped' in anyone's definition. There is a 'but' though." She frowned and stared at the floor. "What I do... I'm very good at it. And I'm not prepared to give it up."

"Not the security. You could do that from my ship."

She snorted. "Not sure how given your primary occupation as a smuggler. But you're right, I'm not talking about the security angle."

"You ready to tell me yet? It stays between us. I swear that."

"I know. I do know."

"But you're not ready," he said. "It's okay. It's enough to know how important it is to you."

"If I admitted the truth to anyone beyond my family, it would be to you."

He smiled at that, fully. Nice to know where he ranked in the hierarchy of her trust. Pretty damned high if he was placed just short of her family. Having her trust meant a lot to him. As much as having her heart would mean. Maybe even more.

"It's not criminal, is it?" he asked. "Cause, you know, that *would* fit in perfectly with our work."

She laughed. "God, I could love you."

She didn't flinch when she said it, and his heart swelled and squeezed at the same time.

"Same," he said, with just as much surety. Because it was true. He could love her. If he didn't already. He could love her for the rest of his life. "You're not staying aboard, though, are you?"

"I haven't actually decided, to be honest," she said. "I'll consider it. It would be safer for Clare O'Malley to not live on Narava."

"What about Mary Margaret Reilly?"

"Not even sure who she is anymore. Emma Reilly has been out of the loop for a long time now."

"Not so hard to let all of that go, then," he said. "Become

someone else. We'd make sure the new persona stuck. Emma and Clare could vanish."

She sighed. "But Emma still has family she would miss. And a career, a passion, she doesn't want to give up."

"You sound decided," he pointed out.

"I'm not. But I am leaning." She swallowed visibly but met his gaze steadily. "I'd miss you, though," she whispered. "If I don't stay aboard *Ebisu*, I will miss you. Very much."

"Same," he said, seriously. "But I won't ask for what you can't give."

"That's what I've always liked about you, Tygran. You take me as I am. And don't expect anything different."

"I like you as you are. Why would I want any different?"

She stood and settled next to him on the bed, then kissed him. It was soft and gentle, full of emotion. And acceptance.

And maybe even love.

CHAPTER THIRTY-THREE

She considered his offer all the way back to Narava. He never pushed her, never even brought it up again. Just one more reason she adored him. He gave her the space she needed. And the time to face what she needed to face.

It took her almost the entire trip to really accept that she would never be completely free of the Leeches now. She'd intended to disappear Clare after this last assignment, but now she had no choice. And what if the Leeches discovered who she really was and went after her family? Her sisters could be susceptible to the Leech infection, too. She couldn't allow her family to be in danger because of her choices.

Running away on the *Ebisu*, with Raf, would solve those problems. The Leeches would have a hard time discovering her real identity if she separated herself almost completely from her previous life.

But...

She'd worked too hard for that life. She *loved* her career. She'd struggled, did things she never thought herself capable of, and had clawed her way to the top of her profession. She was *just starting* to see the heights she could reach. And there was so much more she wanted to do, so many more stories to chase, so many more goals to achieve. The idea of giving all that up hurt, physically. An ache of loss, a kind of grief, wound around her heart. She'd wanted this career for almost as long as she could remember. She'd been born to do what she did. How could she just give all that up?

She couldn't. That was the problem. She couldn't. And she didn't want to have to. She refused to let the Leeches steal her future. Fuck 'em. She was used to disguising her identity. She could vanish into another persona, become someone completely new, and they'd never find her. She'd be safe. Her family would be safe.

And Raf wouldn't feel obligated to keep her in his life.

She knew better than that thought. His offer was about more than obligation. She couldn't deny he had real feelings for her, as she had for him. But the obligation would always be between them if she took up his offer. Whatever they might have, whatever they felt, could only ever be real if they ensured neither of them felt trapped by it.

She was more and more sure she was in love with Raf. But she couldn't be caged by that love or it would sour. She needed her freedom, her independence.

And so did he. He loved his life of independence aboard his ship, with family of his choosing, going where the jobs took him.

If they were going to work as anything more than a short-term affair, neither one of them could be forced to give up that freedom.

She sat in the canteen as they came out of the final jump

into Naravan space. Raf was busy making sure they could land safely, without alerting anyone to their real identity. She'd provided the necessary clear landing codes when he'd taken this job, but getting on-planet without accidentally giving themselves away took concentration. So she stayed away and waited for the all's clear.

As she did, she considered exactly what to tell Raf about her decision. She needed him to understand her reasoning, so he didn't think she didn't want him. She did want him. More than he could know. She just didn't want to feel trapped. And she didn't want him to feel that way either.

Beyond that worry, thoughts of having to confront the Leeches nagged at her. She was pretty sure she could avoid them long enough to get the interview done. Then she'd start the process of disappearing.

She was going to miss the Shifter support group, though. And Ti'ann and Nathan. She'd allowed herself to make friends this time, on this assignment. A mistake. Saying goodbye—or rather not being able to say goodbye—was going to hurt. But better that than bring the Leeches down on the people she loved.

As she considered all the things she'd need to do after they landed, Ahab and E came into the canteen. She watched the body language, and knew yet another worry. They'd spent a lot of time together on the return journey. She'd only ever caught bits of their conversations; they were very careful. But she had heard the Leeches mentioned. Ahab wanted E to help him in his crusade.

The thought of it left her conflicted. She had no love for Leeches and more reason than most to fear them. Dead Leeches didn't bother her much, though she wasn't proud of that. And if they came after her, she wouldn't hesitate to kill them to protect herself. But that was self-defense. Not hunting them on purpose to slaughter them. After years with a Shifter support group, she could no longer turn a blind eye to eradicating an entire group just because she was afraid of them.

Unlike Shifters, though, Leeches were more than capable of fighting back. Shifters were such gentle beings, they had been nearly helpless in the face of human fear and violence. At least in the past. Lost City Shifters had changed that. But not before humans had nearly succeeded in exterminating the species. Leeches came from humans, had the same capacity for violence that humans had. She could never see them as helpless victims.

And yet, sending E after the Leeches… Was that any better than turning him loose to destroy the Shifters? The Leeches could defend themselves against a single human man with a vendetta. E hunting them was another story. E could succeed in slaughtering a lot of them if he was focused on the task. But did they deserve extermination just because they were scary and had become so dangerous?

Having E hunting them would distract them, maybe keep them from infecting more women or even coming after her again. She wasn't opposed to that idea. But E waging war on the Leeches would eventual draw attention. Rumors would start. His nature would eventually come out. Then where would they be?

And was any of this her responsibility? Just because she knew what would happen, was she responsible for stopping it? She'd never felt that way on a job before. She reported news so others could make informed decisions. She was supposed to be neutral. Until Lost City, when she'd been all on board for preventing the government from destroying it.

With a scowl, she realized once she'd crossed that line and gotten so involved with a story, she was susceptible to doing it again. Case in point, she wanted to say something, to warn…someone about this alliance forming between E and Ahab. But letting the galaxy know about E could endanger the Shifters again, just when they were on the verge of saving them. She rubbed at her temples to lessen the slight ache developing.

"You okay?" Ahab asked, breaking into her thoughts.

She softened her scowl. "Yeah. Fine. Just… Returning to Narava means facing a few things."

"The Leeches?"

"I'm worried about them finding me, yes. Especially with your lab destroyed. Any idea how long it will take you to rebuild?"

"Depends," he said. "It'll take money."

"Money you don't have yet?" she asked.

He shrugged without answering directly.

She turned her attention on E. "You don't have to return to Narava. Are you sure you don't want to remain on *Ebisu*?"

He tilted his head down. "There are things to do first."

She narrowed her eyes. "You're not going after your creators, are you? I thought we'd all decided that was a bad idea. E, you can't risk what might happen if they take you back."

His expression never changed. "They will not find me if I do not wish to be found."

That was the problem. What if he wished to be found? He, Kira, and David had spent a lot of time talking during the return journey. From what Clare had overheard, she got the impressions stories of Ennoren hadn't exactly clarified a purpose for E, but maybe she'd been wrong. Maybe E wanted revenge on his creators for the sake of his human half who would have so detested what was done with his body. Having E go after the scientists at SRC was an even worse idea than focusing him on hunting Leeches, though.

"We just want to keep you safe, E," she said. "And prevent war."

There was a vague softening around his mouth and eyes. Still not real expression, but a loosening of tension maybe. "I would not like to see Nathan Longfeather and Ti'ann Jones involved in a war. Nathan Longfeather wouldn't like that either."

"No. No, he wouldn't," she confirmed, maybe a little too quickly. E's preoccupation with Nathan and Ti'ann seemed to be the one thing that kept him on their side. She was eager to encourage his concern for what happened to them.

Kira and David walked in just then and diverted Clare once more. "You two ready for your interview?"

"As well as can be expected," David said. He held Kira's hand. "Still not sure about all this."

"Don't worry," Clare said. "My friend is reliable. You'll be safe. As soon as we've meet with Monroe, we'll get you to the secured studio."

"Where are we meeting James and the others?" Kira asked.

"We decided it would be safest to take you directly to Lost City. The Shifters and Nathan have that area secure. We considered landing in your backyard again but Jasmine was afraid that would draw attention."

"Again?" Kira asked.

"The *Ebisu* collected me and E from your house, so Nathan and Jasmine could provide the Kierna'Rhoan coordinates. Raf was able to sneak in the same way as when you first left Narava. But Jasmine was afraid we'd be pushing our luck bringing you back to your old house. Even if Raf could land without drawing attention, again, you wouldn't be able to get out of the house's security without setting off monitoring alarms."

"Still watching the house." Kira sighed. "I'm surprised they're bothered."

"You two pissed off a few very powerful people." Clare shrugged. "Even though you have more friends than enemies on Narava now, we have to be cautious of your enemies."

"It's fine," Kira said with a head shake. She sat at the table, across from Clare. "I'd rather go right to Lost City anyway. I know Xep can barely contain the excitement of meeting the lost lines again. There will be no living with Xep until we get there."

"We've arranged a secure landing location with Nathan," Clare said, "outside the public face of the city and the area monitored by the government. We'll be met and taken into the city through a secret entrance that no one beyond our support group and the Shifters knows about. They felt more comfortable keeping much of the exits and entrances private. So the public only knows of two."

"Smart," Kira said. "So from Lost City we'll go to the secured studio in Capital for the interview?"

Clare nodded.

"Then what?" Kira asked.

"Then whatever you want," Clare said. "You'll be safe

inside Lost City, so that will be a good place to return to after the interview. You could stay there for as long as you want to stay on Narava. When you're ready to leave, we'll arrange a ship to return you."

"Raf again?" Kira said.

"If he's available." Clare tried not to show any emotion to that answer, one way or another. "We didn't hire anyone for the return trip just in case."

"Word of our possible arrival less likely to get out that way," Kira said.

"Really, we just weren't sure you'd return," Clare said, "and we didn't want to jump the gun. Now that you have agreed, we can see if Raf will make the return journey."

Kira and David exchanged a look. "I'd prefer it was Raf," she said. "He's becoming our personal pilot."

The comment made them both grin. Clare tried to disguise her smile, knowing Raf would find the comment mildly annoying because it was true.

The internal comm buzzed at that moment and Clare answered. Raf's voice warmed her even as her gut started to dance with anxiety and anticipation.

"We're cleared to enter the planet's atmosphere," he said. "Is E there?"

"He's here," Clare confirmed.

"Now's the time for him to shift. We're queued up to go through the detector rings in the next few minutes."

Clare glanced at E. He shifted to a metallic storage box without comment. She shivered and turned back to the comm. "Okay. Done." She glanced at Kira. "Xep?"

"Shifted as soon as we dropped into the system," Kira

said. "Didn't want to take any chances. The storage box that is Xep is in our cabin."

"Xep has shifted too," Clare told Raf. "We're good to go."

"I'll let you know when we're on final approach to the landing site," Raf said. "Longfeather transmitted the final coordinates as soon as we hit the system."

"Thanks." She clicked off the comm and studied Kira and David. "So far so good."

Kira snorted. "I'll feel better when we're inside Lost City. I'm glad we're going there directly."

Clare sat but found it impossible to keep from tapping her foot. She was used to tension and a low level of anxiety when a job was nearing fruition. Usually she loved that feeling—it mixed with excitement and a bit of greedy anticipation of the accolades. But this time, as they waited to hear news of passing through the detector rings, then further news on the approach to Lost City, all she felt was a gut full of apprehension.

If this went wrong, if someone had discovered Kira and David were returning to Narava and they got killed, it would be all her fault. She'd be responsible for the deaths of cult icons—people she'd grown to admire and like—all in the name of furthering her career.

She closed her eyes and swallowed down a sudden rise of bile.

It would all work out just fine. They'd planned this very carefully. No one on Narava that knew about her efforts to bring Kira and David back would ever give them away to their enemies. She'd get her interview, her boss would be overjoyed, and no one would get hurt.

She kept up that mantra as they passed safely through the detector rings. She continued to chant it in her mind as they made the approach to the planet. She breathed it as the *Ebisu* glided to a low flight path to stay undetected. When the ship finally set down without any warning claxons sounding, Clare felt like her bones turned to liquid. She folded over, breathed deeply with her head between her knees, then sat up and looked around.

Kira and David were holding hands, looking as tense as she felt. E and Ahab were sitting to one side of the canteen, deep in quiet conversation. Clare blinked. She hadn't even noticed E shifting back to his natural form.

A moment later, Xep entered the canteen, also in natural form but for the mouth in a golden-skinned face. Whirling green-blue eyes seemed wider than normal. Clare had never mastered the skill of reading a Shifter's expression when they were in natural form, but she got the impression from Xep's body language that the Shifter was as excited to be here as the others were tense.

Xep confirmed her impression a moment later. "I'm looking forward to seeing the city very much. Will we have to wait long before we're allowed entry?"

"No," Clare said, finally standing, though she had to brace a hand on the table until her knees felt steady. "We'll go directly into the city. It'll be safest. You won't be able to stay for long periods of time without risking infection by the parasite that's altered the Lost City Shifters. But Val has arranged for alternate accommodation for you when you aren't in the city."

"Do you think you might want to stay?" Kira asked quietly. "Even when we're finished here?"

Xep stared at her for a quiet moment, long enough that Clare knew they were talking mind to mind. Aloud, Xep said, "I will return to Kierna'Rhoan when the time comes. But… maybe not forever."

Kira nodded in understanding. Clare watched the exchange carefully, taking mental notes, memorizing. She might not be able to use the moment, but if she could, it would add a lot of poignancy to her story. An exiled Shifter, able to return to its home planet without worrying about extermination… That story might be necessary, she thought as they all made their way toward the exit. To bring a personal, relatable face to the continued argument—though Xep wasn't human, the desire to "come home" and be safe was something humans could relate to. The story might even help.

She considered how to broach the topic as they met Raf and Sonia at the landing ramp.

Raf circled the others to reach her and took her hand. "You ready for this?"

"I am." She forced a smile, though she was sure her nerves were showing. "So long as the others have done their part, we should be good."

"Once you all are safely in the hands of Monroe and Longfeather, we'll move the *Ebisu* into hiding." He handed her a small comm card. "Secured and untraceable," he said. "When you're ready to be in touch again."

She stared at him, realizing they hadn't settled anything, and she wasn't sure when she was going to see him again. She'd been so focused on the landing, getting Kira and David safely into Lost City, it hadn't occurred to her this might be goodbye with Raf.

Her gut clenched and fluttered for a whole new reason. "I've been so worried about… I forgot…"

He smiled. "We're not going anywhere. Yet. I have some business here. But no immediate jobs. We can wait. You need a ride back to Kierna'Rhoan, we'll take you."

"The longer you're on-planet, though, the harder it'll be to avoid the authorities."

His smile turned cocky. "Na, we're good at that part. Here all the time and never once gotten caught."

She lowered her chin and gave him a look. "There's always a first time."

He kissed her on the nose, a surprisingly sweet gesture. "You just take care of yourselves," he murmured. "I'll be waiting when you're ready."

She faced the lowering ramp, pressing her palm to her stomach in a quick, settling gesture even as she ignored the tightening in her chest.

Showtime, she thought, and led the way down to meet Nathan, Monroe, and the others waiting to escort them safely into Lost City.

CHAPTER THIRTY-FOUR

Everything went perfectly. Without a hitch.

As Clare let herself into her apartment, she could barely believe everything had gone so smoothly. The interview went out live without so much as a technical hiccup. And it was good. It was going to change everything. She hoped for the better, though that wasn't her call. But Kira and David were about to shake up the debates. Again. And she couldn't wait to see what happened—so long as it wasn't a war.

She took a breath as she locked her door and then stared around the little space that had been her home for the last four years.

Time to say goodbye to Clare O'Malley.

Her boss had already started the process of setting up her next persona. Only she and her boss knew the new name, the new cover story. It had taken a lot of willpower not to say goodbye to the Shifter supporters, to Ti'ann and Nathan. But no one could know she was about to disappear or they might wonder why.

They might come looking for her. The Leeches might try to get her location from the people she'd come to care about. Everyone would be safer if Clare just vanished without explanation.

The thought still broke her heart a little. But maybe one day she'd be able to meet up with Ti'ann and the others again.

She pulled out the comm card Raf had given her and considered it as she crossed to her bedroom to pack the few personal things she'd take with her into her new character. She hadn't contacted him yet. There'd been too much going on. Kira and David had decided they felt safe enough surrounded by the Lost City Shifters to stay on-planet for another couple of weeks—long enough to do follow up interviews and maybe even speak before the senate via a secure holographic presence. Since they'd made such a powerful enemy out of one of the senators, appearing in person seemed imprudent.

And Xep… Xep had fallen in with the Lost City Shifters like they were old friends. She'd barely seen Xep or Val after they'd been surrounded by the lost lines and swept off to talk with the Supreme Councilors.

Raf wouldn't be needed for transportation back to Kierna'Rhoan for at least another two to three weeks, Naravan time. Could he wait that long without taking another job? Could he stay on Narava that long without running the risk of being discovered by the law?

She ran a thumb over the card without actually pressing the call. She needed to contact him, but she was dreading their conversation. How did you tell a man you loved him but couldn't hide on his ship for the rest of your life? How did you admit to wanting to keep him but knowing you had to let him go?

She'd spent all her spare time trying to figure out how she could have her freedom, her life and career, and still have Raf. He needed his freedom, his life and career, too. She would never ask him to ground himself for her. But she wasn't sure where that left them.

With a sigh, she set the card on a small table just outside the bedroom. She'd pack first, then she'd call and arrange to meet him. This was a conversation they need to have in person.

After so many weeks, her bedroom was warm and inviting. She really was going to miss this place. Pulling a rucksack out of her closet, she set about collecting her personal items. She'd nearly finished when she heard a noise in the living room, like the sizzle and pop of something electronic shorting out. Had there been a power surge?

She carried her rucksack into the living room to check on the noise. The bag hit the floor with a loud thud, dropping from her nerveless fingers when she saw the three Leeches standing in her living room. One held the comm card from Raf, now a burnt and useless misshapen hunk of plastic. All three smiled at her, flashing their sharp, white teeth in their skeletal faces. From behind them, a human assistant stepped forward, holding a pressure syringe.

Without even knowing she was going to do it, Clare screamed.

Blaster shots from the corridor just outside her apartment startled everyone in the room. As the Leeches turned to the noise, Clare dove back into the bedroom, dragging her rucksack with her. She scrambled through the bag until she came up with her small blaster. From the living room, she heard the hissing of Leeches and the low voice of the human man with the syringe.

She angled around the edge of the door frame in time to see the human heading her way as two of the Leeches eased toward the apartment's front door. She didn't waste time waiting to see what they'd do. She fired, in quick rapid bursts, taking out the man with the syringe first, then hitting the Leeches one at a time. Unfortunately, her blaster wasn't strong enough to stop the Leeches for long, even set on high stun.

She took all of two seconds to decide killing them was an option and clicked over to kill, then fired again. The kill setting still wasn't actually fatal to Leeches, but it was hurting them as they dropped, one by one, still hissing. Two of them, though wounded, dragged themselves toward her cover. Bile rose as she kept firing.

"Die, damn it!" She wanted to screech with disgust and terror, but she bit back the reaction so she could focus on shooting. She didn't waste any energy, hitting her targets dead on with each shot. Finally, after ten or more dead center hits, the two moving Leeches fell still.

The screech was rising in her throat. She swallowed it back and stepped out of the bedroom with her weapon raised and tracking the bodies on the ground. The human was just stunned, so she eased down and took the syringe from where it had fallen next to him. She kept her gaze on the bodies sprawled around her living room the entire time, jumping at the merest twitch.

She could only see the legs of one Leech from behind her couch, which made her even jumpier. She couldn't tell if he was awake or unconscious. Another blaster shot from the outer hall reminded her there were more dangers outside her door. She had to get out of here.

She edged back to her room, snatched up her bag since it contained things that could be traced to Emma Reilly, put the syringe inside, then started angling toward the front door, keeping her attention on the bodies. When a Leech's hand lifted and dropped, she hit him again with a blaster shot. A quick glance confirmed she still had enough energy in the blaster to shoot her way out of the apartment if she needed to, but only if the escape was quick.

She considered the layout of her building and decided the fastest way out would be the fire door exit and the stairs at the far end of the corridor. So long as that exit wasn't guarded. A knot lodged in her throat because she couldn't make herself believe that exit *wouldn't* be guarded. But she had to try. She was dead—or a Leech—if she stayed here.

At the door, she listened to the activity outside. Another blaster shot sounded making her jump back a foot. That had sounded really close. Damn. She held her gun trained on the door, readying to open it, but before she could, it slammed open, banging against the wall.

She fired a split second before she realized the person in the doorway was a friend. Shock kept her frozen as she watched E avoid the shot faster than any human could have.

Her shoulders dropped and she let loose a wobbly, breathy shout. "Damn, I almost killed you, E." She huffed. "Glad you can move that fast. Also, you are really scary."

E gave her a look she couldn't read, as usual, and said, "You are not injured?"

"No. The noise outside distracted them so I could get to my blaster."

As she spoke, Raf and Ahab eased into the room, both with weapons raised. She blinked and without thinking about how silly she would feel about doing this later, she threw herself into Raf's arms.

"What are you doing here?" she said against his neck as he hugged her close, his hold as tight as hers.

"I came to see what you'd decided to do. Finding a couple of Leeches outside your apartment door was something of a shock. Watching another Leech attack them was even more surprising."

She pulled back to look him in the face. "Huh?"

He nodded to E. "I was in the middle of trying to shoot my way in here when E strolled up, looking like a Leech, and took them both out." Raf's eyes crinkled at that sides and his brows lowered. "With his bare hands."

"Ah." The concern on Raf's face made sense now. "Yeah, he's scary," she said. "But we knew that already."

"Still. Very glad he's on our side."

"Would you like me to kill these remaining Leeches?" E said without any emotion at all.

"Uh, they're still alive?" Clare asked.

He nodded.

Before she could make that call, Ahab spoke up. "I would prefer them alive. I could use them."

That didn't sound much better than killing them. "You're not planning any kind of experiment, are you?" she said. "Because, despite everything, I'm not good with that."

"No experiments," Ahab said. "Just some questions. Then I'll kill them."

She swallowed, not sure she liked that idea either. Killing them when they were attacking seemed a lot less mercenary and wrong. And yet, they'd come after her to turn her to a Leech. These specific Leeches had intended her harm. And they would keep coming. They were the reason she had to change identities and make Clare O'Malley disappear without letting her friends know what had happened. She couldn't say she liked them. They were the enemy.

She looked at the bodies, then at Raf.

He shrugged. "Your call. They're after you this time. If they'd been gunning for me, I'd just want them dead. Living, they can still come after you."

"There will be more," Ahab added. "These can tell us what they know about you. How they found out your name and location. It could help you hide better."

She sighed. This was why she tried not to get so deeply involved in her stories. Damn it. She took a deep breath and accepted the new scar on her soul. "Kill two and keep one. The human… Can we turn him into the authorities? It's illegal on Narava to collaborate with Leeches."

"I'll arrange that," Ahab said. "And I promise to make the remaining Leech's death quick when it comes."

She really wanted to ask how he intended to get information from the Leech, but she was afraid if she knew, she wouldn't be able to live with it. This was costing her enough already.

She did say, "No torture. Please. Just questions. Maybe he'll gloat and give you everything you need." She turned to say something to E, only to realize he'd moved away from their group and into her living room already.

In the time it took Ahab to respond to her question, E had

already killed the two Leeches and was throwing the remaining one over his shoulder. The Leech's hands hung dangerously close to E's body, but he didn't seem to notice.

Swallowing down a heavy dose of disgust, she faced Raf. "We need to leave. All that noise will bring the Guards. It's better if I'm not here when they arrive. And a lot better if you and E are gone."

"She's right," a strange voice sounded from the doorway.

Clare's heart jumped and she instinctively swung around with her blaster raised. She noticed from the corner of her eye that Raf was also facing the newcomer with his blaster up. Then her brain caught up with her vision and she realized she recognized the man in the doorway.

"Holy shit," she said, keeping her weapon trained on him, "you're Terrance Samuels."

CHAPTER THIRTY-FIVE

To Raf, and without taking her attention from Samuels, Clare explained, "He was the supposed inspector that came to the Lost City dig site before they'd uncovered the city. We were all convinced he was a government plant." To Samuels, she said, "What the hell are you doing here?"

He'd dropped off the radar after the incident at Lost City, and it hadn't occurred to anyone, Clare included, to go looking for him. They'd all just assumed he was a lower level minion in the conspiracy to destroy the city.

Samuels smiled, smooth and calm. He was ridiculously handsome and polished in his dark grey suit, the white shirt and purple tie a nice compliment to his black skin and dark eyes. His tailored, classy appearance gave him a more dangerous edge than if he'd been dressed less expensively, like a beautifully crafted, finely sharpened sword, the kind that could split a human body in half with a single swing.

"Clare O'Malley," he greeted. "We didn't get a chance to talk much last time. I think that was a calculated move?"

"What are you doing here?" she repeated, not in the mood to discuss their earlier meeting all those months ago.

Samuels raised his brows and shrugged. Then he glanced at Ahab. "You'll have the money in your account by the end of the day."

Clare felt those words like a gut punch, though a part of her wasn't as surprised as she might have expected. She'd known there was more to Ahab, that he wasn't someone she could entirely trust. This particular turn of events was a shock, though.

"He works for Senator Johnson," she breathed, facing Ahab.

Raf remained facing Samuels, his blaster still focused on the other man.

"He's trying to make sure the exterminations continue," Clare said, still to Ahab. "Are you helping him with that?"

"He pays me for specific jobs," Ahab said, not even flinching at her accusing tone. He didn't look guilty or even upset that he'd been found out.

"What did he pay you to do this time?" she asked. "Not kill Kira and David. You had plenty of time to do that. Not actually kill Shifters. You could have done that. So what was it?" Her chest tightened when she realized he might have been after the location of Kierna'Rhoan. Could he have gotten it? She didn't even want to ask that out loud for fear it would prove true.

Ahab shrugged. "I was to follow you and see what you did. Then report. That's all. And I got paid enough to rebuild most of my lab. It was worth it."

She shook her head and faced Samuels again. "So, what do you want from us? What was all this about?"

"Information." Samuels glanced past her to E, who was still standing with the unconscious Leech over his shoulder. "I could actually care less about the Shifter situation," he said, "one way or the other. I do the work that pays best at any given time, just like Ahab. Just like Tygran. But…to do what I do, I need information. Someone other than me passed information of the city to the senator. And that was unacceptable."

He looked back at her, his dark eyes bright. "I've been after *him*. And now I know exactly what he is."

"Shit," she breathed, holding Samuels' gaze. "You can't go public. He's too… People will go nuts if they know something like E is possible. You can't go public."

"Ironic comment," Samuels said. "Coming from a reporter."

The bomb hit exactly as he'd intended. She straightened, but was unable to breathe for a full thirty seconds. He'd outed her casually, purposefully. The slight smile and brief glance at Raf couldn't mean anything else.

She sucked in a gulp of air and nodded. Fine. He'd found her out. She'd love to know how—so she could close off whatever crack had appeared in this identity when she moved into her next one. But she had bigger things to worry about just then.

Because if he could find her real identity, so could the Leeches.

To no one in particular, she said, "We need to leave now before the Guards get here."

And then she had to contact her family. They were at risk now, too. Shit shit shit.

She was aware of Raf still holding his blaster on Samuels, of the fact that he'd just discovered her secret but hadn't reacted to it. She supposed she'd have to deal with the fallout from that later. Right now, they really did need to go.

"Can we discuss what you intend to do with all this great information of yours somewhere else," she said, keeping her focus on Samuels. "None of us will be going anywhere if the Guards get here and see all the bodies."

Samuels lifted a hand. "Of course. I have a car waiting. And a place to talk." He glanced at E, then stepped back into the corridor.

"Can't trust him," Raf whispered.

"I know," she murmured back. "But do we have a choice?"

He glanced at her briefly, his eyes narrowed. Then he looked at E. "Let's go."

To her surprise, Raf put a hand on the small of her back and guided her out into the corridor. They both kept their weapons in hand.

She glanced down at the bodies of the two Leeches in the hallway, then looked away.

If Clare O'Malley had to disappear, this was a great way to do it. Everyone would assume she was either taken by the Leeches, killed in their attack, or on the run because of having killed the Leeches. There would be enough gossip and story to keep people from looking too deeply into her disappearance.

That was, unless Samuels made her real identity public. Then there would be nowhere on Narava for her to hide. Her life here, her career, would be over.

And after Samuels' revelation, she wasn't sure Raf and the *Ebisu* were an option anymore either.

Now what the hell was she going to do?

CHAPTER THIRTY-SIX

Raf kept an eye on Samuels, made sure his homing device was activated, and ensured Clare stayed close enough to protect her if it became necessary. Sonia and his crew would come back him up, but it would take time for them to reach him. Especially now that he and Clare were moving.

In the meantime, there was a lot of very important—and useful—information to get from this turn of events. Terrance Samuels wasn't the only one who lived on information.

Another liar. That was relief. At least Raf would be dealing with the kind of person he was used to dealing with. Dangerous, yes. But intelligently so. No random shooting and killing just because. That meant they had a chance of getting out of this without being killed. Or inadvertently starting a war.

That last was almost as worrying as the being killed part.

As they reached the ground floor of Clare's building and headed into the sleek black Towncar waiting at the curb, Raf glanced at Clare… Emma now, he supposed, since her cover had just been blown. She stared ahead, avoiding his gaze.

Looked like they need another talk. He wondered how long it would take her to understand. He accepted her, whatever she did. He knew the real her, the person beneath the lies and disguises. She couldn't hide that woman from him. And he was mostly positive he loved that woman. Why she would think a little thing like her being a member of the press would change that, he didn't know. Silly woman.

He kept his hand on her as she climbed into the car, then followed her in, all the while scanning their surroundings, watching out for more Leeches. He wasn't all that worried about Terrance Samuels. The man was dangerous, no doubt about that. He oozed a kind of power that spoke of getting his way. And he'd managed to get Ahab aboard the *Ebisu*, which was pretty impressive given how suspicious Raf was.

But Samuels wasn't looking to kill them—at least not immediately—and he wasn't interested in turning them over to the Leeches—at least not yet—so for the moment, Samuels was the least of their worries.

Raf had nearly had a heart attack, seeing the two Leeches standing outside Clare's door. What if he hadn't gotten restless with waiting and come to visit her? What if Ahab and E hadn't followed him? He wasn't sure he liked that they *had* and he hadn't picked it up. But since they'd done him a favor by taking care of the Leeches, he wasn't inclined to get too mad.

The car bounced as the trunk slammed closed, then E and Ahab climbed into the back of the long vehicle, joining Raf and Clare. Samuels was the last to climb in. He signaled the driver and they made their way steadily into Capital City ground traffic.

Raf watched the buildings pass, smiling slightly. He kind of liked that Narava had made it mandatory that most vehicle traveling within city limits had to be ground travel. Air transports were allowed to launch from the edges of the city and from some of the higher, residential areas—especially the rich areas where the residents could afford private air transport. But inside the city, everything was ground level—public and private. He stared up past the buildings at the blue sky. It was nice to actually see the sky in a major city.

Everyone inside the car remained resolutely silent which gave him time to study them even as he kept track of their movements through the city. Samuels looked confident, smooth, and curiously intent. He kept glancing at E, then away, as if he didn't want to reveal his interest in the hybrid. He didn't show any signs of fear, which might be a sign of short-sightedness, but Raf was inclined to think it more likely that very little scared Samuels.

E sat stiffly, looking like he always looked, impossible to read. He didn't seem particularly bothered by any of this, but with E there was really no way to tell.

Ahab looked…uncomfortable. More so than he had in the apartment. He'd shown no signs of discomfort with his part in bringing Samuels into their world, or revealing E to the power broker. But now, the young man's hands kept twitching, subtly, his mouth was compressed into a straight line, the skin around his eyes tightened almost imperceptibly. He was tense.

That was interesting.

Raf looked back at Samuels in time to catch the other

man studying him. He smiled, his cocky, self-assured, perfectly at ease smile that tended to confuse and worry opponents. Samuels raised a brow. Raf's grin grew. Ah, this was fun. If it weren't for the fact that Clare was in danger, that he'd nearly lost her to the Leeches and was still trying to recover from that shock, he'd be enjoying this immensely.

"Raf Tygran," Samuels said. "You have quite the reputation. And a large number of warrants for your arrest here on Narava."

Raf dipped his head as if he'd just received a compliment. "I do my best with what I have."

Samuels' mouth quirked at one side before settling back into a solid, unemotional line. "You're not worried I'm taking you to the nearest Guard complex for the reward?"

Raf snorted. "You want more from us than some puny little reward."

"Not so 'puny,'" Samuels said. "You're worth a small fortune. Probably because it's suspected—confirmed now?—that you transported both Kira Farseaker and David Cario off-planet."

"You think so?" Raf asked. "How much am I worth exactly?"

He wasn't about to confirm his part in Kira and David's escape from Narava, not out loud to someone like Samuels. The man could speculate all he wanted. But if the senator Samuels worked for had any real proof Raf had taken Kira and David off-planet, Raf had a feeling there wasn't a place in the galaxy, besides Kierna'Rhoan, where he could hide.

"Enough to make an individual richer than they might ever imagine," Samuels said.

"Oh, I don't know," Raf said, draping his arm across the

back of the seat behind Clare. "I can imagine a lot of riches. That'd have to be a pretty serious reward to impress me. Though, if it's high enough, I might turn myself in to get it."

Samuels did smile then. "So confident. And yet the Leeches still haunt your every move."

"Yeah, well." Raf shrugged. "I keep telling them they need to give up the chase, but what can you do?" He gave a sad little shake of his head, still carefully not giving anything away.

Samuels, however, was revealing himself. Smart, ruthless, clever, and as dangerous as Raf had assumed. If Samuels wanted to, he could bring a whole hell of a lot of trouble down on Raf's head. There was a threat in his mentioning the Leeches. Raf wasn't going to rise to the bait. But he knew now, for sure, that Samuels had instigated the Leech meeting on FarMore Station. No one else had been involved—Raf's biggest worry. Samuels had set Raf up so he could get Ahab aboard the *Ebisu*. A good plan that had worked. Raf respected that.

If it hadn't put Clare in jeopardy, he might even admire it.

From the corner of his eye, Raf noted they were starting to climb. He wasn't really surprised to see they were going into the same cliff suburbs where the Farseaker mansion was. All the really wealthy people had homes up here, overlooking the beautiful blue of the Dreic Sea. He was a little startled when the house they stopped at was only a kilometer away from the public entrance to the Farseaker home. He wondered if that was on accident or if Samuels was located this close to the Farseaker estate on purpose. Maybe planted here by the senator?

Something to consider.

They followed a long drive, covered by trees and a privacy shield, up to an impressive purple stone house with a large wooden front door. The house was a big, multi-story place, but not nearly as massive as the Farseaker home. It was a different level of wealthy, but still nothing to sneeze at.

When the car stopped in front of the house, Samuels stepped out. As they followed, Raf felt a slight pulse from his tracker. His people knew where he was and were on their way. Until they got here, he was very interested to hear what Terrance Samuels had to say.

The car moved off as Samuels opened the front door and led them inside. Raf gave the place a cursory look—noting the high ceilings and polished natural woods, the precise and neat layout of entryway furniture, the lack of clutter, the clean, citrusy scent of the dust-free air. Then he watched Clare, the way she scanned their new location, the way her curious gaze took in everything at once.

He should have guessed she was a reporter. She watched and listened and collected information like a spy. She'd subtly questioned members of his crew who were used to keeping secrets and learned their life stories. And she had just enough of a complicated background to make people stop looking after the first layer. She was superb. She would have made an excellent smuggler.

Samuels led them down a long hall to an open room at the back of the house. It was large, clean, and once again, free of clutter. A small desk with a computer unit sat to one side, no extra paraphernalia on the desktop. The walls were covered in a very sophisticated-looking combination of paneling and wallpaper. The carpet was lush, pale, and spotless. The back wall was entirely windows, looking out onto a small sculptured lawn.

"Please," Samuels said, gesturing to a grouping of comfortable chairs and couches at the side of the room opposite the desk. "Sit. We have a lot to discuss."

E ignored the offer and paced around the room, studying it. Ahab made himself comfortable in a low-backed chair, and after a beat, so did Clare, setting the bag she'd taken from her apartment at her feet. Raf stood behind Clare, one hand on her shoulder, his blaster in his other hand, resting against his thigh. Samuels smiled at them and took a seat.

Raf could feel the tension in Clare's body and wanted to rub her shoulders to loosen her muscles, but now probably wasn't the time. He hoped the contact would let her know he was still on her side.

Though he'd expected Samuels to start the conversation, Ahab was actually the first to speak.

"E and I have discussed my goals," the young man said. "He'll help me. He's uniquely designed for it. That will get him off-planet. Which should make everyone happy."

Clare straightened and sucked in a breath. Raf narrowed his eyes. E and Ahab pairing up? To go after the Leeches. Looking at E and the scary way he didn't show any normal kind of human reaction to things, Raf almost felt sorry for the Leeches. Something like E could exterminate them.

The ironic fact that E had been created to help with the extermination of another species wasn't lost on Raf. But Raf liked Shifters a whole lot better than Leeches, so he wasn't nearly as concerned with what happened to the Leeches. Besides, the Leeches could defend themselves in a way

Shifters couldn't. And E might keep them so occupied they stopped chasing after the *Ebisu*. Raf couldn't mind that.

"Is that…a good idea?" Clare said. "I mean, yes, getting E off-planet is probably best. If we don't want a war on Narava." She paused, her head turned toward Samuels.

The other man stared back without reacting. And Raf had to wonder if Samuels did want a war. Bad for business, bad for trade, but maybe not so bad for an ambitious man looking to climb the rungs of power. If Samuels wanted war on Narava, Raf had a feeling he could arrange it.

That was almost as scary as E.

"But," Clare continued, "if E is turned loose on the Leeches, news of him is going to get out."

Samuels contemplated E. "What do you want to do?"

The hybrid stopped studying the room and gardens and turned to face Samuels. "I want to find my purpose."

Samuels raised his brows. "You think killing Leeches is your purpose? I doubt that's why you were created."

"They lied to me about why I was created." E paused, his head tilted down and his chin tucked. "Except for killing Shifters. They told me the truth about that. They wanted me to kill as many Shifters as I found."

"Who, exactly, are *they*?" Samuels asked.

The question wasn't what Raf would have expected. He'd assumed the man knew that answer already.

E must have thought the same thing because he said, "You work with them. How do you not know this?"

"I want to hear from you, who *you* know?" Samuels said.

"Ah," E said. "I know Senator Johnson was at the top of the group responsible for me. I was created at Shifter

Research Center. Dr. Ripley was in charge of my development. I was the fifth experiment, the only successful one."

"And the E is for Ennoren?" Samuels asked.

"I was the fifth. E is the fifth letter in the alphabet of the language that came most naturally to me."

"But you were created from Commander Ennoren," Samuels said. "The human part of you comes from him."

E's head dipped down farther but he didn't comment.

"You weren't called on to kill Farseaker and Cario?" Samuels continued. "The senator wants them dead. Badly. Why weren't you ordered to find and kill them?"

"They never got a chance to give him those orders," Clare put in. "He chose to pick his own fate before they could program him."

"They lied to me," E said.

"And honesty is important to you?" Samuels asked.

E gave a slight nod.

"Then I'll be honest," Samuels said. "I worked with Senator Johnson because he paid well. But, as I said, I don't really care about the Shifter issue, one way or the other. Exterminations, no exterminations. Means nothing to me. The senator is a zealot. He and the others… Their grandparents were the ones responsible for destroying the two Shifter cities that were discovered all those years ago. Johnson has inherited the fear and passion. And that narrow focus is going to be his undoing."

Samuels paused and turned to Clare. "This would make a good story. Are you intending to tell it?"

"If it won't get me killed," she said, "you bet your ass I'll break this story."

"Why did the Leeches come after you?" Samuels asked.

She exchanged a glance with Ahab. "Does he know?" she murmured.

Ahab nodded.

"I can be mutated," she said, her voice wobbling only slightly. "Ahab cured me before his lab was destroyed. I have no intention of letting them get at me again."

"So," Samuels said. "Your life is already in danger, whether you break this story or not. Unmasking the senator isn't going to be any more dangerous than the Leeches hunting you."

"Are you offering to give me this story?" she asked, leaning forward in her seat.

Raf smiled at the way she skirted Samuels questions.

"Will you give me the facts I'll need?" she continued. "Go on the record? I can keep your identity anonymous if you'd prefer, though the story would have more legs if you came out publicly."

"No," Samuels said. "I have no intention of turning on the senator publicly. But… I have come to the conclusion he's not strong enough to hold on to his current position. He'll fall. He'll take others with him. I'm already seeing signs that he'll be offered up as the sacrificial lamb—signs he seems to be unaware of."

"If he's going to fall no matter what," she said, "why would breaking the story be dangerous for me? If this is what his associates want?"

"Ah." Samuels raised a manicured hand, palm up. "I said they want him to be the scapegoat. I never said they wanted someone other than their group to arrange that fall. You would move matters forward ahead of their timeline."

"A good thing?" she asked.

"I think so." Samuels nodded. "I think it will ensure a level of unease that should, ironically, keep the status quo."

"But why should the status quo be maintained?" she asked. "The exterminations need to end. Some sort of peaceful settlement needs to be reached with the Shifters to prevent war. Status quo isn't an option anymore."

"The exterminations will end," Samuels said. "The government sanctioned exterminations, that is. But that won't stop a war. There are too many still opposed to and terrified of Shifters. That's not what I meant. I meant the power structure here on Narava will continue on as is. It's delicately balanced now. Powerful, rich families have taken stands on both sides of the issue. The senators are dancing around each other very carefully, none willing to upset the balance for fear of the fallout from the public, but also the backlash from the power brokers outside the senate. War may still happen. Until it does, though, the balance of power keeps Narava running and continuing to be profitable."

"And you like profitable," Raf said, stepping into the conversation. He understood that preference.

"The galaxy likes profitable, Tygran," Samuels said. "Those of us not motivated by zealot emotions, one way or the other, want things to happen in a way that will most benefit our pockets."

"If the senator's role in everything comes out," Clare said, "but comes out before the others are ready to consolidate their power, things will continue as they are now? You're sure?"

Samuels nodded. "I've been monitoring the situation for months. While you've been trying to get to Farseaker and Cario."

Clare huffed out a loud, irritated sigh, and Samuels smiled.

"If I'd wanted them dead," Samuels said, "or wanted the senator to know about your efforts, you wouldn't be sitting here. I've been calculating. And there are some things I think should happen."

"Senator Johnson exposed." Clare started the list. "E off-planet and still secret. Ahab's lab rebuilt?"

Samuels nodded with each correct comment. "I don't have any particular fondness for Leeches," he said. "I don't have the hate our young man here does, but I agree that the Leeches becoming a reproductively active species would be less than desirable."

"And me?" Clare asked. "What do you want from me?"

Raf's hand tightened on her shoulder. He stared at Samuels as the other man stared at Clare.

"You intend to disappear, don't you?" Samuels asked.

She jerked her chin up in a brief nod.

Samuels glanced at Raf. "Off-planet?"

"I'll disappear better if I don't comment on that," she said.

Samuels tilted his head in agreement. "Even without the Leeches, bringing Farseaker and Cario back to Narava would have earned you the vendetta of Senator Johnson. You would have been hunted and assassinated quietly for your part in this. Narava isn't going to be safe for you, whoever you become. Or for Reilly."

She sucked in a sharp breath. "My family?"

CHAPTER THIRTY-SEVEN

RAF RUBBED HER SHOULDER, TRYING TO EASE THE TIGHTNESS. He knew how she felt about her family and a threat to them was worse than a threat to her own life. He watched Samuels closely, waiting for the man's next move, ready to kill him if necessary to protect Clare and those she loved.

"I'm the only one who knows the connection right now," Samuels said, with a little shrug. "The senator knows a woman named Clare O'Malley was responsible for bringing the 'traitors,' his word, back to Narava. Clare is the one who will be hunted. You've been very good at keeping your persona and Reilly separate."

"Then how did you find out?" she asked. "Because if you could, they can."

"I have more sources of information than the senator knows about." Samuels glanced at Ahab then back. "In places the senator wouldn't think to look. If your boss doesn't give in to the pressure to out you—and he's already indicated that he won't even if they throw him in a cell—

they'll find it difficult to uncover your real identity. But Clare… Clare will be in danger."

"Clare's already gone," she said.

Raf noted a lack of expression in the statement. Would she miss being Clare O'Malley, or did she care? Something to ask later. He felt another slight vibration in his tracker and knew his people were close. They only had a little time left.

"So," Raf said, "all of this is well and good, but what are you going to do, Samuels? Keep her secrets, let her break the story about the senator?"

"Once I knew who you were," Samuels said, "I knew that would be the best route. And since Clare O'Malley is already gone…" He smiled. "Well, what harm in Reilly breaking one more major story before disappearing as well."

Raf had picked up that Reilly was the name Clare used as a reporter. She'd told him that was the name her colleagues used for her. But in all this, he hadn't had time to consider that Reilly would have to disappear, too.

"What makes you think Reilly won't continue to report?" Clare asked.

There was a hint of something in her voice Raf couldn't quite interpret. Maybe stubbornness? Maybe fear?

"Because the Leeches might make the connection to your family," Samuels said.

"You thought of this plan before the Leeches were an issue for me. For Clare, who's dead now. Why would *Reilly* stop reporting?"

Samuels shrugged. "Reilly has broken some very important pro-Shifter stories lately. Reilly has a target on his…her back. You might not have realized this yet, but since the news of Lost City broke, and the assassins were unsuccessful in killing Longfeather and Dr. Jones, the reporter Reilly has also been targeted. Fortunately for you, no one beyond your boss knows who you really are. Well, your boss and me."

"Are you threatening her?" Raf asked, adjusting his stance just a little so his blaster, which he'd never bothered putting away, was at the ready.

"I'm offering a trade," Samuels said, keeping his gaze on Clare. "My silence in exchange for Reilly breaking the story I want out when I want it out."

"Silence?" Clare asked. "You won't say anything to *anyone* who'd like to find Clare and Reilly?"

"I have no sympathies for the Leeches," Samuels said. "Why would I tell them anything?"

"You're funding one of their biggest enemies," she pointed out. "They would have every reason to come after you. If they found out."

Samuels raised his brows. "So. We have a mutual secret to keep. You don't reveal me to the Leeches—which I don't think you'd do anyway—and I keep your true identity to myself."

"But then there's no incentive for me to break the story of the senator," she said. "No threat you can impose."

Samuels laughed. "Threat? Do I really need to threaten? You're a reporter. This story is huge. Are you telling me you'll pass?"

"Of course not," she said without pause. "I'm all over this story. I will break it tomorrow if you want. But what do you get out of all this? Just a maintenance of the power structure? What's really in this for you, Samuels?"

He smiled. "I have my reasons. Nothing to concern yourself with. But don't worry. None of those reasons involve starting a war with the Shifters."

Raf studied the other man. He didn't trust him. But then Samuels didn't expect their trust. They were working off mutually beneficial deals here. The man's "reasons" were worrying. But that was someone else's concern. Right now, their concern was getting out of this with Emma Reilly's identity still secret. And of course their lives. Surviving would be good.

The slight vibration from his tracker sped up. His people were near. In the house if he guessed right. He smiled at Samuels.

Samuels narrowed his eyes.

From just outside the large, open room, Sonia said, "So do we shoot him, Captain, or do you want to make this deal he's talking about?"

Raf dropped the smile and effected a serious expression, his mouth pursed as he considered the power broker sitting so casually in his chair—seemingly unconcerned with the appearance of the *Ebisu* crew.

"Hmm," Raf murmured. "What do you think, Clare? Do you trust him?"

"Of course not," she answered immediately. "But I want this story. I want it bad. And I think… I think he could be a good source."

Samuels raised his brows at that assessment. A reaction that made his next words surprising. "I can be that," he confirmed. "I have always been a good source of information."

"So," Sonia said. "Shoot him or leave him?"

"We'll leave him," Raf said. "For now."

"I would like to know how you got through my security," Samuels said, still not showing any signs of being bothered by having blasters pointing at him.

"I've been taking hacking lessons," Sonia said.

Raf barked out a laugh. He couldn't help it. She was taking those lessons from one of the best hackers Raf had ever seen. Leave it to Sonia to get a useful skill from a love affair—just to be able to deny it's a love affair.

"All right," Raf said, with an expectant glance around the room. "I think we're done here. Samuels, you keep our secrets, we'll keep yours. Reilly gets one last absolutely legend-making story, which should take down Senator Johnson. All's well on Narava. And we all go our separate ways. Does that about sum it up?"

Samuels dipped his head to the side in affirmation.

"Where's the money in all this?" Sonia asked.

"None this time." Raf exchanged a look with Samuels. "But maybe in the future."

Samuels' mouth lifted in a slight smile.

"What about E?" Clare said.

Raf looked at E. "You want to work with Ahab? Stay off Narava and kill Leeches?"

"I want to find my purpose," E said. "I was designed to protect and hunt."

"And kill," Clare said under her breath.

"I will protect human women from the Leeches," E said. "I will rescue those who do not want to mutate. I think that is a good purpose."

Raf opened his mouth to comment, then shrugged. E had a point. If he stuck to rescue operations, he would be doing good work.

Clare glanced between E and Ahab. "You won't be attempting to kill all the Leeches?" she asked E, sounding leery.

"I will protect humans," E said firmly.

Ahab didn't show much reaction to that, so Raf assumed they'd already worked this part out. He was good with E taking on a protective role. Especially because it was safer than just about any other purpose E might choose. The fact that it would complicate the lives of Raf's enemies was a bonus.

"So," Raf said. "Guess that'll do for now. Sonia, Clare… Shall we?"

He gestured Clare toward the waiting guard of *Ebisu* crew. When she was safely surrounded by his people, he faced Samuels again.

"Just to be clear," Raf said. "When Reilly and Clare O'Malley disappear, they're gone. No one is going to go looking for them. No one is going to hunt up Reilly's family. No one will make the link between the two public."

Samuels folded his hands in his lap. "No one will ever find a trace of Clare O'Malley, or the reporter Reilly. Or any links to her family."

"Good," Raf said. "Because if they do, and I hear about it, there's gonna be consequences to that action." He held Samuels' gaze, letting the man see just how deadly serious he was, that the threat wasn't an idle one.

"I imagine there will be," Samuels said. "I suspect once Senator Johnson has to face the pubic for his actions, there won't be anyone interested anyway."

"Kira and David," Clare said suddenly from the middle of

her guard. "What of them? Will they be allowed to return to Narava without threat?"

"There will always be someone interested in killing them," Samuels said. "But I think after that interview, after the discovery of Lost City, their...status on Narava has changed. Cario has always been a hero as far as the public is concerned. Showing up on camera with a pregnant Farseaker will only add to their cult icon status. They should be fine."

Clare nodded and let out a long breath. Raf hid his smile. Given everything she was in the middle of, she was still concerned for Farseaker and Cario. So much for the heartless journalist myth. At least with his reporter.

Raf strolled to his people, turning as they started to filter out to look at Ahab and E. "You two need a lift somewhere? I'm heading off-planet soon. We've got room for a couple of passengers. Discounted price for friends."

Ahab looked at Samuels then back at Raf. "Thanks. Think that'd be a good idea. I need two days here first. You can wait?"

Raf raised his brows toward Samuels. Samuels nodded once.

"Guess we can," Raf said. "I'll message you a meeting place." He glanced back at Samuels before saying, "You two coming now or...?"

"Got some financial things to settle first," Ahab said. "I'll see you in two days."

Raf studied the three staying behind for a few more minutes, then turned and left. Sonia had a small airship waiting in front of Samuels' house.

"Where you'd get this?" Raf asked as he boarded ahead of her, leaving her to cover their exit with her blaster.

"Borrowed it," she said.

"Permanently?" Raf asked.

"If it'll fit in the hold, I think it could be a keeper. Replace that one you saw fit to dump six months ago."

"Hey, that was necessary."

"Yeah, yeah. We ready, Captain."

Raf grinned and glanced at Clare, settling in a seat next to Delilah, smiling over at him with that gleam of secrets in her dark eyes, ever so slightly hesitant. His grin widened.

"Ready," he said. "Take us home."

CHAPTER THIRTY-EIGHT

CLARE NIBBLED AT THE REMAINS OF A PREVIOUSLY LONG NAIL during the journey to the *Ebisu*. She didn't argue about returning to Raf's ship. It was the safest place for her for the time being. She still had to contact her boss, collect the information Samuels was going to send her, get the final story of her career as Reilly out. But first, she needed to face Raf.

He'd supported her through the confrontation with Samuels. Despite the news that she was a reporter. He'd even threatened Samuels to keep her safe. His actions gave her hope, but she was still nervous as all hell when they boarded the *Ebisu*.

The ship was hidden in an isolated place in the mountains between Lost City and Capital. A place so generally inhospitable, no one ever came here. This time of year, the weather across the bare, rocky hills was actually quite nice, a little cool but with some warmth in the earthy-scented air. There was nothing but black and gray rock, jagged and flaky. But at least they weren't freezing.

She did wonder how Raf found a flat, stable place to land as most of the flat spaces in these mountains tended to crumble into deep pits and ravines. But the ground underfoot was the solid rock of the mountains themselves rather than the overlayer of false rock ash, which meant the *Ebisu* wouldn't be falling into a big hole. She hoped.

Raf gave a few orders to his crew then took her directly to his cabin. Her stomach danced and tightened. She pressed her palm to her abdomen, trying to remember the last time she'd felt so unsure and nervous.

Once the door was closed, they stood silently facing each other across a meter of space.

"So," she finally said, pointing to herself. "Reporter."

Raf nodded, pointed to himself and said, "Smuggler."

A smile tugged at the corner of her mouth, despite her worries. "Most people don't like reporters. Especially if those people have secrets."

He shrugged. "Depends on the reporter."

"You're not mad?"

He huffed out a breath and shook his head. Then he closed the space between them and pulled her into his arms.

"Mary Margaret," he said, ducking his chin to look into her eyes, "when are you going to get it through that smart, beautiful, thick head of yours that I accept you as you are. I thought I made it clear it didn't matter what your last secret was, why you were living under a false name. I know who you are in here." With one finger, he tapped lightly at her chest, over her heart. "That's what counts."

"Don't call me Mary Margaret." But she smiled when she said it.

He smiled back. "Fine. Emma." And he kissed her.

She sighed into the kiss, relaxing, savoring, taking all the acceptance and desire he gave, returning it with her whole heart. For the first time in years, she let Clare O'Malley go completely and returned to being just Emma. No covers, no complicated back stories to confuse and mislead those around her. She was just Emma Reilly, the ambitious woman who worked as an undercover reporter, hated her real first name, and had to eat a very specific diet to offset a genetic condition. Emma Reilly who loved her family. Who was unfortunately susceptible to the Leech mutation. Who wanted to be the very top of her profession.

And who loved Raf Tygran with her body and soul.

As she eased back from the kiss and met his beautiful blue-eyed gaze, she let her heart break and even that pain made her feel completely herself.

"I love you," she said.

"I know." He grinned, but the smile fell away a moment later. "But you're not coming with us, are you?"

She shook her head. "How did you know?"

"I saw the avarice when Samuels offered up the story on the senator. I understand that. It's almost a need, isn't it? To want that something—whatever it is—with so much desperation. You couldn't give that up any more than I could give up the freedom of the *Ebisu*. At least, not yet."

"Not yet," she agreed. "But one day, I'll stop. One day, I'll have had enough of this work. I'll want…something else."

"I'll be waiting."

She tilted her head. "Will you? Can you?"

"For what we have? For love with someone who knows

me completely? Yeah, I can wait for that. Besides, who says we have to wait all that long."

Her heart tripped over itself as it sped up, just a little. "Meaning?"

"I figure, given what you do, you might need the occasional services of the galaxy's best smuggler."

"True." She nodded and tried to suppress a ridiculously huge grin.

"And then there's vacations. Everyone needs a few weeks off every now and then."

"Also true." She rose on her toes to kiss him again. "Are you sure?" she whispered against his mouth. "I won't tie you down, make you commit if you don't think you can stick with it."

"I'm in, Emma. You're it for me from now on. And I will do damage to any man who thinks he can change your mind. You need to know that before you commit to me. I'll be jealous and possessive, even if I'm not around all the time."

She actually giggled. She wasn't sure why. Something about Raf being jealous pleased her, even though her pleasure in his jealousy was a bit embarrassing.

Forcing her face into a serious expression, she said, "I'm going to be possessive and jealous too. I'm going to bribe Sonia to report all your activities to me. If you step out, we will have words."

His hands moved in long slow strokes up her back, his expression all soft and indulgent. "I expected nothing less. And unless I'm completely off the mark, I suspect Sonia will take that job without requiring much money—not for free mind. She is a pirate."

Emma laughed and kissed him again.

"We have a couple of days," she said against his mouth. "You're not leaving yet. I need to disappear for a while before I can reappear in my new persona."

"I think this is the best plan I've ever heard. I think we need to solidify this new deal of ours with some action."

Her heart thumped in a quick rhythm as her limbs softened and her stomach tightened with need and desire. "What did you have in mind?"

He waggled his eyebrows and kissed her again. This time with a passion that took her breath and ensured her heart was his completely. A desire unlike any other in her life rose up to fill her.

She stripped him slowly, savoring every inch of his hard body, lingering attention on every scar. The story of him still fascinated her and she knew she'd never get enough. As she licked across his hip bone, he sucked in a breath, his hand tightening in her hair, his faint groan filling her with such sexy satisfaction it was almost enough on its own. She took him into her mouth because she wanted more, tasting and savoring the length of his cock, knowing she was driving him just a little crazy and inordinately pleased with that knowledge.

When he launched up and pulled her mouth up to his, she laughed, sinking into his kiss. He returned her exploration, kissing over her most sensitive spots, lingering on her inner elbow, her waist, her inner thigh. She was drawn tight and ready when he closed his mouth over her heat and licked into her. She held out as long as she could, stretching out the pressure and pleasure, the build and tightness. He eased away when she got too close, moved back when she relaxed a fraction. And then he pushed her all the way, sending her careening into that quiet, electric light show of pleasure.

She was still panting when he kissed her mouth again, and all of her emotions piled up into a thick wave of love. She rolled him onto his back, took him inside, and relished the pleasure on his face with her every stroke, setting a slow, deliberate rhythm she knew would drive them both crazy. Hands on her hips, he held her gaze, his blue eyes open and unguarded.

He broke eye contact only when he finally had to let go, and she delighted in that too. Watching his pleasure sweep through him, knowing it was all hers… She'd never expected anything like this in her life. The completeness of it all took her breath away.

She loved this man. For everything he gave her, for the freedom and acceptance. For the time and the understanding.

She was his now. For the rest of her life, she'd be Raf's, no matter what. She'd never loved anyone like this before and never would again. And she knew deep in her soul, even without the words, he loved her.

That was enough. He was enough. Just as he was. Because he loved her for who she was, too.

AFTER ONCE AGAIN RETURNING KIRA AND David to Kierna'Rhoan, Raf found himself back on Narava. The planet was maintaining a delicate stability after Senator Johnson's arrest, but business still continued. Exactly as Samuels had predicted. In the Docks, a visitor might never guess the planetary government remained on tenterhooks.

And in the wake of the breaking scandal, Reilly had become a true legend. A legend that rivaled all other journalistic legends. The mysterious reporter's subsequent disappearance had become a story all its own, which only solidified her epic status.

Raf hadn't seen her in two months. His brief stop on Narava to collect Kira and David hadn't allowed enough time for a night with her. They'd messaged every day of that two months, at least when he was in reachable locations. But he was a little desperate to see her in person now.

He strolled through the Docks with the outer casualness that ensured no one messed with him because only the very dangerous walked that easily through the city at night. He found the strip club in an area he rarely frequented. Still, his reputation proceeded him and he was given entrance without any difficulty and only a minimal bribe.

As he passed through the crowd to the bar, he hunted for a cap of curly red hair, only to remember he wasn't sure what her hair looked like now. She'd told him she'd had to change her appearance completely for her new persona. But she hadn't told him exactly what to expect.

He found he was both excited and a little worried to see what she'd had to do to keep working.

Settling on a bar stool, he ordered a Binnean brandy and swiveled to study the throngs. Currently on stage, two human women and a human man performed an acrobatic dance which was so impressively athletic it went beyond erotic into something more. Almost art.

He sipped his drink as he watched the performance. This wasn't the club she'd worked in when undercover before. He knew that. So he wondered why she'd picked this particular location. When he spotted a handful of t'Pree clan Binneans huddled off to one side, he hummed under his breath, the cogs of possibilities turning in his brain.

A tap on his shoulder distracted him. He turned to see a sexy-as-all-hell woman with long, straight brown hair pulled into a sleek ponytail, hazel green eyes surrounded by long dark lashes and slim arched brows. Her lips were full and red. Her lush body encased in a sophisticated, form-fitting skirt and jacket. Her legs looked fantastically long and shapely in spiked heels high enough to put her eye-to-eye with him. And the delicious line of freckles across her nose was faint under her sophisticated, flawless makeup, but still there.

"Well hello," he said, letting his gaze travel the length of her, taking her in. Wondering where she had hidden her blaster…

"Hello, Captain." She put out a hand to shake his. "Thank you for agreeing to meet me."

Her voice sounded a little different now, too. Deeper, cultured, with a huskiness that rippled down his spine. He liked it.

"Ms. Bianchi, I take it," he said, for the sake of their audience, using the cover name she'd given him—at least the last name. She hadn't revealed her new first name yet. He was inordinately curious about that, though.

She smiled faintly, politely, but in her eyes he saw his woman. Gods, she was good. Except for the freckles, and that tiny twinkle in her eyes, she *inhabited* this new persona. If he didn't know her so well, love her so damned much, he might have been fooled. But she could never hide herself from him now.

"Drink?" he asked.

"What you're having." She slid onto the barstool next to him, crossing those long legs.

He forgot himself for a moment, staring and remembering the feel of her legs wrapped around his hips. He shook himself to dispel the fantasy, then ordered her brandy.

She ignored his reaction. "I've been informed you have an acceptable ship, something that will suit my needs."

"I understand you've got a job for that ship."

She smiled again and blinked very slowly as she held his gaze. "There've been rumors," she said. "Binnean clan war."

"I've heard those rumors." He passed her a glass.

She sipped her drink without breaking eye contact. "Interesting, aren't they?"

"Very."

"My employer would like me to look into the trade implications. They have certain contracts with t'Pree clan that might be jeopardized by conflict."

"And your employer is?" he asked, wondering if she'd actually tell him yet.

"They prefer to remain in the background of my inquiry."

He swallowed his knowing chuckle, but gave her a slow grin, loving the way her eyes danced but nothing else in her expression changed. "You're a private investigator then?"

"What I am is a person who solves problems, Captain Tygran. Is that going to be an issue?"

She was so serious and so much this other person, he was awed. His heart thumped harder, thrilled with her anew. "No problem," he said. "So long as I get paid."

"I need transportation to Neros Seven first. Then on to Binnea."

"Humans aren't allowed on Binnea," he said, mostly to see where her story went.

She gave him a pitying look, which might have been insulting if he hadn't known it was part of the act. And also that he'd been asking for that look with his comment.

"I have a meeting with a t'Pree tek-la on one of the trade stations above the planet," she said, her tone just slightly condescending. "Of course."

"Of course."

"My employer has agreed to your fee. It will just be me traveling. Is the job of interest to you?"

"Oh, certainly. And as it so happens, we were heading in that direction anyway, Ms. Bianchi. So the *Ebisu*, and her captain, are at your disposal." He held her gaze. "But first, I like to know who I'm transporting. Mind telling me your first name."

She stared back, not a hint of anything personal in her expression when she said. "Mary. Mary Bianchi."

He almost choked on his drink and it was all he could do not to grin like a fool. Under his breath, so only she could hear, he murmured, "I love you, Mary Margaret."

Just as quietly, she whispered, "I know." Then louder, "It's Mary. Just Mary." She pursed her mouth in a prim expression he didn't believe for a moment.

"Mary it is." He raised his glass to her.

Her answering grin was sexy and full of heat. He returned it in kind, his pulse thumping in anticipation.

This was going to be one hell of a fun job.

If it wasn't abundantly obvious, Raf Tygran is my Han Solo. (And if you're a Star Wars fan from way back, I'm sure you caught that already.) From the moment he introduced himself in PROMISE, I knew he was my Han. Raf became his own character, with his own story arch and personality. But he is heavily influenced by my adoration of the original space pirate.

Funny side note, I adored both Han Solo and Indian Jones when I was a little girl. But I was ten years old, looking at a movie poster for Blade Runner, before I realized that Han Solo and Indian Jones were played by the same actor. I think that speaks highly to Harrison Ford's acting skills—at least as far as this little girl was concerned. And one day soon, I will write my Indian Jones tribute character.

Now, despite knowing that Raf was my Han, when I got to the declarations of love in this book, I honestly didn't add the "I know" the first time around on purpose. It's just what came out because that was so something Raf would say. As soon as I typed the words, though, I was so amused with myself, I knew Emma would have to say those words back to him. It was only right. Leia got her chance. Emma needed hers.

I also acknowledge that this is a bit of an unconventional ending for a romance novel. The characters are together, but in a long-distance relationship. I couldn't think of any other way to end the book that wouldn't require one of them giving up an important part of themselves. And I didn't want to do that to them. This was their only way to be happy and to have their HEA. And it is, by the way. In my head cannon, these two are committed to each other for the rest of their lives, even through the ups and downs of having two adrenaline junkies in a relationship.

And here's where my head cannon turns to Firefly. Because I could see the continuing adventures of the *Ebisu* and her crew going forward. I'm not going to commit to that series just yet. But it is there in the back of my head, niggly at me. Maybe one day. Only this time, the captain and his woman aren't dancing around denying their feelings for each other! I can save that tension for other characters.

Those of you who have followed this series from the initial publication of PROMISE (when it was still called The Promise of Kierna'Rhoan) in 1999 will note that the stories come out with a great deal of time between each release. Sorry about that. Each one has needed its own time to gestate. And I can't see that changing I'm afraid. But I do have another story lined up to write soon—this one dealing with that impending Binnean War. So the series will continue in its sporadic and patchwork kind of way. I hope you'll keep checking back for more of the Naravan Chronicles. It's a complicated world, but one I enjoy playing in. And I hope you've enjoyed reading it!

Isabo Kelly

ABOUT THE AUTHOR

Isabo Kelly is the award-winning author of numerous science fiction, fantasy, and paranormal romances. She also writes best-selling paranormal romance under the name Kat Simons. Her life has taken her from Las Vegas to Hawaii, where she got her BA in Zoology, back to Vegas where she looked after sharks, then on to Germany and Ireland where she got her Ph.D. in Animal Behavior. Now Isabo focuses on writing. She lives in New York with her Irish husband and two beautiful boys, working as a full time writer and stay-at-home mom.

Don't miss out on new releases from Isabo! Sign up for her Newsletter here: http://eepurl.com/caxHa9

For more on Isabo and her books:
Website: http://www.isabokelly.com
Facebook: http://www.facebook.com/IsaboKelly
Twitter: https://www.twitter.com/IsaboKelly

Kellyn's Sacrifice

The Last Guardian

Bonfire Night

For more information on Isabo's books, visit:
http://www.isabokelly.com